DEATH of the
LAVENDER ARTIST

A LOU NAYLAND NOVEL

BY SCOTT R. HARTSHORN

© 2021 SCOTT HARTSHORN

ISBN: 979-8-9853351-3-2

THIS IS OF COURSE A WORK OF FICTION, FILLED WITH IMAGINARY PERSONS, PLACES AND DEEDS. THEREFORE I WOULD LIKE TO APOLOGIZE TO ALL MY FELLOW CITIZENS OF OKLAHOMA CITY FOR, AT TIMES, REARRANGING OUR BEAUTIFUL CITY, INVENTING INCIDENTS THAT APPEAR TO HAVE EXISTED BUT NEVER HAVE, AND FOR TAKING EVENTS OUT OF CONTEXT AND OUT OF TIME FOR THIS IS A STORY.

ALL RIGHTS RESERVED. NO PART OF THIS BOOK MAY BE REPRODUCED OR TRANSMITTED IN ANY FORM OR BY ANY MEANS, ELECTRONIC OR MECHANICAL, INCLUDING PHOTOCOPYING, RECORDING, OR BY ANY INFORMATION STORAGE AND RETRIEVAL SYSTEM, WITHOUT PERMISSION IN WRITING FROM THE AUTHOR OR PUBLISHER.

SCOTT HARTSHORN
QUAHUNT@AOL.COM

MARLA JONES, BOOK DESIGN
405.354.7422

DEDICATED TO MY CHILDREN, ANDREW AND EMILY.

SCOTT HARTSHORN

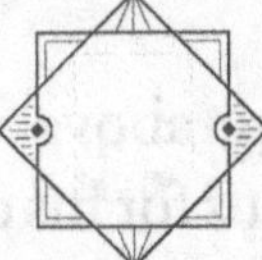

chapter one

It was on a peaceful evening in the third week in November of 1935. The bright white moon was climbing in the eastern sky over Oklahoma City, the quiet capitol of Oklahoma. It had been a hot day but as midnight approached the temperatures across the Sooner state dipped dramatically, due to a cold front blowing in from the Rockies. The cooler mountain air swept over the warm southern streets of the Big Friendly, causing a dense yellowish fog to form and settle across the boulevards of the 3rd Ward.

Weather and the late hour had emptied the streets, with not a soul in sight. But the sound of the rhythmic beat of a Harness Bull's boots striking the cobblestone pavement echoed down the foggy avenues. A beat cop emerged from the fine mist of rain beneath the dimly lit street of South Broadway. The light and drizzle created cottony halos around the street lights, like the fluffy seeds you blow off dandelion heads in the spring.

The officer stopped abruptly next to the red brick wall of the Victoria Hotel. He canvassed the area slowly while tilting his hat back and looking up at the well lit windows on the second floor of the hotel. A window near the rear of the building was partially open, allowing him to clearly hear the raised voices of two males arguing. Attempting to hear their discussion, he crossed the street and stepped up onto the far curb to achieve a better view of those inside. He could clearly see a middle-aged man with tints of silver running through his curly black hair. The man sat calmly on a stool before a bleached tightly stretched canvas and was speaking to another man somewhere unseen in the apartment.

◁○▷

The cop didn't know it but the fop sitting above was the a renowned artist James "Cowboy" Warren, famous for his depictions in oils of southwestern landscapes and images of working class laborers in their daily toils in the rugged Oklahoma oil fields and cattle ranches.

"Turn slightly to your right," he told the attractive man with reddish blonde hair sprawled across a finely stitched leather couch turned at an angle before the gas fireplace. The rakish young man, dressed only in a pair of blue dungarees, was barefoot and shirtless. He turned slightly, eyes closed, clasping a half-a-glass of cheap Chianti. The artist used a broken piece of charcoal to sketch the outline of his well formed model onto the stretched cotton canvas. The markings soon resembled the outlines of the half-nude athletic body of his muse on the couch, Paige Swalia.

The artist's eloquent strokes flowed over the canvas. "Paige," he asked, "did you see the article in the Oklahoman today about that crude middle-aged sodomite Jack Cloud?" He smirked to himself and simultaneously admired the shirtless Paige, slumped upon the divan. The heat from the gas fireplace caused small beads of sweat to form across the model's well-developed chest.

The two men had, until recently, indulged in sexual intercourse almost every afternoon in the second floor studio for these past four months. If anyone else caught wind of their clandestine meetings, they would have been arrested. Their passion had devolved into the low-key domestic intimacy of holding each other as they drank wine and listened to the radio, brushing against one another as they walked down Broadway before the curious eyes of pedestrians. Just being in the same space still excited the middle-aged artist. But he had recently sensed a change come over his youthful muse.

The strawberry-blonde Paige opened his eyes slowly and spoke through the mist of a bottle and a half of the Florentine vino. "That's somewhat hypocritical coming from an old queer like you," he said with a determined tone.

Warren stopped his sketching. He peered over to the youth and asked, "Did you know the man?"

"No," replied Paige. "But I know the guy involved in the incident with Mr. Cloud." Paige finished his glass and sat up to face the artist still sitting before his easel. "The young man's name is Edward Chambers, but most of the bachelors at the rooming house call him Eddie. He's only eighteen-years-old. A boy really. And he's fresh out of the Sand Springs Home for Boys outside of Tulsa. Or so I've heard. Anyway, he's an aimless youth that prowls the bachelor houses in the 3rd ward."

"So he's an eighteen-year-old working man of sorts and therefore the whole affair was consensual," Warren interjected.

"Most likely, yes." Paige sighed as he searched around for the bottle of wine.

"So who filed the complaint if, as you say, it was consensual?"

Paige lifted a wine bottle off the floor and filled his glass again. "From what's been said, it was that shit wipe County Attorney Mart Brown that swore out the complaint. Not the parties involved."

The artist took a cup of thick Turkish coffee from an Arab table behind him and slowly sipped. He set the cup down, and continued sketching the young man. "How's that possible?"

"For one, Chambers has a criminal record. And second, it appears that Brown has four male neighbors of Cloud who are willing to testify against him." Paige's voice had grown louder as the wine bottle grew emptier.

Warren picked up the tone in his young friend's voice. "Is there something personal about this case that has you upset?"

The young man finished his glass in a single gulp, refilled the glass from the bottle, and stood up. "I hate catamites like Cloud who take advantage of unworldly men like Chambers," he slurred. "It's disgusting actually. Why don't old dirty farts like Cloud find someone their own age? Instead of seducing the innocents like he's Zeus almighty swooping down on the young Trojan Ganymede?" Paige stood half-naked in the sitting room, burning red eyes cutting through to the base of his soul.

"Does this have something to do with us?" asked Warren.

Paige paced about the room, gathering up his shirt and boots. He stopped before the fireplace as the mantel clock behind him ticked slowly away the minutes of the night. He pulled on his shirt, buttoned it. Staring at his lover, his voice rose. "Actually it fucking does. I mean nothing to you, do I?"

The artist folded his hands in his lap and spoke in a soothing voice. "That's not true, Paige. I'm the one who asked you to spend the night with me because I miss waking up next to you. When you leave every night this whole place suddenly becomes empty. Devoid of love or life....."

Paige cut him off. "Lies, it's all just lies. You only like to brag to your old faggot friends that you have a young lover. You don't care about my feelings or my needs."

"That's not true and you know it," the aged painter almost whispered.

"Lies. You know it's true. You're only using me as a cheap model. When you've finished this piece, you'll move on to another man that's far too young for you to be your inspiration." Paige laced up his boots and tucked his cotton blue shirt into his tan work pants.

Warren stood up and walked over to the young man and put an arm around his strong shoulders. "Please don't speak like this. It breaks my heart. You know I love you. You're the only thing that makes me happy."

Swalia stood up and shoved the old artist away, heading to the door that led down the back stairs. "No, you're a catamite just like Cloud and I want nothing further to do with you!" He took hold of the brass knob, yanked open the door mumbling under his breath, "Nada to vada in the larda, what a sharda!" Just as the mantel clock chimed midnight, he slammed the door behind him and stormed down the baker's dozen of stairs, out the side door, and onto the deserted street below.

◁○▷

The Cowboy stands staring at the closed door. He feels a pain growing over his chest and into his left arm. Nausea sweeps over him and his heart begins to race. He's never felt the heartbreak of the end of a relationship so physically before. He walks slowly to the couch, and drinks the remainder of his lover's wine. He lays down, crosses his arms, clutching himself, as the pains of age slowly dissipated. He reflects on his situation.

Even now it still seems like I've got forever, yet I've got no time at all. I've got nothing really, even though it seems I've got everything. I smoke cigarettes and the hands of the mantel clock still tick on, yet they seemed to not move at all. They hardly budge out of the last place I saw them. But there they are counting off a half? two-thirds? all of my life? Maybe I do have forever, yet that's no time really at all."

I've still got forever to find real love and somehow I can't seem to do anything with it. He looks up at the ceiling, seeking answers in the stars beyond, desperately seeking an answer to the unanswerable. Then suddenly it becomes clear, a plan, the answer to my woes.

As the wine's effect settle over him, he fades off to sleep.

◁○▷

On the street below, the officer saw the young man exit the hotel and walk off north along Broadway. He shrugged his large shoulders and shivered in the growing dampness and reflected as he continued south about his rounds.

The Bull knew he had grounds to detain the young man, but felt it would serve no purpose. The senior officers on the force were all well aware of the bachelor housing located along Grand Avenue and Broadway. Whose tenants were overwhelmingly young, single, under forty and queer. But for the most part they all kept to themselves and caused little trouble.

The city Bulls had more trouble along "Battle Row" on North Grand because of the number of fights it handled daily and the nightly activity at the Vendome, the most luxurious brothel in town, owned by Ethel Clopton. Every officer knew the brothel caused ten times more trouble than any of the queers in their hotels and tea houses so most cops thought it best to let them be.

chapter two

Deep in the heart of the 3rd Ward of the Big Friendly that spring of 1936, looms an apparition, standing over 6' tall, with broad sinewy shoulders and a slender crooked nose. He slips into an alcove of an attractively decorated living room inside the small wood framed house on the corner of Robinson and Reno. His vacant dark eyes dart back and forth, searching the room like a predatory cat possessing the heart of a soulless demon. The menacing figure pushes deeper into the shadows and glances causally about the room awaiting the events of the night to unfold.

The room stands out with its modern décor, the furnishings bright and decorative. A large art deco rug dominates the center of the room. The brightly colored red and black triangles clash and dominate the eye. The carpet is surrounded by a broad expanse of highly polished beautiful wood flooring laid in long strips. The armchairs are squarely built and placed at an angle to the corners of the room. A multifaceted Tiffany lamp sits on the sharply cut table poised at the end of an elegant couch. Over the fireplace hangs a large framed oil painting of the god Pan seducing a maiden in the forest, in brilliant yellows and reds framed in gold. A modern writing table sits squarely in the middle of the large front window. Every detail of the apartment—the picture, the rug, the blown glass vases, and the wall hangings, all point to a luxurious taste on the verge of effeminacy.

The mantel clock ticks precisely away. "Seven minutes short

of midnight," the ghostly figure observes. "Perfect." He stands transfixed, wiping his mouth with the back of his hand, eyes bulging. He slowly becomes conscious of the growing, heinous hunger of the hunter rising up from the pit of his stomach.

Anticipating the pleasure of the first blow, tremors of excitement race through the stalker's limbs as he tries to suppress the desire swelling to the surface. "Calm," he thinks. "Mustn't rush it. Better to draw out the pleasure of the hunt."

Just then, the kitchen door gently swings open and a beautiful young man emerges through the swinging four panel door. He is wearing a faded green flannel robe, untied, revealing his nakedness, and clearly exposing his manhood.

The hidden figure follows him with his eyes, his arms falling limply to his side. He gasps for breath, and his eyes close as he sways forward in the alcove. A finely tuned forearm emerges leisurely from inside the young man's robe as he flips the light switch to the living room. None of the bulbs respond. He makes his way through the gloom aided, only by the filtered light of the street lamps through the side windows.

The hidden phantom's heart beats wildly, like a racing mustang, increasing the primitive hunger raging inside him. He slowly wraps his fingers tighter around the long lead pipe and watches furtively, mouth partly open, as he scratches the back of his hand holding the pipe.

The young man stumbles ever closer towards the alcove.

The stalker inhales as his victim stops and turns slowly attempting to gather his bearings. "Now!" he thinks. He strikes the man from behind and savagely batters his prey's head and shoulders again and again with the heavy pipe. His beastly cravings explode as he pummels the face of the now lifeless body. His animal-self screams inside his head, causing a deafening drumming in his ears. The room spins before him in streams of white light as a shot of power races through him like lighting.

His senses return and the specter of death suddenly becomes aware that his arm aches like hell and a man lies dead on the floor before him. Crimson colored blood pools about his feet. The killer stands over the motionless form, bloody pipe in his hand. A perverse smile crawls across his face. But it changes as quickly as an Oklahoma spring, replaced by a look of abject terror. "I'm a monster!" He swallows and fixates his eyes on the corpse. "But maybe he deserves what he got. He's only caused hurt to the souls of others." But did he really deserve to die for breaking someone's heart? He questioned himself.

Panicked and scared, scared as a man can get and go on living. He swallows and fixates his eyes on the corpse. He whirls and runs out the rear door of the now desecrated house, to the alley beyond, and disappears into the darkness of the night.

chapter three

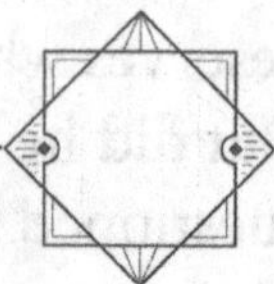

Lou Nayland, former minor league baseball player, and now underpaid private detective, looked down at the people scurrying around the noisy streets like ants during the height of the morning rush. Everyone seemed oblivious to the noise, failing to distinguish between pleasurable sounds and the painful sounds. They simply followed their routine, their own feet wearing ruts that grow deeper and deeper until there is no way to escape the trap of their own device. From his view above, the street resembled a sleeping beast covered with ticks that he could ignore until one bites too deep and he must awake to scratch.

Shrugging his shoulders at their fruitless acts, he walked to the front office, donned his overcoat, and walked out onto the crisscrossed red tile floor of the hallway that ran to the elevator shafts at the end of the hall. The brass doors of the elevator swept back as he approached, and the pretty curly haired dishwater blond elevator operator, Linda Keally, appeared below her brilliant red, round blocked service hat. In a tone that came across as especially flirtatious given her slight trailing lisp she inquired, "Going down Mr. Nayland?" Linda was an attractive blonde, whose luxurious hair shingled into a thousand short curls that ran into one another. Her baby blues were sardonic over a face of freckles that gave her the appearance of a delicate spotted flower. She possessed the type of voice that resonated in your mind long after she was gone. You know, one of those lingering sounds, like the echo of a train whistle ringing in the morning air.

I nodded, smiled an amused grin and thought her goodness made it hard to determine if she really was flirting or if it was just in her nature to be good people. The polished brass doors slid open at the ground floor as that pleasant thought rambled through the grey matter between my ears. I thanked Linda, tipping her with a buffalo nickel. She smiled thanks.

I crossed the Italian marble floor of the Hightower Building, head through the frosted glass front doors out onto Hudson towards my green coupe parked across the street. The pleasant breeze blowing down from the northwest chilled me and the other pedestrians on the street, reminding us that winter still had a little bite left in her. The cold wind even penetrated through the back of my grey wool hounds-tooth suit as I attempted to unlock the car door. Such gusts during the month of April usually harbored ill omens, either bringing the last snow of the winter or the first thunderstorms of spring. They would build over the Texas panhandle, climbing to the limits of the atmosphere and then blow east developing into the dreaded twisters that wreak devastation upon the small rural communities.

It had been a very long, but profitable week. Irene was out of town for a few more days seeing her mother so I had decided to leave the confines of my office early, in hopes I could find some other form of happiness out at the ballpark. The Tribe was playing an exhibition game against the St. Louis Cardinals at three o'clock. The Cardinals, true major leaguers, had won the 1934 World Series. Expectations were running high this spring for the hometown ball club. Especially after manager Bert Neihoff and his crew roundly defeated the Beaumont Exporters last September to win the Texas League pennant.

Grinning, I turned the engine over, revved it momentarily to warm her, and made a u-turn into traffic, turning west onto Main. Out of the corner of my eye I caught the large black and white sign marked SPEED 20 MPH, so I let off the accelerator as I headed toward Holland Field. The stadium west of downtown, that housed the well- manicured home field of the minor league Oklahoma

City Indians. When I had passed the county jail I flipped on the radio and tuned it in using the punch button for 1520, the KOMO radio station, to listen to the afternoon news.

Famous local artist James "Cowboy" Warren was found dead this week in Tijuana, Mexico on a lounge chair next to the pool at the Agua Valiente Casino Hotel. Early reports suggest he died from an apparent heart attack. Mr. James had been vacationing in Tijuana, Mexico for the past several months.

Warren was born on the 5th of January 1889, in Danville, Illinois, a son of a self-made man who made his fortune as a cotton miller in the latter part of the century. At the age of thirteen, James left school and joined his father and elder brother William in the business. The entire family was civic minded and were greatly involved in the local administration and the political establishment of Frederick, Oklahoma and the surrounding area.

Mr. Warren married twenty-year-old Bertha Francis Howard, whom he called Bertie in 1909. After the death of the couple's only son to the influenza epidemic in 1919, Warren left Frederick shortly after to attend art school in Kansas City. James never returned to Frederick, but rather traveled the west first working as a cowhand, where he acquired his nick-name "Cowboy."

Later Warren rose to fame due to his interesting and introspective paintings and sketches of American Indians, cowboys and oil field workers in Osage County in the early 20's and subsequently in the Borger, Texas oil fields a few years later.

Mr. Warren will be remembered as a southwestern artist of considerable note. He was 47 years old at his passing and leaves behind no living relatives....

I turned the radio off and put my mind back onto baseball.

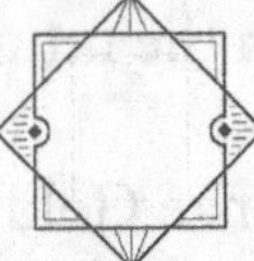

chapter four

Spring baseball games always excited me. I suppose it all started when I played little league baseball and my father coached me and my friends. I looked down at the key chain hanging in the ignition. A small piece of brass jingled pleasantly as I drove. It had been engraved with inscriptions on both sides. The side facing me read 1916-1917 Football 7-1, Basketball 18-1. Without flipping the piece around I knew it read S.H. S. Coach Rupert Nayland. It had been given to him by the senior Class of '17 in thanks for their magical final year in school. When he died three years later, it was one of the two things my father left me.

Shoving down the frog attempting to grow at the back of my throat, I forced the memories to slip back into the smoke of my mind. I shouldered the wheel over in an attempt to pass "Old Dan" pulling the Meadow Gold Milk Wagon along Main Street, felt the car's rear end begin to slide, and brought it out with a splash of power, nearly kissing the curb. I waved to Old Dan's driver and turned onto Pennsylvania Avenue looking for my usual parking space along the left field fence.

I parked under the line of wild plum trees across the street from the new water plant building. Grabbed my overcoat and walked down Penn towards the turnstiles situated at the front of the stadium. It was one of those fine days in early April with the warmth of golden sunshine spiked by the slight nip in the air of the fading winter. A breeze scampered ahead of me, snatching at scraps of paper, scattering the previous falls leaves, snapping at the pennant flags that billowed over the clubhouse. The first faint shoots of green were peeking from the elms lining both sides of the street. The bursting sticky spear-heads of the pecan trees were in full display as well. I hoped it foretold rain in the future and not snow.

I strode by the freshly painted red and bronze Gold Seal Beer advertisement towards the six little ticket boxes in front of the stadium. "Hello," I said to the young sandlot boys selling tickets. The sand-lotters were local kids that helped Putter maintain the ball diamond in exchange for being allowed to practice on the field. One of the young lads recognized me and smiled as I handed him a deuce of half-dollars. "You got any dangerous cases on your plate, Mr. Nayland?"

"Nothing that would interest you Tommy," I told him

He grinned a huge gap-tooth grin. "You remember my name!" he said giving me my change.

I slid him the two-bits back. "You and the boys get some sweets, but only after you're to run by Putter."

"Thank you, Mr. Nayland!" the boy exclaimed.

I slipped the ticket into my suit pocket and proceeded through the turnstiles. The radio broadcaster for KOMA 1520 sat in his press box directly over the ticket booth could clearly be heard announcing the day's throwers and the start of the game.

> "The batteries: Parmelee pitching, Ogrodowski catching,
> for St. Louis; Brillheart pitching; Fitzpatrick catching for
> the home club! Play ball!"

I cut across the sticky floor beneath the stadium and thought in a thousand years the only thing America will be remembered for will be the constitution, jazz, and baseball. I smiled broadly and headed towards my seat.

"Afternoon Mr. Nayland," barked a gravelly voice. Come to see us or the Cardinals?" It was Putter, the aging head grounds keeper for John Holland Jr. Who had recently taken over the club after Senior had died during the past winter. Putter maintained the Holland Field as the best-kept diamond in the Texas League.

I stuck my hand out to shake. "Hi Putter! I'm here to see our Indians, of course. After last season's championship run, I figure we might even have a chance to sneak one out here today against the gashouse gang."

Suppressing a laugh he said, "You have high hopes indeed Mr. Nayland."

"By the way Putter, I gave one of your boys' money to buy candy for all the lads. Make sure they don't sneak off before they do their chores."

"They wouldn't dare, Mr. Nayland." We shook hands and I headed to the center stairs to my usual seat along the third base line.

I waved to Blue and held up two fingers. He quickly brought over two mustard covered hot dogs. I actually preferred ketchup on my hot dog, but that is considered a violation of the holy rules of the baseball fandom. It does clearly state, "A Hot Dog may only be served with mustard within the confines of any baseball stadium." I slipped Blue a dime for the dogs along with two bits and said "Keep the change!" That was my second generous tip of the day. Not my usual pattern, but I shrugged and told myself I had had a couple of profitable weeks and it felt good to spread it around.

It was an amazing upset over the Cardinals. When the standing ovation for the Indians died down, I maneuvered through the crowd to the clubhouse below hoping to get an opportunity to congratulate Coach Neihoff on his win and talk a little baseball. As I hurried down to catch Coach Bert in his office, the stadium loudspeaker rang out with the distinct voice of the newly hired reporter for radio WKY, Walter Cronkite as he interviewed "Pepper" Martin on the mound.

"Them Indians don't seem to realize who they're playing out here today; they're up against the St. Louis Cardinals, not the Atlanta Crackers."

I smirked. "'Pepper' had the situation sized up accurately. The "gashouse gang from St. Looey" did look like just another ball team to the Indians, and Bert's Braves had done themselves well before the record crowd of 4,500 over-coated spectators warmed by racing away with a 6-1 victory."

The voices of the interviewers faded away as I entered the locker rooms under the bleachers. Water dripped onto my shoulders from the steam pipes overhead. I strode towards the two smoked glass doors at the end of the hall; the one straight ahead read LOCKER ROOM, PLAYERS ONLY in green lettering. The other read BERT NEIHOFF, MANGER. I knocked on the worn oak door.

"What do you need?" The gruff voice of Bert penetrated the heavy door.

Grabbing the well worn door knob, I pushed into the dimly lit office, "Just thought I would congratulate you on your victory today, Coach."

Bert stood up, with his usually pleased to see me grin, shook my hand with an iron grip and belched out, "How the hell are you Lou?"

I attempted to match his grip and replied, "Well, thanks for asking."

He sat back down into his large leather chair while kicking a bench in my direction stenciled in black, PROPERTY OF THE INDIANS. I pulled it over and straddled it, staring back at him with a smile. Bert had a square jaw and large ears, which protruded out at right angles to his head. They made his head appear larger than it actually was. His shoulders were wide and hid the slowly expanding ring of fat falling over his belt. But he was still strong in arms and chest for a man of his advancing age.

While in his office, it was Bert's habit to pick up an old worn baseball and toss it back and forth between his large hands. I had long ago concluded it was his attempt to look casual while speaking to others, a vain attempt to hide his natural intensity. He opened with his standard line, "Still making a living peeping through keyholes and following middle-aged cheaters?"

"I crawl out of the gutters to socialize with hobnobbers like you on occasion. But today I also wanted to congratulate you on a superb win. It was no small feat."

"So other than confirming my brilliance as baseball manager, what's on your mind?" He set the baseball down and reached for a pack of cigarettes lying on the desk. It was empty. It was always empty, but I didn't mention he might smoke too much. Instead I threw him a deck of Luckies from my coat pocket. He drew one from the box and as was his habit began to roll it back and forth between his large fingers. "If I hadn't said it before, I appreciate how you handled "The Toad" matter last summer. That could have blown up the clubhouse and destroyed the club's season."

"I'm glad it worked out for Johnny and Lauren," I replied. "And speaking of the Camps, I noticed "The Toad" isn't on the roster this season. I hope he's still playing."

"Yeah, the Ivory Hunters found him and signed him to move up. It's ironic actually, considering today's win. He signed with the Cardinals this past winter to play in their farm league." Coach Neihoff struck a redheaded stick match on his cleats and lit the well rolled cigarette in his hand. "They put him on their Double AA club up in Columbus, Ohio and from what I hear, granting it's only a few games into the season, he's apparently fitting right in, hitting well from all accounts."

"I'm glad to hear it. He's a good kid. I hope he finds success with the new club," I responded before asking, "Do you know if his wife is with him up there?"

"I believe so," Bert replied, and we both nodded in an appreciative manner.

"Anyhow I just wanted to say hello and congratulate you on the win. Besides you know as well as I there's something about a baseball game that puts the grind in prospective and reaffirms one's faith," I said with a knowing smile.

Bert turned his chair and leaned back. "My mother always said she loved to go to church, but not to hear the preacher. She could read the bible at home, but she could only be in church, in the church. And to me, you, and the others who have played, baseball has some of that same sense of peace. That has nothing to do with ideology, but simply with ritual, familiarity, small truths or of lessons of the day. That we were familiar with before, but may get a little more light placed on them today." He said thoughtfully now looking up and not at me.

I wiped my hands over my knees like I was wiping the dirt away after a great slide into second then placing them on the bench in an attempt to leave. "I've taken up too much of your time already, Coach, and I'm sure that new rookie reporter with WKY will be down here to interview you on your success today. Best I get out of your hair." We both stood and shook hands. "Wish you another great summer. Tell you what, let's have dinner at Cattlemen's before you get too deep into your season. I'll even pick up the tab."

A huge smile lit up his face. "These boys aren't the '27 Yankees, but thanks for your support. And you're on for the steak as well." I closed the door behind me and headed up the short stairs to the clubhouse floor.

When I stepped onto the last step, out of the corner of my eye, I spied the stout body of the Jersey Boy standing in the hall chatting up an Annie. We briefly looked at one another when he nodded a greeting and continued talking to the stunning young bleached blond in a tight sweater smiling up at him. As I strode past, he spoke to the back of my head, "See you in the funny papers, Shamus."

I turned and flashed him a toothy grin before I walking on across the gummy floor of the stadium. I strode towards the exit as the intense smell of buttered popcorn and steamed hot dogs wafted under my nose."

God I love ballparks, I thought.

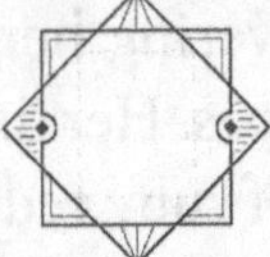 **chapter five**

I wonder if the average citizen has any idea how much trouble a private investigator can get into sometimes. Well, if you happen to have an office on Hudson, with a sign on your door that reads Louis "Lou" Nayland, (no associates thank you), Private Investigations, you know. Like all other P.I.'s I deal in a number of unsavory areas. I started out stealing cars back for the finance company and worked my way up. Catching a clerk with his hand in the till, finding a missing person or maybe listening in on other people's conversations, is now my standard fare. Following errant husbands and wives until I catch them being naughty is my favorite. Occasionally there is some violence and excitement, but mostly it's mundane and the financial rewards in money, small. Periodically, I'm able to convince myself that it's good to be a private investigator and occasionally see my idea of justice triumph. Very rarely do I simply admit to myself that I'm a nosey bastard who likes meddling in other people's business, but gets paid to get it done.

Sure, I have a lot of idle time. I use it up with my feet on the desk, waiting, or checking the race results, or staring at the walls of my office. My large leather chair had been purchased with my last minor league baseball check. My grey tin ashtray is full of as many cigarette stumps as a tray its size could expect to hold. A map of the city hangs on the buff colored wall. In the corner sits a green four drawer filing cabinet and above it hangs a framed certificate licensing Louis Nayland to pursue the calling of private detective in the State of Oklahoma in accordance with certain black letter regulations.

In the opposite corner hangs the 1936 Sinclair Gas Station calendar, newly flipped open to April. A voluptuous brunette, skimpily clad in a blue wrap-around scarf covering her hips and breasts, appears to be attempting to touch her toes. Her dark brown eyes twinkled back at me playfully over a set of ruby red lips. It's a man's office.

But spare time can be as dangerous as stepping over a rattlesnake taking a sunbath. It's just the preliminary, the lull before the storm. You wait an hour, a day, or even a week. The quiet minutes multiply, but sooner or later things come to a head.

◁○▷

I'd been working on an extra long lull that appeared to be going nowhere. I sat in my office that Wednesday morning with my shirt sleeves rolled up and my collar open thinking about but a race horse named Easy Winnings, and whether the Indians could pull off another pennant win, when the ring of the black Bakelite rotary telephone disturbed the quiet and with no but me to answer. I lifted the receiver and said, "This is Nayland."

"Lou, is that you?" asked a familiar husky voice.

In a curious, playful tone, I asked, "Yes, and this is?"

"It's Nancy Swalia, Nancy. You remember? We met at the University library last summer, when I helped you in that murder case."

I smiled to myself. It would have been impossible to forget Miss Nancy. She had slipped into my thoughts many a night since last August. "It's very nice to hear from you, Nancy."

"You told me that if I was ever caught in the rain you would be the man to see," she said, voice quivering. "Well, I believe it may be raining." She paused, "I must see you as quickly as possible. Could you see me now?"

Curious and now concerned, I responded, "Sure, I'll not move from here until you arrive."

"I can be at your office in twenty minutes! I'm on the east side of downtown. Please wait for me. This is very important." Her voice pitching slightly higher as the call disconnected.

I returned the headset to its cradle as I opened the bottom drawer of the desk and pulled out a bottle of Oban and two glasses. Filling the first a third of the way to the rim, I leaned back into the large cowhide swivel chair, and took a sip. I gazed about my office as I waited for Nancy to arrive. My large walnut desk faced the smoked glass partition door on which the landlord had recently stenciled "PRIVATE" in bold black letters. The remainder of my cubby of a room was dominated by three five-foot tall sliding windows that brightened the room when the sun was right. One faced north towards the Courthouse and the other two framed the corners of my desk on the east wall. Hudson Avenue ran north and south five stories below. The street sounds were barely audible at this height. Taxi horns, the roar of trucks and buses, even faint voices of pedestrian's carried up to my office, not unpleasant sounds.

chapter six

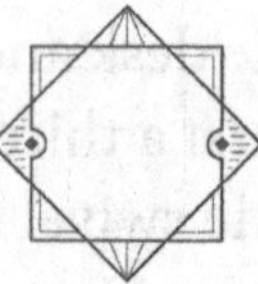

I finished my scotch just as the ringer sounded on the outer door of the half-office I use for a reception room. I heard the door close and the ringer go quiet. I yanked the knot in my tie straight, combined my hair with my blunt fingers as the distinct sounds of a woman's heels clicking across the tile floor and stopping at the door marked "PRIVATE."

The door to the reception area opened confidently, then lost its nerve. I swung around in the swivel chair and looked toward the little waiting room. Some women are beautiful. Some have bodies that make you forget beauty. Here was a woman that had both. She was tall with perfect ivory white skin. Her face was small and delicate , clefted at the chin, with full sensuous lips, wide-set green eyes set below her long lashes which highlighted their effect below her upswept hair, the color resembling a prairie brush fire that fell softly to the sides and touched her freckled cheeks, but her red didn't come from a bottle. The three-strand necklace of pearls hugging her throat seemed to reflect the warmth of her delicately tanned complexion. She had that mature, voluptuous look some women get when they pass thirty. She'd had it for three or four years; it looked swell on her and she didn't try to hide it. She held a chic hat and wore an expensive suit that had been cleaned too often. She didn't have to open her mouth for me to remember who she was. What I didn't know at the time was, she led me straight down a string of murders.

I watched as she gracefully approached. Whether you looked at her face or at her body, packed within the form fitting tight green wool suit, nothing was left to the imagination. The result was most satisfying. I rose, walked around and indicated with a thick-fingered hand the oak armchair in front of my desk and held it.

She sat in the chair as smoothly as a cat walking a fence. Her voice was low and controlled when she said, "Hello, I trust my coming at this hour is not an imposition."

I returned to the chair behind the desk. "Not at all. What can I do for you, Miss Swalia." I said as I smiled without separating my lips.

"Thank you, and it's Nancy. Or have you forgotten me so easily, Mr. Nayland?" she said with a wry grin. Her hard deep green eyes were the color of the Caribbean Sea after sunrise and sat above her aquiline nose giving her a classic Roman appearance. She wore no make-up and no lipstick. None of this took away from her sheer beauty.

"Oh I haven't forgotten." Since she had opened my office door, I'd noticed with some irritation the school boy, unruliness of my own heart. I became annoyed with the disturbance aroused in my breast by her mere presence, so I tried to conduct myself professionally with my potential new client. "Now, what can I do for you, Nancy?"

She fingered the strand of pearls dangling from her neck in a mindless manner. "I'm looking for my brother."

"Are you sure he's missing and not on a lark?" I examined Nancy with some care, for I believed it is important to find out the weakness in people one has to deal with. One never knows when it may be useful.

"Yes and no. You see he's been gone for more than a week now and I'm terribly afraid he'll have gotten himself into some kind of trouble." I registered genuine concern in her voice.

"What kind of trouble could that be?" I inquired politely.

Nancy paused and prepared herself to speak. "Well you see it's—well it's—it just isn't easy for me to talk about it."

I nodded as if I understood her, but pleasantly, as if nothing serious was involved. "Why don't you just lean back in that chair and close your eyes …"

She smoothed her skirt with a motion of her hands and softly replied, "Yes, yes, I'll try, thank you."

Her sweetness made me nervous. My hand shook, precipitating the neck of the bottle to rattle like a castanet against the rim of the glass as I poured a couple fingers worth of Oban into a fairly clean pony glass and placed it in her trembling hand. "Here, take a swig of this before you start."

She held the glass in both hands, it was nearly full. She looked into the precious liquor reflectively, then tilted the glass higher and higher and set it down empty, "That helps. Thanks."

"It usually does." I told her.

Sitting up straight in the hard wooden chair she calmly asked, "Where should I begin?"

"The beginning is usually a good place." I stated as I took a meditative sip of my scotch.

Lines of irritation formed around her eyes, "Don't be cute, Lou."

I pulled a deck of Luckies off my desk; drew one, put a kitchen match to the tip and lit it. I didn't offer her one. She didn't seem to care. Then I puffed smoke across the desk.

"Ass."

"Sometimes," I replied, attempting to instill some levity into the situation "Shall we get down to business?"

"Yes, please," she said with a new-found air of confidence.

I wondered, not for the first time, at the resilience of women as I took a draw off the Lucky and said, "So let's begin with why you believe your brother is missing."

She shifted in her chair, composed herself, and then stated her thoughts with purpose, "Like I suggested earlier, I'm not even sure he is missing, but I haven't heard from him in several weeks. And when I called some of his friends they hadn't seen him either. And Paige-- that's my brother-- would be absolutely livid if he knew I had even approached a private detective to track him down. But this is so unlike him. I felt I had no other choice."

I snubbed my cigarette out in the ashtray and said, "Ok, I got the picture. So why don't you give me some background on your brother. There might be something that will give us a clue as to whether your brother is really missing or just gone underground for his own reasons."

"Our mom is alive and lives in Des Moines," she continued. "Our father died a couple of years ago. He was a doctor. Paige was going to be one, too, but dropped out of med school after the first year and changed to law. He had a good job in Des Moines. I guess he wanted to escape someplace… Anyway, a law school friend convinced him to come down here to Oklahoma City when the oil boom started. Said there was plenty of work and that the city was evolving socially, whatever that meant. Now he's a lawyer here in the city and works for a firm doing mostly oil and gas leases." Nancy paused. "At least that's what he told me he does. He is several years younger than me and since high school we have not been as close as a brother and sister ought to be. But that's mostly due to his lifestyle choices than anything on my part. And though he won't admit it, I've recognized his tendencies from the time we were kids."

I raised an eyebrow in response to her last line, but thought it best to let it slide and circle back to it later. "Do you know the name of the firm he works at?"

"No, sorry I don't."

"You said earlier that speaking about him wasn't easy. Why's that?"

She nodded. "Well some people might say he has a kind of mental illness." There seemed to be some malice in her voice.

I shook my head, frowned sympathetically, and asked, "Does he have mental issues?"

"None at all," she proclaimed.

I leaned back in the swivel chair. "I'm still not clear on what you're saying about your brother."

Her face flushed, "I'm not sure how to say this, but here goes. My brother runs with a somewhat different crowd here in the city."

"Different how," I asked, curious and a little concerned.

"Well, to put it delicately, he ummm… prefers the company of men." She stated quickly.

"Sorry. I'm slow. Come again."

"Let me put it in terms you'll understand, Mr. Nayland," she said brusquely. "He bats from the other side of the plate."

I raised an eyebrow a trifle, and a muscle tightened in my cheek before I asked, "You mean your brother's a pansy?"

Nancy blushed and nodded. "But my father never knew. And my mother, I believe, only suspects. She's very religious, so she can't really wrap her mind around the possibility."

I nodded slowly. "But what makes you believe he's gone missing?"

"Even though we don't hang around socially and very rarely see each other unless it's Christmas or something, he still calls me every Sunday night. Just to check in and ask about mom."

"So when did you speak to him last?" I questioned.

She looked down at her handbag and picked nervously at it. "Three Sundays ago. That's why I'm getting so worried."

"Ok, do you have an address for him?"

"Possibly. He lived in the Victoria Hotel last fall with an older man, a well-known artist by the name of James Warren," her voice trembling slightly.

"Have you called on him to inquire about your brother?"

"I can't you see, because I heard he died recently in Mexico somewhere."

"Yeah, I think I heard about that on the radio." I stated out loud and then asked, "Do you have anything more recent?"

"Just that he had found a place at the Century Rooms somewhere on South Broadway. He has been rather reluctant of late to speak with me about his personal life so I can't be sure that's where he went." She stated with some uncertainty.

"Did you go to the Century Rooms to determine if he was still in residence?" I inquired.

"I did," Nancy replied, as a natural confidence slowly appeared across her face. "It's a cheaply run establishment for young professionals. I didn't like the manager at all. He a horrid little man; balding, unwashed with distinct pock marks scarring his face. He said Paige moved out a couple of months ago and he didn't know where to. And he didn't care. He seemed more interested in another slug of gin than conversing me. I can't imagine why Paige would even have taken up lodgings in a place like that."

With a boyish grin I asked, "Really, did you just say a slug of gin?"

A blush crossed her face. "That was my impression anyway."

Something about her made me too warm under my clothes. "That's fine, precious," I said. "So, your brother moved on from the Century Rooms, but you don't know where he's gone to." She nodded her head in agreement. "And I gather you're afraid he's living in even deeper sin as a gunsel to some other old rich man in some penthouse here in the city, is that it?"

Nancy's cheeks flamed red and she exclaimed, "Well for goodness' sake!"

"Or am I being too coarse?" I asked.

A scowl appeared on her freckled face before a smile replaced it, "You're teasing me aren't you?" she said somewhat flirtatiously, "And I don't think anything of the sort about Paige. If Paige heard you say that, you'd be sorry. He can be mean and he's not soft by any stretch. I believe something terrible has happened. Call it a woman's intuition." I remained silent waiting for her to continue. "Aren't you going to take any notes?" she asked. "I thought detectives wrote everything down in little flip notebooks."

"I'm the comic, not you, precious," I said, "You just tell me the facts and I'll do everything I can to help you."

She smiled again. "Really, that's about all I can tell you. Oh, this might help. He did let slip one time that his group of friends refer to themselves as members of 'The Gardenia Club.'"

"That's something," I said. "Did it occur to you to report him missing to the police?"

Nancy suddenly appeared annoyed. "I wouldn't dare ask the police. Paige would never forgive me for involving the police. He's highly suspect of their actions when it concerns him and his friends."

"Alright, maybe not that directly, but did you call the jail to see if he had just been locked up?"

"No, but if that were the case, I'm sure his friends would have told me," she insisted. "They're quite a tight knit group of men."

"Did you call the hospitals? Maybe he got knocked over by a car and lost his memory or is lying unconscious in one of their beds or is too badly hurt to talk."

She leveled a glare at me, apparently not admiring of my logic. "If it was something like that, we'd know," she said. "Everybody has things in their pockets to tell who they are, and if that had occurred I'm sure someone would have called my mother."

"So, what do you think happen?" I asked firmly.

She gazed at me with a mocking smile. "If I knew that I wouldn't need you, would I?"

"You're right of course," I said. "Can you give me a description of your brother? It might help."

She put a finger to her lips. "Let's see, he's nearly thirty, reddish-blonde hair, medium height, slender but well built, has no facial hair, a small mole under his right ear, always immaculately dressed. Usually wears a brown or tan hat, has a sound knowledge of art, but owns none. Has no family other than myself and mom."

I grinned. "You'd make a hell of a detective if you ever leave the library." I thought she winked at me as she said thanks. That excited me so I questioned her some more. "Do you have a picture of him?"

Nancy reached into her purse and pulled out a black and white snapshot of her and her brother standing on a front porch. I told her that it would do to start.

"Will you be able to find him quickly, do you believe?" she asked with the calm expectancy of one who never fails to get what she has demanded.

"If he hasn't gone off on his own accord, I believe I can determine his whereabouts," I said in solid confidence.

She picked up a small clutch purse that had been sitting on her lap and said, "Now as to your fee…"

Though my heart was still doing its boyish dance, I tried to speak clearly and professionally. "I get thirty bucks a day and, of course, expenses."

I sat silently in the swivel chair toying with a brass letter opener as Nancy opened her pocketbook, a unique, expensive, brown leather bag, but like her suit, it had seen far too much duty. She fumbled inside and drew out a small roll of cash. "That seems fair. Will two hundred be enough to start?" she asked as she peeled four fifties from the roll and placed them on the blotter before me.

"It looks like you've bought a boy." It was a statement of fact, unenthusiastic, spoken in a tone of voice that made my sentiments clear though unspoken. After I'd placed my right palm over the negotiable paper and slipped it into my pocket, I stood and escorted Nancy out of the office.

But at the door she reached up and kissed me on the cheek. "For good luck." In our closeness, I took in her faint odor. It was an overwhelming fragrance like the smell of nostalgia from half-forgotten summers. She disappeared into the drab little waiting room, and a second later I heard the door to the corridor open and close.

I shook my head in an attempt to clear away the effects of Nancy's presence and kiss as she closed the outer door behind her. The room seemed to have become darker.

At my desk, I reached for the scotch bottle, poured half a glass and considered the possible roads of inquiry. Knowing that clear detective work was one-third luck, one-third intuition, and one-third hard work. Old timers rated luck and intuition as a standoff, which is to say one is as important as the other. Miss Swalia's brother's stomping grounds were new territory for me. And though my intuition had stood me in good stead before, I knew this case would require hard work and a greater than usual amount of luck. I quickly determined I was indulging in profitless, idle theory and decided I would start by seeing Brice Jackson in the morning.

The Indians weren't playing tonight so I figured I'd roll the dice and see if I could track down Paige's place of employment. I reached for the city directory and found the number to the Bar Association and dialed the number. The register secretary at the bar informed me that Paige Swalia was currently listed as an associate with the firm of Allen and Jarmen. She added that their offices were located in the Ramsey Building at 200 West First Street. I knew the building. It was a smart looking number built in '31 that rose up thirty-three stories from the street. When it was originally built by the oilman W.R. Ramsey, his goal was to be the owner of the tallest building in Oklahoma City. By 1936 he owned the fourth tallest building in the city. The law offices of Allen and Jarmen were located on the third floor.

I picked up my hat, headed to see my girl Linda in the elevator, then briskly walked the four blocks to Allen and Jarmen's offices.

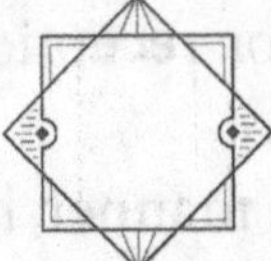

chapter seven

Aiden Allen's office was located on the northeast corner of the art deco Ramsey Tower that over-looked the recently built Biltmore Hotel. So I rode the chic art nouveau elevator up to the third floor and stepped out into the finely carpeted hall that led to the two separate law firms located on the floor. To the right were the offices of Black and Black. On my left were the frosted glass oak doors of Aiden Allen and Partners. It appeared that each firm took up half of the third floor. I pulled the brass handle on my right and stepped into the well- furnished offices of Allen and Jarmen.

Each of the partners occupied a corner office. In between were two smaller offices for the firm's young associates and the fourth was a conference room. At the core of was the secretarial pool, mail and file room, and the receptionist's area.

An attractive paper pusher sat sorting envelopes. She was in her early thirties, with thick brunette hair over heavy-lashed brown eyes that said she was good when she was bad. Her nose was strong, but not enough to overshadow a perfectly formed mouth. She exuded sex, like the juice in a grape, young enough it hadn't gone sour. There was fullness, a rare bursting ripeness to her that made you think of Reubens and Fragonard, or maybe some erotic work by the sculptor Augusta Savage.

Her black, dotted Swiss dress had a full skirt and square neckline. A little prim for someone of her age. That is, until she leaned in toward you and the front of her dress sort of fell away. She knew what she was doing alright.

When I approached, she put down the handful of envelopes and brass letter opener and said, "May I help you?" Her voice was as rich and ripe as the rest of her.

I smiled my nicest smile, the one I keep for receptionists and old ladies. "I'm here to see Aiden Allen, please."

"Your name please?" she asked in a carefree manner, her brown eyes twinkling.

"Lou Nayland," I stated with a bit of a wry smile.

"May I tell him what it is regarding?" she purred in a low voice.

"It's a private matter, and I prefer to tell him in person."

"Please have a seat Mr. Nayland and I'll see if he can speak with you." She picked up the receiver, pushed a clear button until it lit and spoke into the phone softly explaining my request. She reset the horn, a frown replacing the playfulness on across her face. "He has ten minutes. If you'll come with me." She stood and walked across the reception area, slightly exaggerating the swing of her hips, and escorting me down a brightly lit corridor to s frosted glass door at its far end. She opened the door and I stepped into the office.

Allen sat behind an immense mahogany desk on which stacks of folders were heaped. He was a pasty-complected, bespectacled man with a tired oval face beneath thinning silver hair worn swept back from either side of his face. The shoulders of his dark suit were dotted with dandruff. He remained seated, sorting out some papers. Finally he looked up. "Please have a seat Mr. Nayland. I'll be right with you." He laid down his pen and in a deep cultivated voice asked, "How may I help you today?"

I pulled out my buzzer and slid it across the desk so he could clearly read the license. He nodded, so I proceeded. "I'm looking into the disappearance of Paige Swalia."

"I didn't know he was missing." Neither his tired face nor his rather distinct voice held any emotion.

I frowned and cleared my throat. "To be honest I'm not sure myself, but he's failed to contact his sister for the last three Sundays. She has grown concerned and asked me to look into it."

"I see," said Allen. "Well, allow me to alleviate some of your concerns. He began his vacation starting last Monday. He said he would be traveling to see his family in Iowa for a couple of weeks. We don't expect him back until Monday the nineteenth."

"That's helpful. And concerning."

"How so?"

"His family hasn't heard from him, the ones here or his mother in Des Moines."

"I wouldn't be too concerned about that, Mr. Nayland. Paige is a young man. He may just be off with a companion and felt it wasn't his employers business to know where he was traveling and with whom. You know us lawyers, Mr. Nayland. We tend to keep the privilege of privacy close to our vests and away from intrusive eyes."

"You may be right, but I have a few more questions if you have time."

"I can give you five more minutes, so go on."

"May I ask if you're satisfied with Mr. Swalia's work here at the firm?"

"Exceptionally so. He's punctual, competent, maintains the requisite billable hours, and gets along well with the staff. We have no complaints whatsoever."

"His sister will be pleased to hear that. One last thing—is he currently working on any cases that are out of the ordinary, or involve new clients who may have a grudge regarding his work or lack of results?"

"No, I can't say that any of his files would meet those criteria. He strictly works on researching oil and gas leases for wild cat firms and smaller oil companies."

"Well, thank you for your time and information, Mr. Allen. I'm sure I can reassure his sister that he his traveling for pleasure and that she should hear from him next week." He reached across his large desk and we shook hands. I walked out his office, winked at the receptionist, and then caught the elevator to the ground floor.

I walked back to my office to finish notes on a tail job for a recent divorce case I was set to testify in next week. Then I headed home.

chapter eight

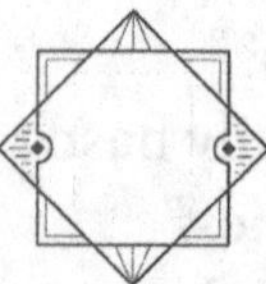

The following morning, I called the county jail to speak with the undersheriff, Brice Jackson. After two rings a crisp strong feminine voice answered, "Sheriff's office." I instantly recognized the women's distinct tone. It belonged to Jackson's girl Friday, Effie Darling. She was an attractive brunette with the energy of a locomotive, a mind like a Swiss watch, and the ability to never let a secret of the office escape her lips. She would have been desirable but for her eyes, which were cool and direct and quizzical. She controlled access to Jackson as well as a Buckingham Palace guard.

"Good morning, darling. Is Brice in?" I inquired.

"Maybe. Depends who this is," she said with an air of efficiency.

"Tell him it's Lou Nayland."

"I'm sure he's too busy to speak to a lay-about like you," she replied curtly.

I tried to project a pleasant smile through the line. "That's probably true, but could you ask him anyway?" I got no response, but heard the click of the hold button.

Roughly four minutes later, Jackson's distinct voice came on the line. "This better be important. It's too early in the morning to dance with you, Nayland."

"It may not be important, but it might be satisfying. I'm calling to buy you lunch at your favorite spot. Interested?"

Silence filled the line, broken swiftly with the sound of Jackson's distinct drawl. "We-ell, you buyin'?"

"Yeah, I'm buying." I knew he wouldn't rejected lunch at Cattlemen's. He preferred the cowboy crowd of the café to those establishments located downtown serving bankers and the oil executive crowd.

"Good," he stated. "Meet me at the café at 12:30 then." He severed the connection.

Several hours later, found myself at the Cattleman's counter listening to the old cashier's dirty jokes. When I heard the front door swing open, I peered over my shoulder and saw the undersheriff enter the café. A gust of wind carried the smell of money in behind him. He hung his white beaver felt Stetson on the chrome hat racks attached to the darkly stained wood wall then crossed the green, tiled floor of the establishment to the empty stool beside me.

Brice Jackson hailed from Muskogee, Oklahoma. I guessed him to be in his late forties. His face was the color of old leather, burned by the Oklahoma sun, and laugh crinkles radiated from the corners of his eyes which had the far-seeing expression of someone accustomed to the vast distances of the west. Straight up he climbed to 6' 5", which included two-inch heels on his hand made boots. He ran his fingers through his perfectly cropped blond hair that had just recently begun to show grey around the temples. He wore a crisp white gabardine shirt tucked with military perfection into his tan service pants. His dress and bearing, along with his chiseled facial features, reminded me of the cowboys in a Remington painting, made you think you could faintly hear a chorus of "Home on the Range" in the distance. Undersheriff Jackson was all cop. Charged with knowledge and ambition to go with it, the best police example of police efficiency we had in these parts. It's not often that you saw an official badge hobnobbing with a private dick outside the reach of the law. But Brice had the sense to know I could touch a lot of places outside the reach of the law, and he could do plenty for me that I couldn't for myself. What had started out as a modest business arrangement had turned into a solid friendship.

He lowered his large frame into the seat next to me. "Hello, private dick," he stated in his usual coolness.

"I prefer private investigator, thank you very much," I responded, rather pleased with the statement.

"Still digging into bins, revealing ladies' sins, Mr. P.I?" Jackson asked. He waved the waitress over.

The usual bleached-blond hash slinger wasn't working the counter. Today the head waitress, Mary Van Gorder, ran the shift. A German immigrant who had come to the States, with her three children, after her husband had been killed in the Battle of the Somme in 1916. Nearly six foot of Germanic womanhood, she was a real looker with sandy blonde hair, a well endowed chest, and a heart of gold. Mary took in every stray dog or waif that crossed her path. She treated them all like her own, including handsome, but slightly directionless young men, who usually gave her more trouble than the stray dogs or waifs ever did.

"Afternoon Lou," Mary said with a wink. I had done a favor for one of Mary's waifs several years back. He'd got caught shoplifting and ever since we'd had this ongoing flirtation that had never developed into consummation. But we both enjoyed the exchange.

"Hello, gorgeous. Keeping all your strays in line?" I asked.

"You know me. I'm doing my best."

Brice quietly waited for our repartee to cease before stating, in his clear southern drawl, "We'll each have sweet tea, Mary." She smiled at Brice, winked at me again, and headed down the counter to retrieve our drinks.

He lit a cigarette, took a long draw, and blew a stream of smoke toward the ceiling. "So is this just lunch, or do you have something particular on your mind?"

"Mostly just lunch, but I've a couple of questions for you after we eat."

When the last word left my lips, Mary appeared and placed the iced teas before us, gave me another wink and asked, "What are you two young men having today?"

Smiling playfully at us, Mary waited until Brice spoke up, "Could we have the lunch steaks with a side of taters, please?"

"Coming right up, boys," she replied, and walked away to turn in the order.

"It'll be a few minutes until the steaks come," Brice said as he spread his large worn hands onto the counter. "Want to cross-examine me now?".

"I'm afraid there aren't many questions, and they may just put you off your victuals, so I'd rather wait."

Brice took drag. "You probably heard they fried that killer of the Lindbergh kid, Richard Hauptmann, last Saturday."

"Good riddim's to the bastard," I responded.

Jackson nodded in agreement and finished his cigarette before stubbing it out in the tin ashtray sitting between the clear glass shakers of salt and pepper. When he stretched and leaned back, I asked him, "What's going on in your shop?"

"Just a small vice clean-up job this week. The sheriff sent me and the boys out to Miss Mandy's establishment. You know the place. It's four or five miles out on Reno, just past the old Cobb farmhouse. Got her a nice little clapboard two stories up behind a stand of blackjack trees."

"I think I know the place," I said. "She a hustlin' lady, Brice?"

"We-ell, I reckon so, but she conducts her affairs mighty decently. She ain't running it crooked, and she ain't takin' in no roustabouts or oil roughnecks. If some of these preachers around town weren't rompin' on me, I wouldn't bother her a-tall."

"Did the sheriff want her to lay off a while or move on?"

Brice scratched his head, scowled. "We-ell I dunno, Lou. He just told me to go out and size her up and make up my own mind on how to handle it. Said he would back me up whatever I did."

"What did you decide?" I asked.

"Despite her line of work I discovered she was still a lady. So I told her just to lie low until the preachers moved on to another sin." I'd have liked to have seen that conversation knowing Brice as I did. To Brice, anything in a skirt was entitled to the politeness of yes ma'am and no ma'am. Here in the Big Friendly you're a man first, a man and a gentleman, or you ain't nothin'. And God help the soul if he ain't. He went on. "She told me she understood and would go visit her mother in Topeka for a couple of weeks." Mary dropped the steaks down in front of us. Each one held a large, charred sirloin, steak stretching to the edges of the plate. The taters were deep fried to a crispy golden perfection and sat precariously on the edges of the steak, in a vain attempt to avoid falling off the plate. Mary set a basket of hot, homemade, buttered rolls between us, gave me another wink, and hurried off to her other customers.

I finished first, but remained silent, as befits two men who know each other intimately and watched the sheriff as was his habit use the last roll to clean all the steak juice from his plate, and delicately stuff it into his mouth.

Mary approached and asked, "How was it, boys?"

"If God could do better," Brice replied, "he's kept it to himself."

She skillfully stacked and picked up the plates winking at both of us in turn. When she sauntered off Jackson lit a cigarette and pulled the ashtray back in his direction, leaned back on his stool and said , "Well."

I pondered my opening question. "I'm not sure you can even help in this case, but I figure you're the best place to start, so here goes." With an embarrassed smile I began. "What do you know about the goings-on of the queer community here in the city?"

Disbelief crossed Brice's face as he shook his head at me. "Hell's fire, you've reckoned right that a question like that would plum put me off my steak."

I nodded my understanding. I knew how the sheriff felt about "Margeries" but continued on. "But do you think you can help me out?"

"Maybe," he said.

"I'll take whatever you've got."

Before speaking he took a long drag off his smoke and gazed at the assortment of pies sitting in the pie case across the counter. "To be honest, I didn't think we had any of those 'New York Nancys' down here in the Big Friendly until the other night."

"What happened the other night to change your mind?" I inquired.

"There was a beat down job in an apartment in the Southern Rooms establishment on Monday night. It looked like a killing to me."

"Why do you think it's a murder?"

"Because the victim got beat brutally to death, in his livin' room," he stated in his cold professional manner.

"Does the dead guy have a name?"

"Officially, no. We have a name to the man who took the lease, but we haven't confirmed that he is the same person we found dead on the floor."

"Interesting," I said. The tumblers in my head hadn't expected such a dramatic answer to my question and my grey matter was too slow to have a follow up inquiry.

"It appears someone jimmied a side window and concealed himself inside waitin' for the victim." Brice hesitated for a full minute. "The attack appears to have been especially violent from the wounds sustained by the corpse. Planned brutality intensifies the magnitude of a murderous act."

"Why do you think the victim was a pansy?" I caught myself stroking my chin for spots I'd missed during my morning shave.

"A feeling. Mainly deduced from how the place was decorated and some clothes we found in the closet, but mostly on something Doc said to me on his way out."

I took a sip of tea as I tried to take in what he had said. "You got any leads as to why this young man got himself killed?"

"Not a goddamn one," he stated with more than his usual intensity. "And now that you ask me about Nancies, I like the case even less. Good thing the city Bulls are handlin' it and not my office."

"The city cops got the case?"

His face reddened slightly. "Of course they do. It's within the city limits. That's why I ain't got more to give ya on it. But I'll tell you what—Doc Rowell was the one called to the scene. Might be best if you drop in on him for some answers."

"I like Doc," I said aloud. "And we've worked together before. When he's in the mood he's been helpful."

The big sheriff snuffed out his cigarette and stood up to leave. "And if I was you, I'd run uptown and get a haircut from Flatten. You need one and he's usually well dosed on the under-grounders misdeeds here abouts." He turned towards his hat and the door.

I stood up, thanked him, and then put a ten under my glass for Mary and our lunches. It was too much, but big tips seemed to be my habit this week, and I knew Mary could use it for her waifs and dogs.

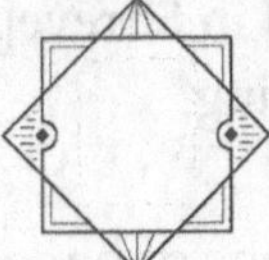

chapter nine

It was a bright, crisp spring day, just warm enough so you'd know summer was coming. After a quick shower, I slid into the coupe, inserted the key, pushed the starter, revved the engine and pulled out onto 11th Street. I pressed the pedal and pointed the Ford towards Mid-town to have breakfast at Sieber's Café.

At the counter studying the menu, a short, thin man came over to stand in front of me. The little man wiped the already clean counter with a dish rag. "Morning," he said pleasantly. "Eat a lot, will ya? I need the business."

I grinned. "How you doing, Neal?"

The day shift manager replied, "Great. How about a steak? It's a steal at two bucks."

I chuckled. "Okay. But it better be good. Throw a couple of eggs on the side and let's get started with a coffee, black."

After two cups of joe I downed a couple eggs, sunny side up, along with the two dollar steak. I propped the morning paper against the coffee pot and folded it open to the sports page where I read the latest interview of the Indian's manager concerning the upcoming season.

Niehoff Tabs Indians 'Pennant Contenders': Niehoff refuses to come out with a flat-footed claim for the 1936 pennant . "We looked exceptionally good against the Cardinals," he summed up the Tribe's appearance against the St. Louis Cardinals here

Wednesday. "Of course we were behind good pitching. That always makes a club look good. Still, the boys had a lot of spirit out there. And the way I see it, the only clubs in the league that have materially strength are Dallas and Tulsa. Dallas looked mighty powerful to me in the games we played in Shreveport. It's a question of whether the Steers have the pitching."

I put the paper aside and popped the last piece of bacon into my mouth. Still working on my second cup of coffee I became eerily aware of someone standing over me. It was Norma, the longest serving waitress at Sieber's, and she had a motherly look upon her face.

I set fire to a cigarette, snapped my Zippo closed and pocketed the lighter along with the deck of smokes back into my coat. I walked over to the coat stand and gawked back at Norma as I put on my coat, buttoned the top two buttons and slipped on my grey felt fedora. Before I slipped out the door she exclaimed, "Why, you don't even carry a gun!" Did she think she was giving me a piece of news?

I smiled. "No, no guns, no knives and no blackjack. Why should I?" In truth, the statement wasn't accurate. I did sometimes carry a sap when I thought I might find myself in a tight situation with the wrong sort of people. But that was seldom the case and saying it out loud ruined my point.

"But you're a detective—a private detective, I mean. And weren't you in a gun fight or something several months ago on the main drag of the Deuce? Sounds to me that your line of work can be dangerous."

I exhaled smoke, turning my head aside to spit a yellow tobacco flake off my lips. "It can be at times, Norma, but we don't have that many crooks here in the Big Friendly. Anyway, people are people, even when they're a little misguided. You don't hurt them, they won't hurt you. They'll listen to reason."

She shook her head, wide-eyed with awe. I strolled back to the lunch counter and put down two bucks for breakfast and a tip. Norma gave me a huge, toothy smile as I walked out to my Ford parked next to one of the City's new parking meters. I hadn't fed it when I'd gone in—for the simple reason I'd been on my personal own tax revolt since the city had installed the previous summer.

I slid in behind the wheel, kicked the starter, let it warm for a moment and then headed towards Flattens Barber shop. The sky opened up and began to wrap itself around the city with a fresh spring rain. I turned on the worn wipers only to find they were fighting a losing battle against the rain.

Parking in front of the shop on North Walker, I turned up my collar and raced the downpour to the front door. The wind and the rain blew bitter and cold, pelting the road as I hurried across the street. I grabbed the knob, and stepped in, using my back to push the door closed against the driving rain. The shop's doorbell tinkled several times as the storm clawed at the windows of the shop like an angry cat. I shook the water from my Wilton, removed my coat, and hung them both on the cast iron rack behind the door. The place was devoid of its usual suspects awaiting a cut, and the old men who dropped in to gossip and play checkers.

Flatten shook head at me under his recently cropped blonde flat top. "That's some entrance Lou. You lookin' for a cut?"

A copy of Roscoe Dunjee's Black Dispatch lay on the barber chair. I picked it up and handed it to Flatten. "Kind of revolutionary reading for an Aggie."

"You of all people should know that I like to gather my information from all quarters. Best you have a seat directly."

I dropped myself in the middle chair and sat quietly, legs crossed, while Flatten threw a barber gown over me. When it'd cleared my head, I noticed Flatten had installed a new dart board in the place. On my layover in London, returning from the Great War, I'd seen dart boards in all the pubs, but the one hanging before me now didn't appear to be the same English game. This board was about two feet square, faced with cork, with a large circle marked on it, and twenty-six radii and a smaller circle, outlined with fine wire, divided the circle's area into 52 sections. Each section had its symbol painted on it, and together they made up a deck of cards; the bull's-eye, a small disk in the corner, was the Joker. There was also a supply of darts, small cute things about four inches long and weighing a couple of ounces, crafted of wood and feathers with a metal needle-point. The same as any standard dart board.

"I see you've installed a new dart board, but it's not the one I've ever seen in pubs."

Flatten smiled at my reflection in the mirror. "It's better than that old man's game. You see on this board you stand off 10 or 15 feet, you take five darts and hurl them at the board and attempt to make a poker hand, with the Joker being wild. Up to four can play."

"Sounds like a lot of work to play a hand of poker," I said.

"True," Flatten said before continuing, "but it allows us to gamble in the open without getting hassled by the coppers."

"I'm impressed with your imagination and enterprise," I said, and meant it.

He squinted at me in the mirror while simultaneously placing a cotton sheet inside my collar and snapping it closed. "Are you here for a trim or information?"

"Can I have both?" I inquired, a smirk growing across my face.

"I suppose, but my worldly expertise no longer comes cheap. It will cost you more than last time," he replied as he pulled a comb out of the blue liquid barbicide and a pair of scissors off a barber's towel.

"I'm sure it will, because this new case is even more delicate than the last one you helped with."

He began to trim the back of my neck. "I don't see how that could be true. You almost blew all the Nobs off the hill with the last one."

I shrugged under the gown. "Maybe, but this time I'm looking for the brother of this really hot tomato. I would like to impress her with my skills."

Flatten spoke to the back of my head. "Doesn't sound to be much of a case."

I looked at his reflection in the mirror, "Her brother is a poof and that's not exactly a crowd that runs out in the open here in the Big Friendly."

"What's a poof?"

"You know, a 'Nancy' boy."

"Then why did you call him a poof?"

"It's a term I picked up in France from my Scottish clerk. He told tales that all the sailors in the Royal Navy were queer and that the Brits referred to them all as poofs. Either way, I need to know about their activities here in our dusty little town."

Flatten held his tongue for a minute as he trimmed his way around to the sides before speaking. "You're right. This might be a more delicate situation than I had initially thought." But his eyes told me he was preparing to weave me a tale. So, I relaxed and settled deeper into the chair.

But before he started, I gave him another piece of information that Miss Swalia had imparted. "I don't know if it's helpful, but my client made reference to her brother being part of the Gardenia Club. She didn't know what it was or even what it meant."

Flatten smiled a knowing smile as the last word of my sentence dropped. He continued the trim job and began to enlighten me on his knowledge of the subject. "I've heard from our young friend Danny regarding the bachelor community.

I sat up quickly and looked directly at his reflection. "Are you talking about that Irish boy who works as a butcher over at the Kamp's slaughterhouse?"

"I am."

"He's a pansy?"

Flatten nodded in the affirmative then asked, "Do you want the information, or are you going to keep interrupting me?"

"Sorry, yeah, let's hear what you got then."

"As I was saying, Danny told me a select group of our local queers refer to themselves as members of 'The Gardenia Club.'" He went on to explain that Danny and his associates had established this secret society, lifting the term from a line in the Dash Hammett novel titled The Maltese Falcon.

"You mean that hard-boiled detective novel about a bejeweled bird or something?" I replied.

"Yep. And from what Danny says, the story line has multiple queer characters running through the entirety of the book."

"Guess I should buy a copy and read it more carefully" I stated.

"Maybe you should. Anyway, Danny tells me that there's a villainous character in the book by the name of Joel Cairo. When he appears in the detective's office and presents his business card to Sam Spade's secretary, she sniffs it and declares with an air of unspoken knowledge, "Gardenia," and then hands it to Sam Spade. Then a meticulously dressed, highly effeminate Joel Cairo appears with perfectly coiffed hair, manicured nails and a slender walking cane."

"Wonder how the author slipped that by the editor's censors?" I exclaimed.

Flatten shrugged. "Danny also told me that this Spade character is basically anti-queer, and that it is an underlying sub-plot throughout the whole book. But that's not really relevant to your question is it? Anyway, the local boys picked up on the Cairo character and now call themselves members of the Gardenia Club as an inside joke."

"Not sure that's all that helpful because I doubt they go around our fair city announcing their membership. What else have you got for me?"

Flatten unsnapped the gown collar and straight razored my neck as he continued. "I've gathered from Danny that the queer community here in the city is mostly made up of clock punching blokes working as bank clerks, city employees, restaurant workers and general laborers. They frequent the downtown rooming houses and hotels along Grand Avenue and Broadway which cater to long term tenants of single men." I didn't interrupt him with questions, but let him weave his ongoing tale of information. "From what I've been told, the most popular is the Grand Hotel. You know the one —it's run by that Greek immigrant named of George Tramejon." I nodded in acknowledgment and he went on. "Seems the Grand has the highest concentration of these bachelors and they use the in-house coffee shop to meet and socialize."

"Is that the only place these men stay or meet?"

He filled a large horse brush with powder and proceeded to dust down the back of my neck. "No, there's also the Victoria Hotel on South Broadway, along with the Southern Rooms around the corner. Then there's the New Empire Rooms above Oban Chester Patterson's casino. Apparently, a fair number of them rent rooms upstairs and frequent the casino with their playmates most Thursday nights. Also, the Century rooms on Front Street, as well as the tearoom at the Biltmore Hotel, but I didn't get the impression from Danny that the queers stay in the Biltmore long term. He said most of their crowd only goes to the hotel's tearoom for Saturday's breakfast special."

"That's a start." I lifted myself up from the chair and handed David a Lincoln for the cut and the information.

When I headed toward my coat and hat, he added, "I think you should talk to Danny himself, but he won't be very forthcoming if you approach him at work. Let me give him a call and see if I can arrange a meeting somewhere he feels comfortable."

"That would be helpful, thanks," I said. I pulled the door open and the bell tinkled overhead.

"Tell you what. Give me a call at about 5 o'clock and I'll see what I can do."

"Thanks again, and I'll call you at five." The rain had stopped and there was a parking ticket under the windshield wiper. I pulled it off in disgust, registered the cops name that had issued it and stuck it in the glove compartment. More time wasted in police court. I sat there a minute, hands on the wheel, then started up the powerful V-6 motor. I decided I would head over to Doc Rowell's office to see if he had anything on the murdered kid Brice had told me about. I needed to kill time before I called Flatten back for a time and place for my meeting with Danny O'Brien.

chapter ten

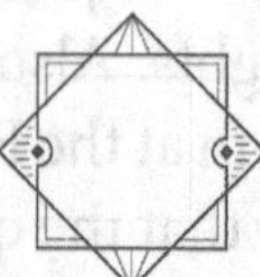

Rays of sunlight danced across the dashboard of my little green Ford as I pulled into a parking spot next to Doc Rowell's art deco white stucco office building, located on the southwest corner of Harvey and 10th Street. I walked to the rear door and knocked.

Waiting there, I recalled what I knew of Doc Rowell. Though he was only thirty years old, the medical community held him in high regard. Due largely to the fact he possessed the hands of a great virtuoso, both on the piano and in surgery. It was also said, within the criminal element about town, that he was the man to see if you accidently acquired a gunshot wound and hoped to see the sun rise again. Along with the added benefits of his service and silence, he charged a reasonable price.

The heavy steel door finally opened, and Dr. Steve Rowell's rugged face appeared and a questioning smile of recognition crossed his lips. "Lou, what are you doing here?"

"I have a couple of questions about a stiff I heard you are currently working on. His death might be connected to a case I'm investigating," I stated professionally.

"Come on in. If I'm not mistaken I think, I have your guy on the table right now. I was about to start the initial autopsy. So grab a seat inside and we'll talk as I work, if that works for you."

Though I'd been in Doc's autopsy room before, it still gave me the willies. I walked past the sheet covered corpse stretched out on the slab to a small stool at the head of the table. I sat and stuck my legs out straight in front of me, crossing my ankles. My eyes wandered over the steel countertops, the glass-fronted cabinets with their clear glass containers, the hanging scale, and a tray of surgical devices on a wheeled stand. The doctor had installed a special ventilation fan to help deal with the more odoriferous dead; floaters, jumpers, and those exposed to the elements for extended periods. The fan had little effect, though. The room smelled of antiseptic and death, with a sweet underlying aroma of blood.

Doc grabbed his lab coat, gloved up, and approached the cold metal slab. He pulled the sheet off the now lifeless body. I pushed the stool closer to the slab to get an unobstructed view of the corpse. The body lay naked and though its wounds were extensive, they appeared less so since the entire body had been washed by Doc's assistant. The face was horribly damaged with multiple wounds. The damage to his head was obscured by his jet-black hair and his torso was marred only by the deepening mottling of the skin. My throat went dry.

Doc took advantage of my presence to a lecture on autopsies. "See Lou, a systematic, thorough inspection and evaluation of the decedent should be performed by a forensic medical expert. And it must always begin at the top of the subject's body, then move towards the feet, to avoid the possibility of missing injuries or evidence." He rattled on as he painstakingly examined the deceased's hair searching for fibers or other trace evidence. He then picked up his scalpel from the tray and began to skin back the scalp, working with the calm efficiency of someone who had handled countless corpses.

As he began to cut, I thought, This is a mistake. I'm not sure I want to watch this. But, trapped by my own appalling fascination, I remained rooted to the spot.

Doc continued. "See here?" He pointed to a spot on the back of the head and paused as if expecting an answer. Getting none, plunged on. "There's a shallow track angled downward from the skull base toward a gash overlying the third and fourth cervical vertebrae as well as multiple areas on the skull with impact blows to the front and back."

I swallowed with difficulty. "What's that tell you, Doc?"

"It suggests blunt force trauma, but let's not jump ahead of ourselves," He examined the other wounds on the back of the victim's head. "Now look here," he said to no one in particular. He pulled the scalp back, continuing with his lecture. "On the ectocranial surface of the right parietal, there's a classic example of a depressing fracture. Concave center with emitting cracks outward." Doc picked up a hand lens and looked closer. "Aah," he said, "I was mistaken. It's not a single depressed fracture but rather multiple. If you look closely, there are two points of impact."

My stomach turned slightly. "I'll take your word for it."

Doc shook his head in amusement and went on." I see now that the fracture radiating up from the secondary impact ran up to, but didn't cross, the fractures diffusing from the first."

"So?" I questioned.

"Follow along, Nayland," he rebuked. "It means there were two or more blows to the back of the head."

"Can you determine what he was struck with?"

"From the size and shape of the concavity, something cylindrical, like a tool handle or a heavy pipe." He used both hands to rotate the body so it was now facing up then continued his lecture. "This was a real beating. See the damage to the nasal-maxillary region?" I nodded, though I wasn't really looking. "That's extremely extensive. The bones are shattered below the nose and the teeth are virtually obliterated." He then rolled the corpse onto its side with some effort. Most people don't realize that dead men are heavier than a broken heart. "There are no injuries on his torso or lower extremities," he concluded.

Doc walked to the steel sink, removed his gloves, tossed them into the stainless metal sink and began to wash his hands. When he had dried them, he turned and said, "It appears our young man here was the victim of a very personal and violent act. Almost vicious beyond reason."

"In what way?" I asked.

In a firm, clear voice, he said, "This is no breaking and entering job gone badly. This was an intentional, hideous act done by a person with true malice of the heart."

"And you determined that how?" I inquired.

"It's the repeated blows to the head, especially to the face and mouth area. That's usually a sign of a very personal and vengeful assault. I believe it was specifically intended to be disfiguring. Textbooks suggest it's a tendency mostly seen in cases that involve a woman assailant or gay men. Whether that guideline is applies to this case, I couldn't say at this time. Either way this is no random act of violence. It's clearly an act carried out by a premeditated, cold blooded murderer."

A buzzer sounded somewhere from the front of the building, so Doc excused himself. I stepped over to the desk in the corner and borrowed Doc's phone to call Flatten back. David picked up on the second ring. "Flatten, Nayland here. What did you get for me?" He told me he had caught up with O'Brien and that he agreed to meet me tomorrow morning in the coffee shop of the Biltmore Hotel at 9:30. I thanked him, hung up, and waited for Doc to reappear.

When he did so, he walked over and covered the corpse with a white sheet and asked, "Need anything else?"

"Do we know who he was?"

"Officially he's a John Doe. Unofficially we believe his name is Denny Galligan. At least that's the name found on an Oklahoma City driver's license, issued three months ago. The coppers found it inside a wallet lying on a dresser inside the apartment." Doc picked up the clipboard off the surgical stand and read out loud. "The ID said he was twenty seven years old, five foot ten, black hair with brown eyes, a hundred and seventy-five pounds." Doc eyed the corpse lying under the sheet. "I'd say he fits the description."

"I think you're right," I said.

Doc seemed to hesitate, like he had more to say. "And I'll tell you something else, something I won't put into my report, nor will I disclose it to the police, unless I'm forced too of course."

"What, Doc?"

"It concerns a piece of evidence I discovered on my initial examination of the young man," he stated with seriousness. "The young man was sexually active, very active. And not with women, if you catch my drift."

"That's interesting, but are you sure he wasn't forced?" I questioned.

"Not that I can see. At least not recently." His tone dropped. "Seems he was an enthusiast."

"Queer?" I exclaimed.

"I prefer the term rantipole myself, and don't knock it until you've tried it, Nayland. I've heard rumors of some stevedores that will treat you like a princess here in our own little city." He grinned before adding, "I have one last thing that might interest you, something that won't appear in the newspaper."

"What's that, Doc?"

"Our victim lived long enough to write something with his own blood on the floor. Ora pro nobis!"

"Now you're over my head. What's it mean?"

He lowered his head like an exhausted bull. "It's Latin for pray for us. Now and in the hour of our death…"

I sat stunned momentarily. "Thanks Doc, that's something to go on. By the way do we know what time he may have died?"

His professional demeanor returned. "From the rigor of the body when I came on to the scene, I would guess sometime between 11:00 pm and 1:00 am the night of."

"That might be helpful. I appreciate your time, your honesty, and your trust. I owe you one," I told him as we shook hands and I left him to his practice.

I sat in my car thinking, and I was relieved I wouldn't have to call Nancy and tell her that her brother was dead. I had been present for such conversations. I knew the look. The pleading eyes. Tell me this is a mistake. A bad dream. Make it end. Say it isn't so. Then, comprehension. And in a microsecond, their world changed forever.

I pushed the starter on the car and headed towards Front Street. Flatten had accidently dropped me a lead without even knowing it.

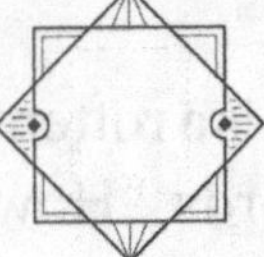

chapter eleven

It was 7:00 pm, the start of the day for most of the casino regulars. I walked down the cast iron steps along the backside of an apparently lower-end boarding house located just off Reno and Front Street into the New Empire Casino situated in the basement. The fat cats of the city liked the New Empire and made it successful. They came for the good food, mostly honest games, beautiful women, and drinks that weren't watered down.

The building's exterior's disguise didn't reflect the interior's design. The clip joint was one of the finest upscale gambling dens to be found in the city. It was owned by a local shyster by the name of Oban Chester Patterson, the undisputed King of the Underworld. Since the teens, Patterson and his democratic political friends had held a virtual monopoly on bootlegging, gambling, prostitution, and narcotics in the Big Friendly. He collected his percentages in the form of monthly "retainers" for legal services from all the associated operators of bars, betting joints, restaurants, and rooming houses.

I pushed my way through the large steel door. Terry Baltes came forward to meet me. Terry was dressed in a black pinstriped suit, it didn't improve his appearance. He looked like a misshapen wrestler with his big shoulders, long arms, short legs and the meanest face in mid-town. His appearance was not aided by the solid row of gold teeth decorating his upper jaw. His job was bar entry, or exit, with the simple touch of the electric footswitch that locked the sturdy metal door at any hint of trouble.

"Hi, sleuth." Baltes made a career of insulting people. His bull-like bray was enough to scare off the usual riff-raff.

I grinned and grasped his lumpy shoulder with real affection. "How's Terry tonight?"

"Lousy. Entertaining the low-rollers like you is a rotten business." His gold gleamed in a grin which belied his words. "How you like? It's new." He stroked the lapels of the pinstriped suit.

"It looks the part," I said.

He clasped my hand. Shook it with enthusiasm and told me he had to get back to his post.

As for robbing the place, I concluded it would take eight good men and they would certainly have to kill Terry and at least one or two more employees to succeed. But then decided you probably couldn't find eight non-squealing killers in the Big Friendly to do such a job.

I continued to scan the crowd when I caught sight of Spider Erion approaching me from a row of flashing slots. Spider, well known in the city as a punter par excellence and the possessor of an inexhaustible fund of racing yarns, is one of those few and very fortunate individuals who possess the best of everything in life. I'm always impressed with the man who can make a living out of gambling.

"Hi-yah, Lou."

"Hi-yah Spider," I said cheerfully.

"How come I haven't seen you around, Lou?"

"I've been around. Where have you been?"

Spider lowered his voice. "I ain't been around."

"No?"

"I've been in stir. I was a victim of circumstances. The District Attorney framed me, not knowing I was guilty. Ain't that a coincidence?"

"Yeah, a coincidence. Care for a drink?"

"Nah. I got to meet the wife to see a movie. Maybe next time. Be seeing you, Lou."

"See ya, Spider," I replied and started down the steps.

When I stepped onto the casino floor a familiar voice rang out from the closest poker table. "Hi-yah, Lou." It was an old buddy of mine by the name of Jay Weber who ran the local car garage. Most people who "knew" him called him Webs. To call him anything other than this moniker was to put him on cautionary alert until he was able to vet you properly.

"Evening boys," I replied.

"Come on, Lou!" Big Paulie yelled out. "We've been holding a chair for you."

I sat down in the only straight back chair open at the table, while tapping Jay on the shoulder and asking, "How are they running, Webs?"

"They've been running by me all day, Lou. What's the bet?"

"You stopped a couple, didn't ya."

"Two bits to you, Webs," Paulie said.

"Well, I'll give you a definite answer to any inquiry along those lines as soon as I see Mr. Wiegal's hold card." Webs threw his bet in. "I call."

"Pair of kings up," Joe yelled out boldly, throwing his cards on the table for all to be impressed.

Webs laughed. "I don't believe that beats three sixes, now does it." He grinned triumphantly at Weigal and then around the table.

Jay scooped up the kitty. "Say, you wouldn't happen to hold any markers on me?"

"Oh, yeah," I replied and reached into my vest pocket for the roll of markers I always carried. Like my father, I was generally unlucky in the game of love, but I played a hell of a hand of poker.

"Look at that. The man holds markers on everyone in town."

"Webs, I've got you for $27.00, $45.00 and $105.00."

"I'll take the $27.00 and the $45.00 and you put the $105.00 back in your bank." Webs peeled off the bills to reclaim his markers. "Thanks, Lou. Always a pleasure doing business with ya."

"No problem, Webs," I stood up from the table, pushed the bills down in my pocket and strode towards the well-stocked bar and ordered a scotch and soda. I leaned on the bar and listened to the platoons of slots getting steady play in the background.

Their whirr-clunk, thunk-clatter dominated the sounds of the big main room. There's a 1 in 2400 chance of hitting the jackpot and those odds remained the same on the first pull as well as the last. Real gamblers never played them. They were installed mostly to entertain the wives of the high rollers who played the games of chance that provided better odds to its participants.

And the best odds for the serious gambler was, of course, the craps tables, where the house held only a two percent advantage over the rollers. Under the noise of the slots, I could make out the chant of the croupiers. I stopped near the craps pit and nodded to the stick-man, a guy called Swift Tony. Every house-run crap game in the world has a stickman, and just about every stickman uses a curved stick to return the dice to the shooter. I'd known Tony ever since I got him out of a scrape involving a bad marriage to a grifter.

Anyone with common sense knew Patterson made his money by from the house percentage from the tables, not by dishy dames in bright costumes and black mesh stockings shagging drinks to the patrons. If luck turned in a gambler's favor, the house had guys like Tony to help keep the money in house. Tony simply comes in with his stick, and with sleight of hand, switches out the roller's dice for two loaded ones, ensuring the high roller doesn't leave Oban Patterson's place with all his winnings.

This evening it, however, it appeared that Tony was running the game somewhat honestly. I lifted my chin in recognition just as I caught a glimpse of Jackson's girl Friday, Effie Darling, sitting at the roulette table. I watched several turns of the wheel. She appeared to be winning by playing a progressive system on red. Watching her push her bet onto the numbered squares let me know Miss Darling understood the game.

The most important thing to remember when playing roulette is that the game begins afresh each time the croupier picks up the ivory ball with his right hand, gives the four spokes of the wheel a controlled twist clockwise with the same hand and, with a third motion, also with the right hand, flicks the ball round the outer rim of the wheel against the spin of the wheel. All this ritual and all the mechanical minutiae of the wheel, of the numbered slots and the cylinder, had been devised and perfected over the years so that neither the skill of the croupier, nor any bias in the wheel, could affect the fall of the ball. And yet it is a convention among roulette players to take careful note of the history of each session and to be guided by any peculiarities in the run of the wheel. It appeared Miss Darling was also rigidly adhering to such practices as she made notes on a small white napkin under her elbow. I smiled pleasantly at her when she turned her head from the table and eyed me crossing the floor towards the finely carpeted stairs to the private club on the second floor.

Stepping onto the lush carpet of the Press Club I noticed a small bar and a dozen tables with brightly upholstered chairs around each. Unlike down, the room didn't have a slot machine or any kind of gambling. The club was a private operation run by oilmen, politicians, and newspaper men for themselves and a few others who were willing to pay for the privilege. But according to Flatten the Press Club is also used by the better educated and socially acceptable pansies of uptown to meet, greet, and indulge. My dues were paid by a former client who said my fee wasn't enough for what I'd done for him. He had thrown in a five year membership, paid up, as a bonus.

I took a booth in the corner so I could observe everyone that came up or down the stairs and who they may meet. I gestured to the bar boy. He wore a version of the staff's standard white shirt under a black vest with matching pants. The kid was maybe fourteen, towheaded and skinny, with slanting shoulders. And like a Labrador puppy, his feet were too big for the rest of him. "Whaddaya need, mister?"

"Go fetch me a racing form, son."

The lad's large blue eyes tried to look crafty. "What's in it for me?"

I flipped him a quarter for the form and another for the boy's efforts." He palmed it expertly before dashing off. I sang out, "And tell the bartender a scotch and soda." He veered and stopped by the bar for a split second.

As the waiter placed my scotch and soda on the table I noted that all the men sitting at the bar appeared to be Ethel's. When he stepped back behind the bat I observed a reddish-blond haired man step up from the stairs. I instantly recognized he resembled Paige Swalia in the photo I carried. He wore a dapper tan pinstripe double breasted suit and well polished brown shoes. He had slicked his hair back but his resemblance to his sister, Nancy was unmistakable. The well-groomed ginger scanned the room then walked over to the bar, sat on a bar stool and ordered a drink. He appeared lost in his own thoughts.

◁◎▷

The dashing bartender is very handsome and fit, but he isn't really my type, thought Paige. He assumes I'm attracted to him simply because he is keen. The bartender sauntered over with my sidecar, placed it before me, and winked. I didn't respond. I gave him no response as I observed how poorly the room was lit, presumably on purpose. I scanned the room for possible entertainment for the evening. The guy sitting on the bar stool to my left looked under-aged and out of place. He smiled in my direction. I didn't reciprocate. I'm attracted only to older men. No need to mislead the youngster. But after his initial gawk and hesitative, the kid actually cruised me with his eyes. I gave him a hard cold stare and he quickly turned and walked away with his drink.

The gentlemen on my right seemed much more interesting, even though I hadn't caught his face. He was in a fairly intense conversation with the man next to him and all I could see was the great shock of silver-grey hair covering his head. His shoulders were wide and his waistline was perfect as far as I was concerned-- not fat and not fit. A small paunch had begun to creep over his belt, and the butt on the stool had begun to spread on its own. Just my type.

But after calling good-bye to the bartender he stood up and left with his companion after. The voice, a relaxed baritone, sent a wave of excitement through the length of my body. I cursed my luck as I watched him leave the bar. Damn, not even a glimpse of his face, I thought and signaled for another drink.

Sitting alone, with half a drink, I felt uneasy. Like I was being watched. And not for the reason I had come to the club. I studied the room until I caught the eye of rough looking gentlemen sitting in the corner booth, staring intently at me. I didn't feel excitement from this attention. I felt danger. I set my drink down and, without appearing to rush, stepped away from the bar and headed down the stairs as if going to the toilet.

◁○▷

I sipped my scotch and watched the interaction at the bar over the top of my racing form in as casual a manner as I could muster. But the ginger-haired youth suddenly peered over his shoulder and stared directly into my eyes. He quickly set his drink down, slid off the bar stool and disappeared down the stairs. I jumped out of the booth, threw a handful of bills on the table, and practically ran across the room to the stairs. By the time I reached the ground floor with its dazzling sounds and lights, the red-haired man I believed to be, was now nowhere in sight.

"Why did he run?" I wondered. He was no man on holiday. That was clear. And what if it had really been Paige? Why was he so high-strung? What kind of rotten little game had he gotten himself into?

I needed to find him. And before whatever he had stepped into beat me to him. Well, I wouldn't solve it now. I needed some sleep.

chapter twelve

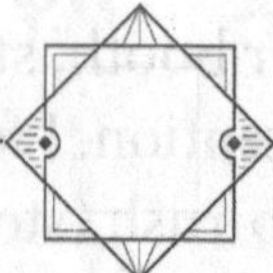

Some time after 8 p.m., I cut across town to my apartment on Northwest 11th Street. The darkness of the night had swept across the city when I pulled into the driveway leading to the parking lot in the rear. I locked the car and walked briskly towards the rear entrance of the two-story brick building I called home. The moon, enlarged and blurred by small swirls of clouds, hung heavy in the night sky. I was struck by the beauty and peace of the night.

When the back door clicked shut, I heard my landlady, Mrs. Giannasi huff as she stared scornfully out her door.

"Evening ma'am," I said in a pleasant tone.

"Buonasera, piccolo bambino malvagio," sang from her lips as she slammed the door on me. I started up the back steps. I figured I had said something to offend her. Either that or one of my clients had tracked me down and had pestered the old bird until she had driven them away by means of a broom handle. She wrongly believed that all my clients were felons.

As I neared the door to my apartment, I noticed that it appeared to be slightly ajar. Light from an interior lamp threw beams through the cracks of the door, creating an artistic pattern across the carpet of the hallway. Inside the light revealed my very small, very comfortable looking flat that I'd made into home by my simply desire to have a home. The furniture was inexpensive, the rug well worn in the center, the pictures on the wall simple photos of baseball players in different field activities and the curtains sun faded. But aside from a stain on the arm of a couch, a damp spot in the corner of the ceiling and mustiness that was part of the building itself, my small cluster of rooms were clean, warm and flooded with livableness.

I reached for my sap inside my waistband. In my weariness, I hadn't realized I had slipped it back into the glove box before coming in. Ear to the door I heard the distant sound of running water. I quietly pushed the door open. No one appeared. I slipped in and wrapped my hands around the Louisville slugger I kept next to the door. The sound of running water ceased as I crept closer towards the bedroom door, spread my legs into a professional stance, and cocked the bat over my right shoulder.

When the bedroom door began to open slowly, I tightened my grip around the wood of the bat and cocked it higher. Suddenly Irene appeared in the frame of the door.

"Hello, darling. Am I interrupting your batting practice?"

I now realized why Mrs. Giannasi had scowled and cussed me downstairs. I stood there looking foolish with the slugger still cocked over my head, but made a vain attempt to appear relaxed and under control. I dropped the bat softly onto the couch and asked, "What's on your poor little 14 carat mind tonight?"

Her evening gown was of smoky-grey chiffon that drifted weightlessly about her. The negligee was artfully fashioned to conceal much of the bare flesh, yet with each sinuous movement of the body, it revealed flashing glimpses of the beauty that was there. Tall and slender, legs long, she had the breasts of youth—high, exciting, and pushing against the neckline of her gown. She was a true Sheba. She advanced slowly, with tentative steps, looking at me with her cool brown eyes that were both shy and probing. Her sun bathed face was woefully incapable of serious guile and betrayed her ever thought and emotion. It was a face that laid her heart bare for all to see, that revealed a temperament that was at once innocent and devilish, fun loving and worrisome, faithful and—what? Not faithful and unfaithful. No, it sparkled with the unmistakable hint of unreasonable loyalty.

These thoughts danced in my head as she came close enough

to make her perfume effective. The scent assailed me, making me more conscious of her basic femaleness than I could remember. Making me more aware of my own manhood, then she threw herself at me like a medium fast pitch, high and inside, her voice low and resonant in the silence of the room. "You know, it's Friday night."

I wiped the stupid look off my face and asked, "Friday?"

She wiggled from my grasp. "Yes, it's meeting night in my social circle—St. Luke's Women's Choir, the garden club and the Salvation Army's potluck fundraiser for veterans of this and that—sooo, no friends left. That is except for my staunch friend Nayland."

"Look, Irene baby. Just because I ahh…"

"I know. Just because brave, private detective Lou put someone's horrible husband in the hoosegow, where he died after being shivved by some inmate, is no reason that we should see each other all the time." Irene paused and smiled. "But mister, there's a reason, a big reason. You see, I like you. A lot. Especially on Fridays. I'm not being too bold, am I?"

I shook my head no. Because in my thirty-plus years in the world, I'd never learned to understand women. No reason I should start now.

"And I did call, both here and at your office. You weren't in all day."

"That didn't discourage you?" I asked.

She shook her head in the negative, and deliberately did things with her body like I was the supreme test of her ability as woman. "If I can't have you, I'll take the doorstep."

"Friday," I replied.

"Yes, Fridays. Now do you want me to serve you some dinner?"

"Sounds good to me."

Irene glided into the kitchen and swung open the door to the refrigerator. "Why don't you mix us a couple of drinks while I finish the pasta sauce." Her eyes, I noticed, were a little too bright, and her cheeks were flushed. She must have had a duo of drinks alone while waiting for my return.

I unlaced my shoes and kicked them off before stepping to the bar cart. When I'd accomplished making the scotch and sodas I said, "You look as beautiful as the dream I had about you the other night." Actually, that dream had been about Nancy, but why spoil what would be a pleasant night together. "Can we eat now?" I asked as I handed her the drink.

"We have plenty of time for these, and maybe one more before the pasta is ready," she replied. "What happened? In the dream?"

"When I tried to reach you, I rolled out of bed. I woke up."

"You made that up," she said calmly. "You never dream about me."

"No," I agreed. "But I might have, mightn't I?"

She turned back to the kitchen, put aside her half-finished drink and stirred the sauce. I knew that I had hurt her and there was no satisfaction in the knowledge. It was like getting mad and striking one's fist against a wall. You could make a dent, all right, but it was your knuckles that bled.

I said nothing, which is usually my only defense when arguing with Irene. I just walked around the room, trying not to think, and just enjoy my first drink of the evening. When I'd made several laps around the room and downed the remainder of my drink, I walked to the cart bar and made myself another. "You know," I finally said. "I think I might enjoy you being my Friday girl."

Irene swished out of the little kitchen and boldly exclaimed, "I never doubted you would." The smile had returned to her lips. "Make me another drink please."

There had been plenty of other women before Irene, but she was the first who didn't object to my way of life. She never questioned a request, but you never know, I told myself while sipping on my drink. Women have been making fools of men ever since Eve opened the first fruit stand.

I took out drinks into the kitchen and helped Irene spoon the sauce over the pasta. When we sat down, I noticed my little friend, the spider, spinning a new web in the corner of the ceiling. It was part of his ongoing battle with my landlady. She would dust away his beautiful design each morning and he would spend the nights reconstructing it. The refrigerator made a whirring noise in the corner, and water dripped uneasily in the sink from a leaky faucet that I had never got around to fixing. The clock on the kitchen wall ticked. The ice cubes melted. Time moved on in silence before Irene asked impatiently, "What should we talk about, Lou?" It seemed as if the silence between us made her uncomfortable and she would like to dispel it.

"How about baseball?" I asked. She gave me a dirty look. I did not look up from my plate of pasta as I took a spoonful of macaroni covered in the rich sauce while holding it away from me so the sauce dropped back to the plate instead of onto my slacks. When I swallowed, I tried again. "I got a new client today."

She took another sip of sweet liquor. "That might be interesting."

"A woman hired me to find her brother."

"That doesn't sound very interesting."

"Her brother is a poof," I added.

"Now that's something you don't hear every day." She finished her last bite and watched me intently.

I felt a surge of satisfaction at having told her something interesting for a change. Irene rarely enjoyed hearing about any of my cases. Her interest was pleasing and, strangely, her reaction brought her a little closer to me. So I went on. "From what my new client said and what I gathered from Flatten, there is a fairly large underground community here in our sleepy little burg. They appear to reside mostly in the 3rd Ward and frequent the rooming houses in the area."

During a lull in my tale, we placed our dishes in the sink and proceeded to the living room. I turned on the radio and refreshed our drinks before I sank into the couch, draping one leg over its fellow. Irene's gown strap fell as she gathered her lithe limbs under her in a manner of cat and awaited further details of my story. I set down my drink, grabbed my lighter and lit a cigarette before I filled her in on what little I had learned so far. I told her how the young gay crowd referred to themselves as members of the Gardenia Club and that they had lifted the idea from a booked called The Maltese Falcon. My details of the case were exhausted in fifteen minutes.

Finishing the last of my drink, I couldn't help noticing the yellow cone of light thrown by the lamp made Irene's her dark face look lovely and eager. I put my arms around he. The sheer softness of the negligee slid beneath my fingers. I ran my fingers through her tawny brown hair and squeezed her gently as she put her head against my cheek. She leaned back slightly so her somber eyes fastened themselves on me, intent and warm as I clasped her hand as I felt the moist heat of her lips against my shoulder. The warm, moist touch of her lips against my skin was the only invitation I needed.

I pulled her tightly to my body, my heart pounding, and bent my mouth to hers. At the contact of our lips, her body became alive against me—moving, writhing—as if it were not directed by her mind but had volition of its own. When our lips parted Irene went docile when I lifted her off the couch and carried her to bed, feeling the tremors starting again through my body as I lowered her into bed, watching as she slid the negligee from her shoulders and down her curved legs, while I undressed. I shut the door behind us as the rise of a mournful refrain from the distant trees filled the apartment.

Then, she was close to me, surprising me with her passion, the savagery of her hunger, her movements, and her caress. The moist heat of her lips burned against my shoulder, her teeth against my skin, and her fingernails against my back, digging, hurting. Then she slide her hand to my cheek, her body arched, strained, and suddenly, in one swift movement, her nails tore across my cheek.

The shock and pain left me speechless. For a moment, I said nothing. Did nothing. Then moved quickly away from her, one hand against my cheek where I felt a warm stickiness there. I fumbled for a handkerchief from my pants on the floor. "Christ , Irene," I said. "What the devil was that for?" I stopped speaking and pressed the handkerchief to my cheek.

She looked up at me and said softly, her voice tight, "I'm sorry, Lou.Believe me, I am. I couldn't help it. It's been so long, and I've missed you, I just didn't think. I'm truly sorry, Lou, it won't happen again. I was just lost in the moment. Please come back to bed."

I nodded in understanding and fell back into bed and kissed her.

chapter thirteen

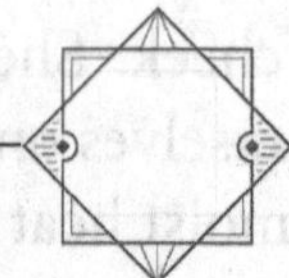

Nancy paced back and forth nervously in the darkened room, peering at a little jeweled gold locket on a thick gold chain. Unfolded, the locket showed miniature photographs, each picture under a thin glass plate. On the left was the cracked, faded portrait of a handsome swarthy man with piercing, soulful eyes, dressed in the high starched collar and cravat of the turn of the century. The photograph across from her father's was a young woman, who Nancy knew had flaming red hair like her own. It, too, had been amateurishly cut with nail scissors to fit the oval frame. Its size prevented much detail.

Decisively, Nancy closed the locket and hung it back around her neck, her mind still racing. Mama had called earlier in the evening, worried that Paige didn't make his usual Sunday night phone call. Mama kept repeating, "Nan, you go check on him for me, promise?"

"Yes, Mama, I will tomorrow," Nancy said, trying to alleviate her mama's fears but she knew that something was terribly wrong. Smoking her cigarette, Nancy realized she needed to quit. She could lose her job at the university library if anyone found out. But when stressed, nothing calmed her quicker than the long smooth drags on her favorite ciggies.

When Paige moved to Oklahoma City, his once secret life slowly exposed itself. When they were children, Nancy knew Paige seemed different from all the other boys in town. Family and friends called him sensitive, soft spirited, a mama's boy. But crueler words were used by the neighbor kids and our cousins—a Nancy, Nellie, a wimp, a pussy, . . . a fag. Nancy hated all these terms. She heard them time after time as the school yard bullies pummeled them at Paige before they pelted him with rocks and fists. More than once she stepped in to save his hide, sometimes even fighting his battle for him.

When she started high school, she rode to school with her best friend Janet. Her dad worked at the bank and "it was no trouble to take the little ones to school. This way they arrive fresh as daisies." But Paige had to walk the long two miles to school by himself. Nancy worried about him. She often badgered her tender sibling to tell her if anyone was hurting him. He would come through the screen door, clothes dirty, sometimes his knees torn or buttons missing from his shirts. Nancy would beg him to tell her what had happened. But Paige always sullenly replied, "Everything's fine. Leave me alone. I can take care of myself."

But Nancy knew better.

One day she returned from school to a quiet house. Paige hadn't made it home yet, which was odd. He usually beat her to the farm and was already doing chores when she arrived. But when she entered the empty house, dread crept over her. Something was wrong.

"Paige, Paige, are you here?" No answer. The dogs danced around her feet, their water bowl empty. That was unlike Paige. He doted on their two collies, often treating them more like younger brothers than cattle dogs. She ran up the stairs, the hounds hot on her heels. Crashing through his bedroom door, Nancy saw his bed was still made, and no book bag hung from his desk chair. "Paige, this isn't funny. Where are you?" she hollered through the empty house. "Paige?"

Nancy had run out to the barn, calling his name. Paige wasn't there. The chickens hadn't been fed. Nancy then hurried down the lane to where Paige walked home from the school bus stop. The dogs ran ahead of her, tails wagging, and then they stopped. The two collies streaked toward the big oak tree down by the fork in the road. A pack of boys, huddled beneath the tree, chanted something. Nancy couldn't hear them clearly at first, but then she heard the ugly words of "Pussy, pussy, meow meow. . . Come on down you pussy." The boys were throwing rocks at something in the branches. Nancy looked up, and there she saw Paige, trapped, scared, and bleeding.

Something inside her broke. She ran, screaming, "Get away from him! Leave him alone!" Nancy flew into the pack of bullies, arms flailing and punching anyone within reach.

From above, she heard Paige's sobs from above, begging her. "Naaaancccy! Go away. Leave please!" His cries unleashed a cold fury in her.

Just then she one of the boys grabbed her, pinning her arms behind her back. The world went quiet. Their venom at Paige interrupted, they focused on her and her budding teenage body. As one of them reached out to touch her soft breasts pushing against her cotton blouse, the collies began snapping and biting at the young teens.

One of them screamed when Rufus took a good bite of his ass.

"Fucking dog, I'm going to kill you!" the kid yelled. Frisky bit the ankle of another and the two border collies created a protective circle around Nancy and the tree, teeth bared and snapping. The unruly teens fell away, cursing and threatening to kill Paige and Nancy.

After several minutes, Paige felt safe enough to scramble down from the tree. The siblings wrapped their arms around each other, both engulfed in tears. His nose was bloody and Paige was covered in welts and the early stages of bruises. He wiped away Nancy's tears, brushing her hand away from his battered face. His jeans torn, Paige realized how much danger he was in.

Nancy never forgot that day. Mortified by seeing her two children in tatters, Mama wanted to call the sheriff. But Papa said no. Mama protested, but Papa stormed out of the house and went to the barn. Nancy knew he hid his bottle of whiskey out there. Mama was a devout Pentecostal and allowed no liquor in the house. But Papa liked his drink. And when he drank, he got mean. The children dreaded these times. If they were lucky Papa passed out in the stables, bottle by his side. Some nights though, Papa roared through the house like a man possessed. This was one of those nights.

The darkened house creaked in the wind. A soft breeze blew through the window. The constant chirping of the crickets filled the night air. As Nancy lay in her bed, she heard Mama pacing the floor downstairs. The silence was broken by daddy's drunken tirade as he crossed the yard. Suddenly screen door screeched as daddy nearly pulled it off its hinges, cursing at its flimsy frame. Nancy heard Mama trying to shush daddy. "Henry, quiet down. The children are sleeping. It's been a long day. "

"Shut up!" he bellowed. Nancy heard angry voices and then the sharp sound of a slap. Mama's cries carried up the stairs. "Please Henry. No!" Another slap. "I'm gonna teach that boy once and for all. No son of mine is gonna be a pansy. He's gonna learn how to be a man if I have to whoop it into him. Now get out of my way, woman."

The house rattled as daddy took the steps two at a time, his large frame shaking the staircase. Nancy heard Paige's door bang open and daddy screaming at him to get his ass outta that bed. Paige whimpered as daddy whipped his belt off.

Paige cried out in terror, "No, daddy, no! Please, daddy!

Daddy began thrashing Paige, telling him he was "gonna beat the fairy out of him" and teach him to be a man. Paige's screams split the night as the whizzing of daddy's leather belt found its target, over and over again. Suddenly the screaming stopped, and an awful thud shook the second floor. Nancy froze then jumped out of bed and ran across the hall to Paige's room. Daddy was splayed on the carpet, blood oozing from his head.

Mama stood over him with the fireplace poker in her hand. She had hit him hard, but not hard enough to kill him. In a voice that sounded more like a growl, she said, "You get outta this house and don't come back." Then she hissed, "I'll kill you if you ever touch my kids again. I promise."

Daddy got to his knees, eyeing Mama and the piece of metal in her hand. He staggered to his feet and walked over to where Paige, still curled up in a ball, whimpered quietly. Daddy looked at his son with cold dark eyes and spat out the words, "You're a disgrace to this family." Then he stumbled down the stairs and out the front door. We heard his old Ford truck drive down the gravel drive, into the darkness, never to return.

The next morning was Saturday. Mama cooked a big breakfast and took a plate up to Paige who was near black and blue from one end to the other. Nancy did his chores and sat with him while he slept. Mama gave him a potion to help ease his pain and let him sleep. Aunt Sarah came by that afternoon and Mama shooed me upstairs. I heard her say "both of the children have a fever today, Sarah. They must be coming down with something." Auntie left shortly after that, promising to check on us later in the week.

We all skipped church on Sunday, which caused the pastor to show up. His voice boomed up the stairs. "Miss Naomi, I hear the kids are feeling poorly. Is there anything we can do?"

Mama replied meekly, "Why no, reverend. Just some sort of grippe or late spring cold. You know how kids are. They'll be fine in a few days. But Reverend," she stammered, searching for the right words, "I've asked you to pray for Henry before and his trouble with the demon liquor."

"Yes, yes you have," he responded. "Is he partaking again?"

Mama sighed and started crying. "Well, Henry got mighty drunk Friday night. He left in the truck, and we haven't seen him since. I'm so afraid something has happened. It's not like him to stay away so long." Later, Nancy could hear the Reverend and Mama praying downstairs. She added her own prayers, hoping daddy stayed away for a while.

During the week, ladies from the church stopped by, bringing food. They sat on the porch and visited with Mama. No one mentioned daddy. Some of the men worked the fields to keep things going in daddy's absence. Country folk were good that way; helping each other in times of need. After a few days, I quit hiding upstairs. But Paige, he hardly moved. He didn't eat anything except a little broth and toast now and then. It was like the life had gone out of him.

A week later, the sheriff came with news. I stood next to Mama on the porch, arms wrapped tight around her, as Sheriff Pitt told us that daddy's truck had been found wrecked in the neighboring county. The inside was covered in blood but they couldn't find any sign of daddy. Mama's knees giving way. The kind lawman helped me take her into the house. He sat her in the kitchen chair and put tea on for us. When the kettle boiled, he shared a cup, offered his sympathy, and said he would keep us informed.

As soon as he left, I ran upstairs to tell Paige. For the first time in days, color rose in his cheeks. He sat up in bed and had me repeat everything the sheriff said. That evening, Paige came downstairs to eat dinner. He talked freely and openly, his words flowed like water. Over the next few days, as his bruises and welts, Paige roared back to life.

Puberty found Paige that summer. He shot up almost 4 inches, causing Mama to complain he was outgrowing his clothes. His once puny body filled out; his pigeon chest hardened into muscle as he did the work of two men every day. In the heat of the summer, his body tanned dark by the sun and his hair turned the color of wheat. Yet, once in a while, Nancy caught a glimpse of the boy Paige once was. He couldn't hide his "Nelly side" from her forever.

When daddy didn't return by fall, Mama decided it was too much for us to run the farm during the brutal winter months in Iowa. We couldn't count on the neighbors' help because it took every ounce of their energy to maintain their own farm and livestock, let alone help a widowed woman. We packed all our belongings and moved to Des Moines to be closer to Nana and Pawpaw.

chapter fourteen

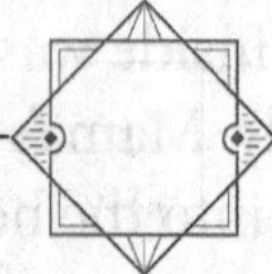

I woke in the morning disoriented to my own surroundings. I laid in bed a moment, my brain filled with fuzzy shadows. Then I heard someone walk softly across the floor, coffee bubbling in the percolator, and the sound of bacon sizzling. Soon I heard water running in the bathroom and the rhythmic scraping and swishing that meant Irene was brushing her teeth. What the devil? Why is she up at this ungodly hour?

I yawned, stretched, and came alive as Irene walked in. Several locks of her silky brunette hair had fallen over her left eye. She wore my worn flannel robe, left open just enough to make out the well-formed edges of her breasts. She was just as lovely in the morning as she had been last night, I thought.

She curtsied. "Breakfast is served, sire." And she headed back to the kitchen.

The bed springs creaked as I stood, slipped on a pair pants and followed her. The sun had not risen, which meant I was up too early for my liking, but I knew Irene had to return to the boarding house to prepare breakfast for her own tenants. So I made no complaint about the hour.

When we finished eating, Irene went back into the bedroom and changed into a tan dress made of thin chiffon, which clung to her with an effect of dampness. Her hair was tied back with a kerchief. She'd deliberately left off most of her make-up, but it didn't spoil her looks any. "I'm trying to look like I can only afford to do my shopping in a thrift shop. I don't want my tenants to think I'm a woman of means." She giggled.

"They'll never believe it," I retorted. "You have too much style."

"Aren't you nice," she purred. She stood in front of the mirror and surveyed the effect, making last minute adjustments here and there, then slipping her wired rim glasses upon her nose and giving me a fresh warm smile. "Sorry lover, but momma's gotta go make a buck," she stated. She gave me a lingering honey cooler on the lips.

It had been a while since I made a women genuinely smile. I pulled my wallet off the nightstand and fingered out some bills. "A lady always needs taxi fare and grub money."

She tucked the bills in her pocketbook and headed out. As she pulled the front door behind her I heard her call back, "See you Friday."

I headed back to the kitchen for a second cup of joe. I threw several cubes of sugar into the dark brew and reached up to the towel rack over the stove and grabbed a pair of grey socks that Irene had washed out and left there to dry. A good woman, I thought, then I shuffled back towards the bathroom.

Stepping out of the tub, I ran my fingers through my hair, toweled myself off, and shaved. I put on a clean union suit before I sat down on the bed and lit a cigarette. I finished dressing then went out to the kitchen and placed the empty cup with the dirty dishes in the sink.

It was ten minutes of nine when I walked into the Biltmore. Noisy people, mostly out-of-towners trying to look like their own version of a Westerner, milled about the lobby. Middle-aged businessmen sprinkled the lobby singly and in groups. The single ones either read newspapers and thought about business, or waited nervously, trying to hide a twenty-year married look. The ones in groups talked and laughed too loud, in a vain attempt to push off the haze of one too many the night before.

I entered the Tea Room, found a table, ordered a coffee and lit a cigarette while awaiting Danny O'Brien's arrival. When the coffee arrived, I blew on it, took a sip, killed time watching people come and go. You know, the men and wives sitting with one another, the tall fat dame lecturing her short scrawny man, the Lunger covering his mouth with a handkerchief in a failed attempt to hide his condition, the teeny, little tomatoes and the big fat guys, the dolls with lantern jaws, and the swells with no chins, the fake city cowboys, and the real ones, standing side by side, the bowlegged wonders, and the knocked-kneed bums.

I continued to sip the excellent Turkish coffee and had the ashtray half-full when I made out the distinctive brushy red hair of O'Brien standing in the doorway scanning the room. Those that know Danny O'Brian know he is Irish, curious, brash, cocksure and colorful. And punctual. He is a bulky muscle man of around thirty, a head taller than most with big bony hands with red hair and freckles covering their backs. Everything about Danny was reminiscent of his native Ireland. He had grown a beard since I had seen him last. He wore it cut short, but the flaming auburn was still noticeable and darker than the fiery red of his head. I waved, and he came over and sat down.

"Good morning Mr. Nayland."

"Morning, Danny. Care for anything?" I asked.

"Aye, coffee is fine."

After the waitress had refreshed my cup and put one before Danny, I began. "Flatten tells me you might be able to help me out on an investigation."

"I'll help if I can Mr. Nayland, because for centuries untold, every generation of O'Brians has produced at least one priest, but my generation broke with tradition. There's just me. But in honor of my family heritage, I am a natural born confessor. People tell me things," he said with his good Irish Catholic manners.

"Danny, I'm looking for a young man by the name of Paige Swalia. Do you know him?"

"Aye, I do sir."

"Do you know him well?" I asked with a degree of urgency.

He's Irish-grey eyes flashed pleasantly. "Aye, quite well I say."

"Care to tell me the story?" I asked.

"We were very close during the high months of summer last year."

"Did you shared accommodations then?"

Danny seemed to hesitate as he blew on his hot coffee. "Aye, in a way. Our situation was more than just sharing a place. You know what I mean, right sir?" I nodded, because there are times it's better just to say nothing. "David said I could be straight with you and that you were an upright Joe who could be trusted. Is that true, Mr. Nayland?"

"Danny, in my line of work, discretion is essential. And yes, you've got my word, nothing leaves here today. I promise," I stated firmly. "And Danny, trust goes both ways."

"Then I'll trust you, sir." Danny licked his lips nervously. "You see, Paige and I were, umm, intimate, as one would say."

"You're telling me you were lovers?"

"That's a dangerous question Mr. Nayland. A queer man risks a guaranteed sentencing in the Oklahoma Penitentiary if caught. But yes, I was, in every sense of the word, sir," he said with a degree of confidence. "We shared a room in one of the boarding houses. While we didn't have sex every night, we did have familiarity every day, the low-key intimacy of holding each other as we listen to the radio, of brushing against one another in the beds we pushed together at night, even the simple fact of having each other in the same space."

"Can I ask for how long?" I delved.

"Several months I'd say. At least until that old bugger artist made him his gunsel and moved him into his posh apartment."

"You mean James "Cowboy" Warren?" I asked.

"Aye, that's the one, sir. And now that Paige is gone, I realize how much I miss picking up after him." A sadness crossed his face as he attempted to take a drink of coffee.

I drank mine in silence, waiting for him to come back to the present before asking, "Do you know where Paige is now?"

His composure returned and he said, "No. Last I heard, he moved out of Warren's place into a room in the New Century."

"I heard that, too, but he's not there anymore," I told him before questioning him further, "Have any of your friends seen or heard from him lately?"

"Aye, the lads told me he was still working at the law firm, but another told me that he quit showing up about two weeks ago. So I just figured he had gone to see his mother in Des Moines or something like that."

"No one in the family has heard from him in a while." I told him.

"That be bad news, Mr. Nayland. It's not in Paige's nature to avoid work, and it ain't like him to not to be in contact with his sister. He called her every Sunday evening when we were together."

"If his work and family don't know where he is, is there someone else that might? Say another member of the Gardenia Club?"

"You've heard of that, have you?"

"I have. Can I ask if you're a member Danny?"

"You can, but I'm not. It's a small exclusive club. I'm not even sure how one gets picked or who's a member."

"Ok, who might possess a more in-depth knowledge of this private club or may know the current where-abouts of Paige?"

"There be Billy Tipton, he might know," he said with a sense of hope.

"Do you know where I may find him, then?"

"That's easy, you see he's a musician and on Saturday nights you can usually find him playing sax with a band or scouting for talent in the Deuce," he said quickly before rushing on. "Your best bet would be the Aldridge Theater tonight, because Gladys Bently is performing."

"Who's this Bently," I inquired.

"Gladys is a blues singer from New York. She performs mostly in Harry Hansberry's Clam house, but tours the South each spring and she's at the Aldridge tonight. She's famous for her extraordinary talent as well as being a black, lesbian, cross-dressing singer."

"The connection escapes me."

"I'm just saying every gay and lesbian person in the city, including Billy Tipton, will be trying to get into the place tonight. And as a favor to you and David, I'll send a note around and tell him you would like to meet him and that he should help you out if he can."

"You know him that well?"

"No, but his wife, Non Earl, is a good friend of mine. If she told him to meet with you, he would. Because we both know that the best way into a man's social circle is through his wife."

"So, you can arrange for him to come to my table tonight at the Aldridge?"

"Aye, if I can find her, he'll come talk to you."

"That would be helpful. But I've got one more question. Do you know a man by the name of Denny Galligan?"

"Aye, I do. The Irish crowd is fairly small around here."

I tried not to force my next question. "Is he a poof Danny?'

"Aye, he be."

"Can you tell me more about him?"

"He's about my age, roughly five ten, dark hair, brown eyes, does skilled labor and lives somewhere on Broadway in a boarding house for single men."

"Does he hang out with anyone in particular that you know of?"

"Strangely enough I do. He played the part of Warren's gunsel before Warren and Paige hooked up."

Interesting, I thought, before asking a final question. "Have you seen this Denny lately?"

"No sir, but we work and live in different parts of town. So I usually don't run across him unless it's in a club or walking down Broadway."

We finished our coffee and spoke on other topics concerning the city before he left me sitting there, watching his back. When O'Brien exited the front of the Biltmore, I stepped across the lobby to the news stand and bought a fresh pack of Luckies and a copy of Friday's evening paper. I handed the dark-eyed girl with short frizzy black hair some lettuce, waited for her to hand me my change and walked briskly to the framed glass phone booth located against the west wall. Slipping inside, I pulled the folding doors closed behind me, dropped a nickel into the top of the black phone box, and dialed my answering service. The clear firm voice of Vicki came onto the line, "Lou Nayland's office. How can I help you?"

"It's just me gorgeous. You got anything for me?" I asked.

"You've got just one message, Lou. It came in at about 8:15 this morning from Sheriff Jackson, but he said he wouldn't be back until Monday on account he was going fishing." She gave me the number though I knew it already.

"Thanks ,Vicki," I said as I hung up. I decided to call Flatten back and dropped another nickel.

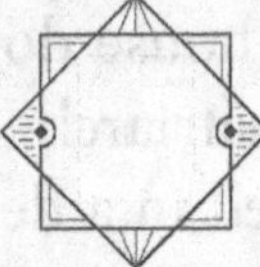

The telephone rang three times before I heard, "Barber shop, how can I help you?"

"Flatten, it's Lou Nayland. I've got a question for you."

"Well, laddie, you tell me the question and I'll tell you what I know, if anythin'," he said with a slight Irish accent.

"First, I need for you to find out if Denny Galligan and Sean MacDougal are members of the Gardenia Club."

"Can do. What else do you need?"

"I saw O'Brien this morning and he gave me the name Billy Tipton. I need to know what you have on him."

He laughed and, unlike most men, his tone had a good solid ring to it, "First off, he ain't a guy. He's a woman by the name of Dorothy Lucille Tipton."

I whistled through my teeth. "Holy shit!"

"Yeah, I thought you might like that. Anyway, our Dorothy came to the city a few years back wearing men's clothing and began auditioning for jobs as a saxophone player, using the name Billy Tipton. As the saying goes, if they didn't ask, Billy didn't tell."

"No one noticed?" I asked.

"Seems not. Billy always dressed in a gray three-piece suit and carried her horn around in a leather case. Kept her hair cut short and neat as a boy. She would play anywhere, anytime, just to keep her music going and to practice getting comfortable in front of a live audience." David paused a second and then pushed on. "Dorothy's new look, however, made her an unacceptable roommate for other musicians. Too weird to be introduced as either a sister or a brother. So she sought an environment where she could shed habits and expectations formed while being raised as a girl. Anyway, by sheer luck, she found herself a room in a boarding house down in the 3rd Ward run by Miss Helen Teagarden, the matriarch of a brood of up-and-coming jazz musicians. Now alighted in a demimonde of show people she felt more at home and her career began to blossom."

"Damn, Flatten. You do know about the damndest people. Got anything else?"

"Of course I do," he stated with pride. "Shame on you for thinking otherwise."

"Go on, McDuff."

"Seems Dorothy, now Billy, began living with a rather notorious and gregarious woman named Non Earl Harrell in a relationship that other musicians considered a lesbian affair. Deuce residents know this and accept this. Recently Tipton made friends with Mary Louise "Buck" Thompson, the daughter of a local radio station owner. He allows Billy and friends to play live on KFXR radio. These dames also wear men's clothing and have girlfriends and live a life of reckless abandon. Those that don't know about Buck and Billy's sexuality, never care to ask. And from what I have gathered, their sexual pandering does not generate much of a "Lavender Scare" in the entertainment and red-light districts. Enough so that Billy was recently hired as the band leader for KFXR's studio band."

"That's all very interesting David, but why do you think O'Brien thinks I should speak with her?"

"My guess is he believes Billy may know the person you're looking for, where he hangs out, and with whom, and where he may be found."

"Possible," I said. "Either way, I guess I'll go down to the Deuce tonight and see what he or she knows."

"That might be a good idea. But Lou, do me a favor and forget where you got this information. When you do meet Billy tonight, treat her like a man. Other than some show people here in town, no one else knows that Billy is really a woman. Let's keep it that way."

"Understood," I said, and hung up the receiver. I shook my head thinking about what I had just heard. "I'll be damned."

chapter sixteen

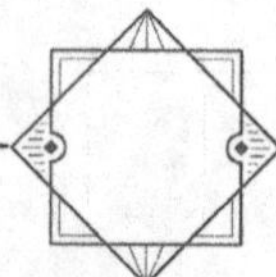

Something happens to the Deuce at night. It isn't a burrow of the
Big Friendly anymore. She withdraws into herself, pulls the shades
down, and begins a life that might seem foreign to an outsider.
She's strange and exciting, tinted with bright lights, and yet she's
elusive somehow.

It is that time of night the natives call dusk-dark, when twilight
blends into night. Second Street was coming alive as I passed
through the chrome circular glass doors of the Aldridge Theater
and stepped into the dimly lit auditorium. I'd donned a blue woolen
double-breasted suit, a handsome tailored, patterned tie, and
shiny black oxfords. The look was dapper and almost dandyish,
appropriate for my meeting.

Once inside, the bouncer appeared from his small fox-den of
an office, just beyond the front door. I observed George wasn't on
duty tonight. A hard boiled man, a virtual masterpiece of ugliness,
drifted into the pulsating light of the red exit sign above the door
and planted his great bulk between me and the crowd beyond. He
was taller than George and carried more weight, most of it in a
hard belly that stretched at the shirt buttons above his belt. His
facial features were bulbous and swollen, his meaty lips thick
and hard-edged, set harshly under a coarse tuber of a nose. He
was an acromegalic, gross and thick, hands and face stretched to
frightening proportions by a hyper pituitary condition. I guessed
the perverting effect of his glands heightened the lobes above

his eyes, creating a caustic expression that magnified the already abhorrent face. Let's just say he was one ugly son of a bitch!

Trying not to stare at the malformations of his kisser any more than necessary, I asked, "Where's George?"

"He ain't working here no more," said the hulk slowly.

"Why did he leave?" I asked.

"On account of Miss Cecelia's passing. Said he couldn't stay ifn' she was gone. Said the place just wouldn't be the same. He upped and moved to St. Looey before last Christmas."

"I can see how he might feel that way," I told the block of a man before me. He gave no sign of wanting to further our conversation, so I tried to push into the club.

"Wait a minute, bub. You got to pay a buck to get in and there's a two drink minimum."

"What's your name?" I asked.

"Moses, and it's still a buck," he said. I thought that a name and a man had never been so mismatched in a century. I smiled, gave him a silver dollar, and went to a table near the back.

The place reeked of stale beer, sweat, and enough cheap perfume thrown in to make your stomach roll. The colored crowd watched with cat-like curiosity as I strode across what would best be described as a dance floor and slid into a booth near the rear. I placed a fin on the table in the vain hope the site of cash would improve the service.

An ofay tomato, wearing a dress that was too tight a year ago, saw me leaning back on my chair with the fin on the table. Deciding I could afford a wet evening for two she swayed over, with her hips waving hello. "You're new around here ain't ya? Best you know up front, this place doesn't cotton to strangers much." Her blue eyes were dull in the dimly lit club. Her eyes had an intriguing aspect about them. Most men wouldn't consider her pretty, but she was young and nice looking. I just didn't have the time or patience to verbally dance with her.

"I'm not a stranger to the management. I might even know these locals better than you."

She wasn't to be dissuaded easily. She pulled a chair closer to me, sat and plastered her leg against mine. "Buy me a drink?"

"No!"

That caught her by surprise, and she quit rubbing. "Don't gentlemen usually buy ladies a drink?" she inquired.

"I'm not a gentleman doll."

She rubbed my arm up and down. "I ain't a lady either, so buy me a drink."

"Blow," I told her.

"You ain't very sociable mister!

"I know it and I don't want to be either."

"Say what's eating you?" she quizzed. "You havin' dame troubles?"

"I never have dame trouble." I stated, "Now scram."

She spat. "I could have sworn you were a nice fella."

'I'm not, so blow sister." She gave me a look that could have stopped a bus and got the hell away from me.

I went back to sipping the watered-down drink and listening to Gladys Bentley and the band perform. The band finished playing Ground Hog Blues and they took five. The musicians walked off the stage towards the bar or to the table of one of their guests. When they had cleared the stage, I noticed a smallish well-dressed man stand up from one of the front tables and head in my direction.

He was not the run of the mill gentleman. He was diminutive, with perfectly coiffed light brown hair glossily slicked back. A face so cleanly shaved, he had the appearance of a guileless choir boy. There was something uniquely feminine about the combination. But even in a proper gay set, this man was flashy. His double-breasted custom men's suit had wide silk lapels, cut tight to narrow shoulders, and flared over slightly plump hips. His trousers were trimmed in silk and fitted his round legs more snugly than was the current fashion. His shoes were English. The ends of his bow tie were tucked under the collar of his hand tailored shirt and he wore a black silk handkerchief in his top pocket. Though Billy was not a tall man, his immaculate dress and dignified bearing made him appear more formidable than he really was. When he stood before me, he spoke with a soft tone. "I presume you're Mr. Nayland?"

"I am," I stood and shook his hand. His grip was delicate but firm. I inclined my head at him and then at the empty chair. "Please, sit down."

"I'm Billy Tipton, and my wife tells me you have some questions to ask of me," he said speaking directly at me in a reasonable tone.

"Just a couple, Mr. Tipton," I told him. "Can I get you a drink, first, sir?"

"Gin and tonic, thanks."

I waved the cocktail waitress down, ordered myself another scotch, neat, and a gin and tonic for my guest. When the attractive ebony-skinned waitress left the drinks, I began. "What brings a man like you into the Aldridge tonight, Mr. Tipton?"

"I've recently been appointed the new band leader at KFXR radio," he told me with some pride. "So besides enjoying Miss Bentley's performance, I'm scouting out possible talent for the radio shows."

"Sounds like interesting work."

"I enjoy it immensely. I suppose one could say I'm a bit of a connoisseur—a connoisseur of music, of wine, and yes, of beautiful women. In short, Mr. Nayland, a connoisseur of life. But you're not here to listen to jazz or the tale of my life. So, let's see if I can answer your questions quickly so I may return to my guests."

"Fair enough," I said, playing with my drink. "Danny tells me you might be able to help me out in a missing person's case."

"Possibly," he said as he effeminately stirred his gin and tonic. It wouldn't be easy to change a lifetime of habits in a few years.

"I'm looking for a young man by the name of Paige Swalia. Do you know him?"

"We've crossed paths in the past."

"When's the last time you saw him?" I asked.

"About a month ago. Who's looking for him?" he asked, with a degree of interest.

"His sister. She's desperate to find him before their mother gets wind of the situation."

"I see. Well, in that case, I'll try to help you, Mr. Nayland."

"Do you know where he's living?"

Billy grinned impishly. "I'm sure his sister told you last fall he was living with an artist by the name of Warren?" I nodded my head and let him continue. "I was told he moved into an apartment at the New Century after that but didn't stay long before he leased a house on Washington Street."

I had already gotten part of that from Nancy, but I played dumb and asked, "Do you have a forwarding address?"

"Sorry, I don't," he told me before taking a drink of his gin.

"Okay, that's helpful, but is there anyone in particular he's is involved with, relationship wise?" I asked.

"Nobody that I've heard of recently. And the impression I got is that he's been single since he left Warren around Christmas."

"Nobody since then?"

"None that I know of," he said with finality.

"I see." I appeared to think. "I've got a couple more questions before I let you go."

"Then Mr. Nayland, please proceed."

"Do you know if there's any connection with Paige and a couple of other guys by the names of Denny Galligan and Sean MacDougal?"

"If you're asking if they had relationships with Swalia, the answer is no. But there is a connection."

"You mean with the Gardenia Club?"

"You have been a busy man haven't you, Mr. Nayland. To be honest, I'm not sure who's is in that club, if it even exists at all. Either way, these are dangerous subjects to speak of even within these protective walls of the Aldridge."

"How so?"

Tipton's eyes quickly swept the whole room twice before coming back to me. "Let me give you a little history which may or may not help you understand the environment in which you tread. Back in 1890 when the young territory was first legislating the penal code, it borrowed most of it from the Dakota Territories. Especially for crimes against nature." I remained silent, allowing him to continue with his story. "That statute stated,

'Every person who is guilty of the detestable and abominable crime against nature, committed with mankind or beast, is punishable by imprisonment in the penitentiary not exceeding ten years… Any penetration, however slight, is sufficient to complete the crime against nature.

"But here in Oklahoma no one was prosecuted under the law until the early 1930's. That's when Draper Grigsby became the new County Attorney and he made it his personal crusade to prosecute cases of sodomy between same sex partners. Hence you might find it difficult to get people in that community to speak to you or provide you with much beyond a superficial response."

"The legality or illegality of their personal habits isn't much of a concern to me, Mr. Tipton, other than how it might aid me in finding Paige Swalia for his family."

"I agree, Mr. Nayland. So what are you interested in learning?"

"If the three of them were not lovers or members of the Gardenia Club, how are they connected?" I asked.

Under his breath Tipton stated, "Just be clear, I said I wasn't sure they were or weren't members of the Gardenia Club. But all three of them were former lovers of James Warren in the past fifteen months."

"Some connection."

"Yes, the community of Nellys, as you would say, is rather small here in Oklahoma City. So there are a lot of relationships that have multiple crossroads."

The musicians returned to the platform and stroked the strings with a little more life than they had previously. I stuck out my hand and thanked Tipton for his time. He picked up his drink to head back to his table then added, "I hope you find him Mr. Nayland. Paige is a nice boy, and I would hate to hear he has befallen some mischief."

Finishing my drink, it occurred to me that despite the risks, queer Oklahoma City residents were certainly boldly expressing their sexuality and seeking out friends and partners, even in the face of assured prison time. With that logical conclusion, I finished my drink and exited the club.

chapter seventeen

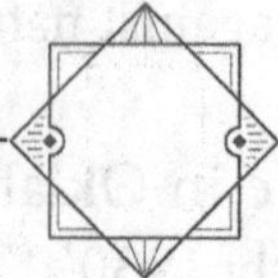

The street was once the kind place people were proud to live on. But in the last few years, it'd lost its claim to pride. The buildings contain too many stories, too few windows, and not enough paint. The American elms lining the lane here and there are shabby and wind torn, as if they have already seen their best days and will shortly to lose what remains of their plumage.

The darkly clad man stands in the shadow of the lamp pole on the corner of the desolate boulevards of Washington and South Robinson. Wearing a gabardine overcoat with the collar turned up he attempts to mask the distinct features of his face. But the glow of the cigarette in his cupped hands highlights his elongated nose and the age creeping around his eyes. He uses the dimly glowing streetlight to check the time. Looking up and down the streets, he heads down the deserted avenue.

He quickly registers each house number as he proceeds down the throughway into the ever-increasing darkness. The streetlight he left behind fails to throw its meager glow this far into the pall of the night. Rain begins to fall from the pitch-black sky causing an eerie haze to form around the shaded bulbs of the streetlights.

Moisture beads on the ghostly figure's hat and coat. He pulls the top of his coat together to prevent the increasing rain droplets from soaking his clothes. He stops abruptly when he sees the number 216 on a freshly painted house to his left. His eyes dart about constantly as he slips across the dead grass towards the rear of the house. He stops unexpectedly. A side window has been left open. He approaches the sill and peers in.

The sound of light snoring reaches his ears as he surveys the room inside. A lone bulb burns from beneath its lamp shade atop a desk. The paneling of the walls, so obviously dating back to the original19th century structure, has been repaired, but now the oak is painted light blue. A huge, framed mirror dominates the wall facing the front door. Carefully arranged flowers sit in vases on each side. Despite the careful refurbishing, the floor attracts the bogie's eye. It is a complex pattern of black, white and red linoleum tile. In the center of the room is a large woven couch where a handsome young man with curly black hair sleeps soundly. Even asleep he exudes an effeminate boyish quality.

The stalker feels the hunger growing inside. He pulls back the cuff of his coat and reads the luminous dials on his Elgin watch. His silent and surreptitious approach to the house has cost him precious time. The assassin continues around the outside of the house to the rear screen door of the porch. He tries to open it quietly, but it is latched from the inside. He fears he may awaken the man within if he applies additional force, so he pulls a large stag handled pocketknife from his pants pocket, flips open the sharp carbon blade and slides it between the screen door and the frame. Slowly, he lifts the latch and drops it without a sound. Inside the rear porch, he tries the back door. It'd been left unlocked. He turns the glass knob and pushes the hardwood door slowly, softly, inward.

The door hinges squeak as he opens the door. The assailant reaches into his pocket, withdraws a tin of oil, and applies drops to each brass fitting. He slowly pushes the door inward and the joints now remained silent. The shadowy figure enters the kitchen and quietly heads toward the living room. He observes a heavy overcoat and scarf draped over a kitchen chair.

When he slips into the front room he sees the yellow glow of a solitary lamp. Thick drapes conceal the front windows of the house. Heavy and lifeless, they hang without motion as the unrecognizable figure stands over the sleeping youth.

The primal hunger rises within the killer. He silently removes a small brown bottle wrapped in a white cloth rag from his coat pocket. His hands shake as he becomes aware of the evil hunger rising inside him like, just like the first time. It makes him nervous, more intense, more concentrated.

As the assassin approaches couch, the youth snorts and turns onto his side. But he remains soundly asleep. The dark figure removes the cork and proceeds to pour a clear liquid onto the rag. He soaks the rag, then replaces the cork and slides the bottle back into his gabardine overcoat. His heart pounds in his chest like kettle drums in a Wagnerian opera. The primordial hunger to destroy his nemesis arises to the forefront of his mind. Its strength matches the hunger in his soul, exhilarating, almost sexual in nature. Excitement pumps through him in anticipation of the brutality to come.

A sickening smell arises from the well-soaked cloth. The killer holds it away from his face, calmly bends down, and places it over the young man's nose and mouth. The dozing man takes several ever-deepening breaths before his eyes fly open. Seeing his attacker above, he struggles to pull the cloth away. But with each breath his strength slips away, until it disappears into a smoky murkiness. His body goes limp and the assailant smiles broadly, relishing the coldness of his vengeful act.

Adrenaline racing through his system and the hunger of his altered-self at its zenith, the murderer walks around the couch. With a mechanical gesture of his index finger, he pushes open the lid to his victim's eyelid. The eye stares back, listless. He lets the lid drop and strolls back into the kitchen.

The assailant strides to the stove and kicks off the gas line attached to the wall. He walks back to the counter and plugs in the chrome plated electric toaster. Pulling a sheet of newspaper from his pocket, he rolls it up, sticks it down a toast slot, and pushes down on the spring-loaded lever.

As quietly as he entered, the specter now slips out of the kitchen, pulling the back door shut. He steps through the open screen door then uses the blade of his pocketknife to re-latch the screen from the outside. The assassin walks back onto the scantily lit street and hikes west along the paved avenue.

The killer distinctly hears a wall clock strike midnight from inside one of the houses lining the street. Suddenly, a huge explosion rattles the entire neighborhood as a large fireball rises heavenly. The nefarious slayer watches what remains of the house as it burns brightly. Eerie black smoke crawls upward towards the starless, gloomy sky above. His eyes begin to bulge in terror as fear creeps inside him, just like the first killing. But now, pressing back against a wall, he seizes control of the fear and pushes it down inside.

A smile crawls across his face and he disappears into the shadows.

chapter eighteen

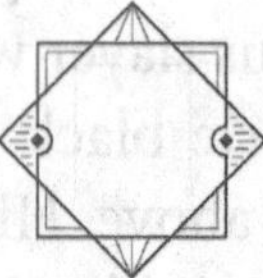

Waking early on Monday morning, I took a hot and cold shower to shake the grogginess out of my system, then shaved off several days of growth. I heard Mrs. Giannasi vacuuming. I felt better as I splashed on after shave. A big plate of bacon and eggs awaited me in the kitchen. I knew the old gal had cooked it up for me because she thought I never ate. I made my stomach behave long enough to start the day with a decent meal. Fifteen minutes later, I patted my meal in place, lit up a smoke and called Jackson back.

Before the first ring ended, Darling picked up the other end. "Sheriff's Office. How can I assist you?"

"It's Lou Nayland and I'm returning Brice's call."

"One moment Mr. Nayland, I'll see if he's in." The line hummed as I waited and flipped through the Oklahoman. On page four was a paragraph concerning the death of Mr. Galligan.

Murder in the 3rd Ward: A crime of mysterious character was committed three nights past at 404 South Broadway, one of the old-fashioned secluded nineteenth century rooming houses which lie between the river and Reno, in the shadow of downtown high rises. Mr. Galligan had recently taken an apartment there. Denny was well known in certain social circles both for his charming personality and his leadership abilities at work. Mr. Galligan was an unmarried man, twenty-seven years of age. Police arrived on the scene early Wednesday morning when neighbors noticed that Mr. Galligan had not collected his morning paper. The police knocked, but received no answer. The officers then forced their way in to find the front room in a state of disorder. Behind the couch, still grasping one of his legs, lay the unfortunate tenant of the house. He had been beaten severely about his head and torso and must of have died instantly. No weapon matching the wounds was found at the scene. Robbery does not appear to have been the motive for the crime, since there was no attempt to remove the valuable contents of the room. Mr. Denny Galligan was so well known and popular that his violent and mysterious fate will arouse painful interest and intense sympathy in a wide-spread of friends.

That added little to what I already knew, I thought, when Jackson's distinct drawl came through the receiver. "What's up Lou?"

I sputtered some questions about his wife and the family until I finally got my words straight and asked him if he was busy. The line was silent so I went on. "If not, how about I buy us some coffee and Danish? I want to know a few things, if you can tell me."

"What kind of things?"

"Stuff the police or a well-informed sheriff ought to know, and the general public shouldn't. Would you rather I find out for myself?"

"Nuts to you, Lou. It's better to have you obligated to me. I'll meet you at Kingman's café as soon as you can make it."

"Fine," I said and hung up. I tucked the paper under my arm and walked out of the Biltmore hotel. The taxis and private drivers were jamming up traffic outside and it took me five minutes to cross over Grand and get into my car.

Brice beat me to the café by ten minutes and was already at a table in the back sipping his coffee. I pulled out a chair and sat down. I didn't have time to waste. The tired waitress came over with our coffee and pastry. I blew on my coffee, sipped it, and made a face.

"Dregs of the pot," the waitress said, and walked off.

I took another sour sip and got down to brass tacks. "Brice, what's the angle on the queer community thriving under the blanket here in town?"

The cup stopped half-way to his lips. "That's a hell of a question to ask me. Because if I answer you with what I've got, then that tells you I wasn't forthcoming the last time we met. And if I don't give you the dope, then it looks like I'm stupid. Or worse, I don't know what's going on under my jurisdiction." I gave him a cynical smile before he pushed on. "There's not much I can tell you because that crew is good at keepin' to themselves. We rarely get complaints from the establishments they hang out in. The men involved don't want to expose themselves to prosecution by making complaints regardin' one another." I nodded my understanding as he pompously continued. "However the police are well aware of the existence of these groups and try to enforce the letter of the law. But remember one thing, politics. There are ways to bog down police investigations, especially if a certain city councilman belongs to this secretive group of men. You understand my meaning?"

I nodded.

"So even if our new County Attorney is on a crusade to rid the city of sin, equal and greater forces appear to be holding him in check. That's why all his cases are against laborers, not lawyers and bank officials. Finally, there's the matter of evidence. No one testifies to bein' involved in crimes against nature unless forced into the corner by our good Mr. Grigsby."

"You were a little light on some of these facts the other day," I said somewhat hurt.

"That's possible. Or it's also possible that I was poorly informed to the depth and width of the activities this particular group involves themselves in. I've been brought up to speed on these matters only recently."

"So, they move about in the clear then?"

"No, I wouldn't suggest that. They get shoved around a little bit by some law figures. And there have been several deaths over the years pointin' suspiciously in that direction."

"They got shoved too hard you mean?"

"Exactly."

"How did the coroner call them?" I asked.

"Suicides mainly. Except the one we spoke of the other day and the one I was callin' to tell you about that happened last night."

"Shit."

"Uh-huh. Would the details interest you? Remember, you didn't get it from me."

"They would, and I understand. So shoot," I replied.

"The cops had another suspicious death last night down on South Washington. Seems another young man was found dead in a house from an apparent gas explosion. It's a copper's case so I don't have many details, but personally, I don't think it was an accident."

I pushed. "Other than your gut, why do you believe that?"

"I've got a mole in the main precinct. He read me parts of their original investigative report. Seems when they canvassed the neighbors, three of them reported that their cats had been strangled and placed on their back porches in the week before the fire. Our copper friends made nothing of it."

"Why should they? People do go around killing cats random like. It's called ailurophobia if you want a five-dollar word for it."

"I ain't buyin' it. It's too much of a damn coincidence," he exclaimed. "I reckon those cats were killed on purpose to prevent them from sounding an alarm when the killer came around later to set that house a blaze."

"That's possible," I said. "Do you have the name of the kid that died in the fire?"

"Yeah, the briquette's name is Sean Mac Dougall, an Irish lad. Worked as a butcher at Kamp's cattle yard."

"How'd he afford the house then?" I asked.

"He didn't. He leased it from a guy by the name of Warren, James Warren."

"The dead artist?" I asked.

"I hadn't heard he was dead," Brice replied.

"The radio said so."

"Interestin'. Was this Warren a poof?"

"Yes, and he had a habit of keeping these boys around as companions."

"Well, if he wasn't dead that would be a connection between these dead pansies. But he's dead, so what do you got now, Lou?"

"Not much actually. Why are you saying the two dead boys were pansies? Did some stoolies spill to get out of your hotel with bars?"

"No, and it wasn't Doc either. He'd never tell me directly something he considers that private, even if I asked him. I have other sources that informed me they were queer. Not my usual stoolies either. They've all clammed up. They don't want to be connected to the Nancies on account of Grigsby using that to prosecute them on trumped up charges."

"Thanks Brice. I owe you another steak."

"You bet your ass you do!" he said, standing to leave. Walking away, he added, "I've got more important things to do than help you in collectin' a fee." His drawl faded away as the door closed behind him.

There was that name again—James Warren. The radio and the paper said he was dead in Mexico, by an apparent heart attack. Had Paige been with him in Mexico? A possibility, I thought. But I needed more information to be certain.

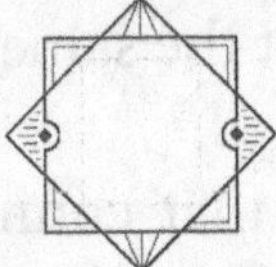

chapter nineteen

I hung up the horn and dialed Doc's number. He picked up after four rings. "Doc, it's Lou Nayland. You gotta minute?"

"Just a few. What'd you need?"

"Jackson tells me they found another young man dead in a house fire last night, roughly the same age as our first victim, by the name of Sean MacDougall."

"Yeah, he's on the slab now."

"You got any details on the materia mortis yet?"

"My guess is smoke inhalation."

"I could've guessed that much. How'd about some details?"

Doc shifted into his lecturing tone. "Subject is charred, with portions of the chest and abdominal wall completely burned away, revealing exposed viscera,—" My stomach turned. I was relieved I wasn't in the room for this autopsy. "—soft tissues of the face and scalp are burned away as well. There are extensive burn injuries to the trunk and extremities of the body, with severe charring of skin and exposed areas of musculature. Clothing remnants are in place, consisting of an armless union suit with the buttons still fastened. Examination of the airways revealed massive quantities of soot deposition."

"Pretty grizzly, Doc. Was there anything else?"

"Like I suggested earlier at the time his body was set afire, Mr. MacDougal had ceased to breathe. I'll confirm that with x-rays later," he concluded.

"Do we know what time the fire started?"

"The neighbors report being wakened by an explosion at the stroke of midnight. Why does it matter?"

"A possible connective thread. Didn't you report that the young man that died from the beating died roughly at the same time?"

"Yes, why do you ask?" he inquired.

"A thought is all. Did you find anything that connected the arson victim to the beaten boy from last week?"

"Nothing as of yet, but check with me tomorrow and I'll let you know." Thinking out loud, he said, "A violent death is such a public event, and that grates on my professional sensibilities. I believe it's my responsibility to preserve the dignity of the victims that come across my table. But there's little I can do once that person becomes a case number. Just a piece of evidence, passed about, whose privacy is destroyed as much as their life."

"I hear ya, Doc. All you share with me is just between you and me, I promise. Thanks for the help and I'll check in with you later to see if you learn anything else."

I hung up and called my answering service. "Morning, Vickie. What do you have for me?"

"Just one message from Mr. David Flatten."

"Read it to me."

"In regard to the two men you inquired about, I've confirmed they were both members of the Gardenia Club," she rattled off. "That's all he left. Sorry, Lou."

"That's something. Thanks, gorgeous."

After I got off the horn, I walked down to my car and threaded my way across town to the New Empire apartments off Reno where the first victim had been killed. It was my first visit to the scene of the crime. I left the car parked on Broadway and strolled down the street toward the two-story wood clapboard rooming house. The house was tall, dingy, narrow-chested, formal and solid, like the century that gave it birth. Shivering, I looked up at the swaying branches. The cool wind had the feel of death about it.

I shook off the sensation and began to investigate the grounds of the exterior of the building. Stopping near a first-floor window,

I attempted to peer inside but the curtains had been drawn. I surmised that several nights before someone had come out of the darkness, stood outside this very window, and stared inside where the young man slept unaware. I walked up the four sandstone steps to the porch. The cops had already removed the restrictive barriers to the apartment. Eight grey steel mailboxes lined the wall. Number 4 had the name D. Galligan printed on its label. I pushed the entry door open and stepped into the main hallway. I knocked on the super's door. The door swung open and a disheveled looking man with sleep in his eyes appeared. He tried to appear larger than he was, and asked, "Whatta you want?"

I showed him my buzzer. "Get your keys."

'Yes, sir, yes sir." He reached inside the door and unhooked a ring of keys and stepped into the hall.

"Denny Galligan's place, I want to go through it."

"But the police have already been through there."

"I know, but let's see it anyway."

He hesitated then he shrugged and started down the hallway towards the apartments at the rear of the building. At the door with a painted black number four he inserted a key into the lock, threw the door open and flitted around in search of the light switch. The crime had been committed in the front room, but no trace of foul play remained, save an ugly irregular spot of dried blood staining a Persian rug. The drugget was a large square carpet in the center of the room with a couch situated over half of it, surrounded by a broad expanse of polished wood flooring in long strips. Over the fireplace hung a fine oil painting of Pan seducing a nymph. Nearby, a stand held sheet music and a guitar. A handsome cherry cabinet stood in the corner with a RCA radio on the top. The room was highly decorative. The walls were painted rose, giving it an effeminate feeling.

I peeled back the rug and examined the corresponding stain of blood darkening the floor below. I knew Doc could tell me more about the blood than I would find kneeling there on the floor, so I continued my search of the house. I pushed the swinging door to the kitchen and vaguely observed the clean countertops, linoleum, appliances in the off-white color the manufacturers call almond, and the bright yellow of the wallpaper and the curtains. Nothing seemed out of place, so I proceeded through the front room to the lone bedroom.

I had the idea poofs were kind of fussy, even when living in a dump. But whoever had searched the room wasn't. It appeared to be a professionally job, whether by the police or the assailant I couldn't determine. It was a real dilly. I grinned to myself. Whoever had caused this wreckage hadn't found what they were searching for. Even after looking in the obvious places, they tore apart everything else, right down to the floor boards.

I kicked aside some of the junk on the floor, but there wasn't much to see—old magazines, a couple of newspapers, soiled underwear, a pen and pencil set that might have been in one of the drawers, and something that was once a suit coat, with all the hems ripped out and the lining shredded. A knife had been used to split the seams of the collar and the button folds, as well as shredding the lining. One of the newspapers was folded open to the obituary column. In the center of the page was the obit of James "Cowboy" Warren. It had been circled in red ink. I thought nothing more of it since the pair had known each other. Everything was covered by a film of body powder from a spilled box, giving the room a cheap flowery odor. The wind from an open window had spread it all over the place. I closed the window and observed the sash had been forced with some kind of wide flat bar. It couldn't have been simpler for the killer.

If anything had been worth taking it was gone now. But I still got down on my knees and crawled about the room in search of any kind of lead. Finding nothing, I leaned against the disheveled bed and tried to put into play the slow tumblers of my mind to think like someone wanting to hide something. A thought occurred to me. Lifting my butt from the floor, I hastily removed the small lamp and alarm clock from the table and flipped it upside down. There taped to the bottom drawer was an envelope. The short note inside told Denny he could reach James Warren at the Agua Caliente Casino and Hotel in Tijuana, Mexico. The postmark was dated January 10, 1936.

The envelope confirmed that Warren had been to Mexico, in January at least. But something nagged at me. Warren's name kept appearing as a backdrop to my investigation, but he was thought to have died at least a month ago, thirteen hundred miles away. My limited grey matter failed to make any connection between a dead artist and the recently murdered men, but my intuition told me there was a link here involving more than just amorous letters to former lovers.

I left the rooms as they were, stopped and thanked the super, before driving across town to Sieber's café for a sandwich.

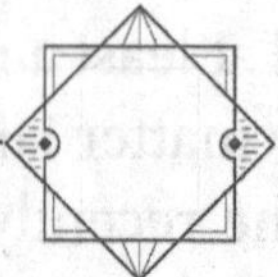

Front Street is a two-way street of rats' nests with the river on one end and railway track on the other, populated with men and women that have the flat, vacant look of defeat stamped on their face. Off Front Street on Reno there's a hotel sandwiched in between other buildings and across the street there's a screwy bar with a funny name filled with screwier people with even funnier names. It was near two o'clock when I walked up a short flight of six steps onto the stoop of the New Century boarding house across from the screwy bar. I took a moment to watch some kids with a broomstick handle and a rubber ball playing stick ball; argue and dodge traffic, a real city game. I thought of the stickball heroes of my youth; guys who swatted the ball a distance of three manhole covers and what those heroes had become-- postmen, supermarket clerks, and me, a private dectective. We all made it big-- at least for my neighborhood-- where civil service was regarded as the pinnacle of success and staying out of jail was no small achievement.

I smiled to myself as I read a sign in the window:

RATES

$1.00 A DAY

$6 & $7 A WEEK

I read the names on the steel mailbox flaps, but nothing stood out. I turned the brass doorknob and stepped inside. The foul smell of too many people living in one place overwhelmed the front hall.

Unwashed bodies, stale beer, fried grease and cigarette smoke assaulted my olfactory sense. I blew my nose into a handkerchief and knocked on the door with "Manager" etched across it.

The manager of the New Century pulled open the door with a look of inconvenience spread across his brow. He wore unwashed clothes, appeared to be in his late forties, but looked seventy with his balding dome, and possessed toad-like features and behind horn rimmed glasses which gave him an owlish look. "Whatta ya want?"

"Just a few moments of your time."

"I ain't got time for you, bub," he retorted and started to close the door.

I stopped it with a well placed foot, "I believe you do Mr…?"

He looked outraged, briefly, then took a swig of Krueger's Crème Ale he had been holding the whole time. "Names Bud Sarkan, if it's any concern of yours."

"If necessary, I can make it my concern, but it would be much easier if you just answered a couple questions for me." I slipped a fin into his dirty shirt pocket.

"Whatta you after, mister?"

"An address is all. I need to know where Paige Swalia moved to."

"You're a copper, ain'tcha? Don't matter, I don't know who you're talking about."

"I carry a badge…and a rod, but I'm a private investigator. You know, like in the movies." Something small and brown streaked along the baseboard and into the shadows. The room behind him came into view. The mingled odors of cigarette smoke and grease hung in the gloom. An ashtray overflowing with cigarette butts sat near a worn armchair. Pinpoints of light glittered through a tattered curtain. This was the sort of place you landed when you could fall no further. A dead end.

Sarkan attempted to sound tough. "A private snooper, eh?"

I can make a nasty mean face if the situation calls for it, "Shorty, maybe just for the hell of it, I'll take you apart here and now. You believe you're tough running a molly house here in the 3rd Ward, but I can make your face look like it's been through a grinder in a packing house, hamburger like, and the more you try to be tough, the more I think of grinding you, the more I like it. The name is Lou Nayland, ace. You ought to know it. I like to play games with wise guys." I paused to let it sink in.

Sarkan's toad face turned beet red around the nostrils. "You got nothing on me dick, so shove off." He attempted to match my voraciousness, but quickly failed him when I slipped the sap from my waistband. Sarkan knew damn well I wasn't fooling around anymore. He knew it, and he was scared.

So I pushed him. "Why are you in such a hurry to give me the bums rush? Bet you've got a record, haven't you Shorty?"

His lips tightened over his rotten teeth. "Fuck you."

I lunged, wrapped my fingers around his throat, and held him against the wall. "When a creep like you gets out of stir, he goes straight sometimes. Sometimes he doesn't. I'm betting that if the cops decide to look around a bit, they could find you had a hand in some crooked pie. And it wouldn't take long to put you back up the river."

"H-Honest, Mac, I don't know nothin' about the boy. And I would tell ya if I did. Look, I ain't no troublemaker and I don't want no trouble either." He glanced up and paled. But the appearance of the sap cocked over him and the look on my face convinced him to share what he knew about Paige. "Alright mister, he was here, but he's gone now."

"Gone where?"

"A house on Washington," he mumbled.

I shoved the leather sap under his chin, "The number. Tell me the number."

Sweat dripped down Sarkan's greasy face. "232, its house number 232. It sits on the west end corner. You can't miss it." I let go of him and placed the sap back into my waistband. I knew Washington Street well. It was where the young Irish kid had gotten fried.

I emerged from the boarding house and walked down the steps to Front Street. A city bus rumbled past the intersection, spewing smoke all over a middle-aged man standing on the southeast corner. The man was of medium height and wearing a dark overcoat and hat. The coat collar was turned up, and he seemed to be reading a newspaper. I studied him a bit. He glanced up as the smoke enveloped him, growled something at the bus, turned casually as he placed his paper under his arm and fumbled a leather cigarette case out of an inner pocket. He put a cigarette in his mouth, dropped a match, looked me over when he picked it up, saw me watching him from sidewalk, and straightened up as if somebody had booted him from behind, lit his cigarette, then went back to reading his newspaper. The stick-ballers must have gone in for lunch. Nobody else stood in the street reading newspapers. I shrugged and told myself I was getting too suspicious.

Walking back to the car my mind drifted back to the apartment manager. I agreed with Nancy's assessment that the landlord was a horrid little man. It was apparent that he took advantage, both financially and physically, of his young tenants. The evil little toad was twisted and foul because of his subconscious fear of his own queerness.

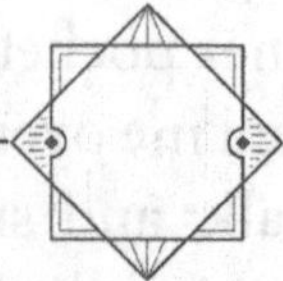

chapter twenty-one

It was ten past four when I pulled onto Washington Street. I let the Ford roll to a stop at the front curb of the house marked 232, the address the weaseling landlord of The New Century rooms had given me after a rather intense interview. The most notable item on the street was the burnt-out structure three doors down. You couldn't really call it a house unless you call a gutted skeleton of burnt timber a house. Either way, a young man had died there just three nights ago. The smell of charred lumber filled the street, but it wasn't the only aroma carried by the spring breeze. A more subtle odor, like BBQ, but different, competed with the burnt lumber.

I pushed the grizzly thought out of my head as I stepped onto the front porch. Had I been less tired or less concerned about what I might find concerning Paige's disappearance and its effect on Nancy, I might observed what should have been a warning to any man. The front door was unlocked and ajar, the letter box flap left partially open and mail was scattered across the floor of the porch. As I pushed the front door open, the door groaned on its hinges. I stepped into the well-decorated room. No one was in the front room, but above the fireplace hung a portrait of a young man, lying shirtless on an oriental couch in front of a fireplace. He had reddish-blond hair and resembled Nancy in both the eyes and nose line.

One thing puzzled me, besides the picture. The wooden door frame was scarred with three deep indentations. They were new, about on eye level, and they appeared as if an incredible force had struck a superhuman blow.

The sound of my own breathing filled the silence as I walked to a small walnut desk in the corner. Nothing lay atop the writing blotter and all the small cubbies were empty. So I pulled the desk drawers open. All were empty.

I'd observed a detective in Fort Worth investigate a robbery once. He said these desks were originally designed with secret compartments. I pulled all the drawers out and stacked them on the floor, then ran my fingers inside their empty slots. Nothing. Until I slipped my hand into the center opening and discovered a finger size hole. With a slight tug the bottom panel slid out. Inside I found a small stack of envelopes, each containing a letter. The envelopes were addressed to Paige Swalia at various addresses from James Warren. Each envelope was postmarked Tijuana, Mexico. The oldest was dated December 31, 1935, and the last, the first of March. Shortly before he died I thought. I placed them into my hip pocket and continued to search the room.

Finding nothing of interest, I pushed the bedroom door open and flipped on the light switch. I stepped back and surveyed the room inside. Nothing moved except the roaches along the floorboards. The bed had been apart and the stuffing was all over the place. The four drawers of the chest lay upside down where someone had used them as a ladder to look on top of the French armoire. It was a professional job of searching, all right.

When I stepped into the room I quickly felt the presence of someone else. I reached for the sap stuck in my waistband. But before I could pull it out, a cloaked specter exploded from the shadows behind me and struck as quickly as a cat upon its prey. The blow knocked me off balance and I careened into the foot of the bed. In the instance before all time and distance ceased, I made out the faint features of my assailant under a stocking mask. Lines of age about the eyes below silver streaked hair, his voice rasping and muffled. I couldn't make out the words he spoke to me. I thought I was going to be sick. The floor rose to meet me and a black curtain shrouded my mind.

Consciousness returned slowly. I laid still for several minutes, my eyes open and staring about the dark room. To the right, an oblong, curtained window gave hints of the sky outside. Sunset wasn't far away. Chimes of church bells clanged in the distance, synchronized to the pounding in my head. I raised my hand to the side of my head and felt the knob there, my hair matted with dry blood. I attempted to stand, made it as far as to my knees, then blacked out briefly.

When my head began to clear again, I rose from my knees and stood on wobbly legs, trying to think. When the fuzzy images before me came into focus. I picked up my hat from the floor and put it on, only to have a stinging pain race down my cheek. I touched the spot. Wet blood covered my fingers. Nausea rushed over me again. I sat on the edge of the bed, searching my pockets. My personals were all intact, including the sap I failed to pull quickly enough. However I swiftly discovered the letters in my pocket were missing.

I walked back to the front room only to discover the painting of Paige was gone and its large frame lay shattered upon the hearth. Weaving out the front door to my car parked on the street, I fought to stay conscious and suppress the nausea creeping up. Two things were different outside the house; first it had begun to rain, and second nobody was reading a newspaper with his collar turned up. Concentrating, I finally opened the door, dropped behind the wheel, and drove in search of medical help.

Sometime later I slumped against the back door of Doc's office and knocked. The nausea had returned, and time ebbed slowly. Suddenly, Doc pulled the door open and I collapsed onto his white tile floor. When I woke up I found myself lying on Doc's autopsy table. My body shivered due to the coldness of the steel beneath me and my head pounded like a set of drums in a jazz quartet. I reached up and touched the side of my head. My face felt numb. I felt the stiff, coarse threads of surgical stitches and saw Doc smiling down at me. "It required eight stitches to sew you back to your ugly self," he stated, seeming to take it as a matter of course. He asked no questions, but said, "I usually get $20 bucks to sew up the malcontents that appear at my door in the middle of the night. But you can owe me." He was either truly that kind of doctor or I was that kind of patient.

While buttoning my blood-stained shirt and attempting to slide my arms into my jacket Doc asked, "Ever consider giving up your line of work?"

I headed towards the door to the parking lot and said over my shoulder, "Did Jesus stop making furniture just because the Romans beat him up?"

As the door closed behind me, I heard him say, "Get out of here, you bum, and time, don't expect such quality service in the middle of the night."

When I arrived back at my place, my head continued to pound. I poured myself a scotch, switched the radio on to a late-night station and sprawled out on the couch. The daze was finally clearing when the sound of the phone ringing brought me back. I picked it up and a nice gentle voice asked, "Is this Lou Nayland?"

"That's right," I said, "Who's this?"

"My name is Draper Grigsby, County Attorney Grigsby. Does that ring a bell?"

"I've heard of you. What do you want? It's late and my head hurts."

"I appreciate the late hour, so I'll make it quick. I need you in my office tomorrow morning at ten o'clock."

"What if I don't feel like coming?"

"Then, Mr. Nayland, I'll issue you a material witness subpoena and a couple of city bulls can help you find my office."

"I'll be there," I said gruffly.

"Thank you and good night."

I whistled through my teeth and hung up wondering what our County Attorney wanted.

Several bottles of Krueger's Cream Ale were cooling in the refrigerator and I finished off, bottle after bottle, sipping slowly, thinking, and wandering around the room. I let my mind wander through the facts I had.

Paige was missing and I'd failed to come up with a lead to his whereabouts or what he was up to. There were two dead young men, both killed violently by an unknown hand. Neither seemed to have any connection to each other except for the fact that they'd both had a relationship with the artist James Warren, but he died months before their murders. It seemed unlikely that the deceased Warren was the missing link. Something about his passing seemed suspicious and required further investigation.

The one clue that showed any promise was the fact they might have all been members in the mysterious Gardenia Club. But no one would confirm that or even admit the club existed. Finally, why was I attacked in Paige's house? For the letters? With Warren dead, who else would care if they connected the deceased men to him? I saw nothing there.

I had the growing feeling that I had the same chance of solving this case as a one-legged man in an ass-kicking contest. And with that unsatisfying thought, I finished the last of the beers and faded off to sleep on the couch.

chapter twenty-two

Tuesday morning, a few minutes after nine, I exited the elevators onto the fifth floor of the Hightower Building and strode towards my office. A white light glowed through the black imprinted words LOUIS "LOU" NAYLAND, INVESTIGATIONS stenciled on the frosted glass of my office door. I halted abruptly, set my lips, looked up and down the corridor, and advanced towards the door in quiet strides. I turned the doorknob, making sure it didn't rattle as my lips drew back over my teeth while I balanced on the balls of my feet, filled my lungs, and pushed open the door.

A swarthy man in a dapper tweed suit waited in my outer room. I exhaled in a gush and tossed the mail onto the desk. "Come on in," I told him. The dandy was the proprietor of a moving-picture-theater on Main Street. He suspected one of his cashiers and a doorman of colluding to defraud him. I hurried him along, promised to "take care of it," asked for and received fifty dollars, and got rid of him in less than half an hour. As soon as the showmen left, the telephone rang.

I snatched up the receiver and heard the soft tones of Nancy's voice. "Lou, it's Nancy. I'm calling to see if you've learned anything yet?" Her voice, soft and intelligent, caused my heart to race like the first time we met.

But I attempted to give a professional report. "I've checked several of his known places of residence and even spoke to that toad of a super, but nobody has seen him or heard from him in a couple weeks. I wouldn't worry just yet. His employer informed me he had taken time off for a two-week vacation and that he is not expected back to work until next week. I have a small lead that suggests he may have traveled out of town of his own accord. I'll let you know as soon as I've learned more."

Nancy didn't respond for what seemed like a long time. "Oh, I was hoping you'd learned something by now. I don't mean to pester you, but my mother is starting to get suspicious, and I would like to have something to tell her."

"For now, I suggest you tell her what I said—that you believe he is traveling."

"Okay, Lou," she said calmly. "But you'll let me know the moment you learn something, won't you?"

"Yes, precious. Now give me a day or two and try not to worry," I soothed.

"I'll try, Lou. Thanks again."

"Bye, Nancy." My heart slumped. This was one client I couldn't let down. But why should she be any different than all my other clients? She simply was and I knew it.

I left my office and walked across the street to the municipal building where the County Attorney's office was housed. A serious looking, but green, assistant prosecutor ushered me into a large finely furnished office on the top floor. The county attorney stood up and held his hand out across a desk the size of a shuffleboard court, which was composed of a thick slab of walnut with the knotholes left in. "Hello, Draper," I said smiling easily.

Draper Grigsby was a blonde man of medium height, perhaps forty-five years of age. He had overly aggressive eyes behind gold wire rimmed glasses, the over-large mouth of an orator, and a weak chin. The type of features that make me think he's the kind of man that likes his food. You know, the ones who put on weight until they're fattish then spend the rest of their life secretly trying to take it off. "How'd you do, Nayland?" His voice resonated with self-righteous power. We shook hands and he indicated with a finger to the straight back chair in front of his desk. I don't like to be told where to sit so I pulled up another. It didn't seem to bother him any. "You brought no counsel with you, Mr. Nayland?"

I grinned. "I won't need one, because you haven't a reason to have a beef with me."

His eyes gleamed with satisfaction as he rocked back in his chair and addressed me pleasantly. "Rumor has it you've been nosing around the 3rd Ward interfering with police business. Is there any truth to it?"

I made a negligent gesture with my hand. "Nothing serious. Just looking for a missing kid."

"Which kid?"

I stared Draper in the eyes. "Anything I say will be used against me?"

Grigsby smiled. "You know that always holds good around here." He pulled his glasses off one side after the other, looked at them, and withdrew a handkerchief to wipe the lenses. He set them back on his face. Then looked through them at me and asked, "Who killed Galligan?" His voice was sharp and intelligent.

"I don't have the foggiest."

His slack mouth twisted sideways in a self-doubting grimace. "Perhaps you don't, but I bet you could make a fair guess."

"Maybe. But I wouldn't." Draper raised an eyebrow. "I wouldn't," I repeated. "Because my guess might be exceptional, or might be crummy. But Mrs. Nayland didn't raise any fool children that lived into adulthood."

Grigsby slapped his hands flat on the desk. "Well in the name of professional courtesy, give it a shot!"

I grinned sardonically. "Sorry, but I'm not dippy enough to make guesses in front of a county attorney and a stenographer."

"Why shouldn't you, if you have nothing to hide?" he drilled.

"Let's start with why I'm here?" I said.

In a more relaxed tone, the attorney stated, "To aid in the investigation of a crime, of course."

"What crime has occurred?" I asked with affected carelessness.

"The murder of Denny Galligan," he responded firmly.

"I know nothing more than what I read in the paper."

His mouth twisted sideways. "Really, Mr. Nayland? I know for a fact that you were poking around the crime scene only yesterday."

"Possibly. But if I was, I wasn't there checking out his death. I ended up there on another matter."

"Don't give me the high-hat, Nayland!" shouted Grigsby. "I want to know what you were doing down there and what your investigation entails?" His voice took on a querulous note.

"Tracking down a missing person," I said, slathering the sarcasm on an inch thick.

"Damn it, Nayland, I'm under a lot of pressure on this. You're running all over town, asking questions, alienating people, upsetting people."

"Somebody has to."

"What's that supposed to mean?"

"Who else is doing anything about it?"

"I resent your implications. We've got this." He withdrew a cigar from the box on his desk and rolled it calmly between his fingers. His expression was that of a man who never fails to get what he wants. "But we would appreciate any assistance you could provide us. So, I'll ask again. Who's missing. and why are you looking for them?"

"You can ask, but at this point you know as well as I that information is privileged. And I have the right and the responsibility to protect my client."

The county attorney struggled to remain calm. "I wish you wouldn't regard this as a formal inquiry. And for the record, I didn't ask who your client's name. I asked who you were looking for."

With professional firmness I stated, "I'll keep that back for now, on both accounts, due to the fact that you're just fishing, and I'm not required to give you anything for speculative fishing trips."

Grigsby placed his cigar on a porcelain ashtray. "This is not an adversarial procedure, Mr. Nayland. I'm only interested in the truth, even though what you just said may be true. I still have the right to ask you what you were doing at a murder scene."

I shrugged. "I told you. I was following a lead on a missing person."

"I need the truth, Mr. Nayland, and I need it now."

"My truth or your truth?" I asked.

Grigsby pulled off his glasses and drilled me with those aggressive eyes. "There is only one truth. "The truth is you have been operating in a very high-handed manner for the past week."

"I'm just working a case," I retorted.

"Is this missing person as queer as this deceased Galligan character, Mr. Nayland?" he questioned with a tone of distaste.

"I have no idea whether he is or if the victim was. I'm just trying to track down a young man for his family. And what do his personal proclivities have to do with anything?"

"It damn well matters, Mr. Nayland," he said, his voice hard with malice. "You see, it's my plan to drive those Nancy boys out of our town. They're immoral and decadent, the very creatures of the devil himself, and I'll have all these sodomites driven from our fair city. I don't need you gumming up the works with your sideshow sleuthing."

I crossed my legs and leaned back in the chair. "I'm sure there are those in this city who believe that's the thing to do, but I'm not one of them."

The county attorney shook his glasses at me for emphasis. "You condone these sinners and their filthy habits?" I let that go by without even swinging. Grigsby sat up straight, squared his shoulders, and growled, "You can't pass. I'm the goddamn law here in this city and that means twenty-four hours a day. I don't pick and choose which laws I see fit to enforce. I'm here to enforce them all!" He slapped the back of one hand into the palm of the other in time with his words. "I have an obligation."

"Aren't you confusing crime with sin?"

"No, I am not, so you listen up. You'll answer my damn question as to why you were at Galligan's yesterday poking your nose about, or I'll lock you up as a material witness.

I felt my brows draw down into a black frown. "I have said it before, you birds on the city payroll think the law ought to be what you say it is. Lock me up, but it won't get you anywhere."

The blood rushed to Grigsby's face. "Aren't you concerned about the influx of these immoral Easterners and their evil influence on the youth of our city? Or are you just generally indifferent to the battle between good and evil?"

I pulled a deck of Luckies from my pocket, put one in my mouth and lit it. I inhaled deeply and flipped a couple of smoke rings out into the still air of the office. They drifted lazily, and one tried to pass through the other. I watched them for a second and then looked straight at Grigsby. "To be honest, I don't care either way, because moral logic always confuses me. So does immoral logic for that matter and so do women. But that's not the point. I have no time for your crusade. I'm just trying to make a living looking for a missing kid. So far I've found nothing in my investigation that has any connection to your murder investigation. Now if you want to go to the licensing board and tell them I'm obstructing justice and ask them to revoke my license, go ahead. Otherwise, charge me or release me."

Grigsby pointed a lone finger at me and roared, "You've had your chance, Nayland! I will move against you with the full power and majesty of this office." His eyes gleamed triumphantly. "I will have your license in my hand by the end of the week."

I stubbed out my cigarette, picked up my hat, and started out of the room. "Go ahead and roll the dice if you like, but I don't want any more of these 'friendly' informal talks. Subpoena me and I'll come back with a lawyer. Because if you want my real opinion, any law that makes a crime out of human love is horse shit. So you can go to hell."

I slammed the door behind me and began whistling Cross Road Blues, slightly off key. Then I strolled out of city hall quite pleased with myself.

chapter twenty-three

In a small wood framed house in west Oklahoma City, Jimmy rinsed out his mouth and examined his even white teeth in the bathroom mirror. Eyeing himself, he moved his head back and forth, admiring his profile. Handsome Jimmy. Handsome Jimmy O'Donnell, he thought. I wonder how I'd look with a mustache. Covering his three-day beard with his hands, he leaned in closer to the mirror and examined his upper lip critically. He scowled and then smiled, showing his teeth. "The hell with it. Gardenia boys and mustaches just don't go together."

While Jimmy peered into the mirror a shadowy figure peers through the small opening of the partially closed bathroom door. Watching Jimmy before the mirror, the dark figure feels the thrill of the hunt growing upward from his groin, causing the muscles in his extremities to tighten in anticipation of the strike. He knows now that he can't stop the brutal act to come. He's accepted there is a true evil force inside him, driving him out into the dark streets to seek his revenge against these young men who had failed him. He no longer fears it. He relished his murderous acts.

Jimmy lathered his face and shaved. Rinsing the suds, he peered into the mirror again, rubbed his now smooth face and smiled. Stepping into the shower, the sting of the water made him feel optimistic about his date tomorrow evening. He hummed, soaping himself and raising a thick lather. Finally, he stepped out of the tub.

The sound of something hitting the floor sounded in the living room, but Jimmy failed to hear it as the wall clock chimed 11:45. Jimmy crossed the white tile floor leaving pools of water in his wake. He reached into the linen closet and yanked out a fresh towel, toweled himself dry, and pulled on his pants that had been lying on the floor. Flipping the bathroom lights off, he headed towards the bedroom to finish dressing.

◁○▷

The hunter slows his breathing, trying to remain silent. An evil smile crosses the stalker's face as he slips back into the darkness to wait. The cloaked figure presses deeper into the closet, heart pounding so loud he fears Jimmy will sense him. But the young man passes the hidden figure, unaware. The killer slowly wraps his hands around the ends of the double knotted woman's stocking he has prepared beforehand. He calmly stalks Jimmy down the darkened hall. The driving evil within his head reaches its apex as he followed Jimmy into the bedroom. The light from a naked night light plugged into the wall dimly lights up the dark room. The young man opens the closet door and slips on a white under shirt. As his head pops out of the neck hole, the specter loops the stocking over and about Jimmy's neck and begins to twist.

◁○▷

Jimmy reached up and tried to pull the stricture from his throat. Light from the lamp danced before his eyes. Jimmy kicked his legs about, trying to throw off his attacker, but he failed to attain any leverage. His attempts to relieve the growing pressure around his throat grew weaker as the assailant appeared to grow stronger. The double knotted chord grew ever tighter, as Jimmy's world grew darker.

◁○▷

A popping sound echoes across the room as the young man's larynx collapses. An uncontrollable hunger streaks through the attacker's body, the deafening sounds of drums rushes into his head. Thunder roars in his ears. The killer's sexual excitement explodes as his victim's breathing becomes more and more labored. The adrenaline raced through him as Jimmy struggled had struggled and then went totally limp. The wall clock struck midnight. "Perfect," he thought. He continued to throttle the man's throat, excitement streaming through his body. Soon, he realizes that Jimmy is dead. His body has fallen and folded u-shaped onto the floor. Calm slowly returns to the killer's body, the thunderous drums in his head finally silent. The muscles in his arm burn from the prolonged struggle of the murder, which further heightens his sexual pleasure.

When he fully recovers, he searches the room, tossing the bed, looking under the mattress, pulling the drawers from the dresser and dumping them across the floor. Kicking piles of scattered clothes about he suddenly glimpses a stack of faded white envelopes tied in a bundle with a maroon ribbon under the bed. He snatches them up and flips through them, His excitement increased as he realizes the letters are his.

He slips the packet of letters into his overcoat and heads for the backdoor. He feels no panic this time. Only excitement. His cruel, altered-self is growing stronger with the conviction that he is doing the righteous thing; a thing justified in his pursuit to cure the world of selfish, cruel men. Especially those who've wronged him.

Euphoria engulfs him as the darkness of the night swallows him.

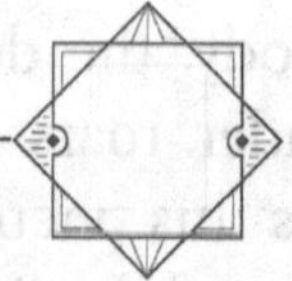

chapter twenty-four

I rolled out of bed the next morning feeling sluggish and exhausted. Stillness filled the room as I sat on the edge of the bed and yawned a couple of times, forcing the fog to disappear from my brain. When the telephone began to ring, I groaned and looked at the radium-painted dial on the alarm clock. It was sitting on last month's copy of Black Mask on the nightstand. It's hands poined at fifteen past six. As a rule I'm not good in the morning before ten or without my first cup of joe and I hadn't had my first cup of coffee yet. The phone continued to ring. I ignored it knowing if it was important they'd call back.

The bed springs creaked as I stood and headed to the kitchen to put a pot of joe onto the back burner of the stove. The phone finally stopped ringing. When the coffee started to percolate, I shuffled back towards the bathroom.

While shaving the phone rang again. I dipped my hands into the hot water and washed the shaving soap from my face. I walked back to the living room and scooped up the receiver on the third ring.

The voice on the telephone seemed to be sharp and preemptory, but I didn't hear too well what it said. Partly because I was still only half awake and partly because I was holding the receiver upside down. I fumbled to right it and grunted, "Yeah."

"Nayland! Did you hear me?" I now recognized the strong southern drawl of Sheriff Jackson on the horn.

"Yeah. What the hell do you want at this god forsaking hour?"

"Did I wake you?"

"You damn well know you did." I growled. "What do you want?"

Brice's accent was hard to discern this early in the morning, but I vaguely recognized some of the words. "We've got another one…. he's been strangled….dead."

"Damn." I slumped down on the couch. "Who's been strangled, Jackson?"

"Another one of those Nancy boys. That's why I called you," he stated firmly. "You're getting to be an expert in this area."

"But why are you calling me? Aren't these killings a city beat thing?"

"Would be, but this one is west of town several miles, in my jurisdiction. And since you've been sniffin' around you might know somethin' useful. So get your ass out here."

"Shit. All right, where's out west?" I asked.

"Head west on Reno, past the lake, and then start look for the squad cars parked next to a farm house on the north side of the road. It's about a mile east of Myra's place. You can't miss it."

I thought for a moment then said, "Give me thirty minutes." I hung up the phone, went back to the bathroom, and finished shaving.

I toweled off my chin, ran my fingers through my damp hair, and stepped to the closet to dress. Because of the chill I slipped on a thin white union suit, brown socks, suit pants, and dark brown shoes. When I'd finished tying on a brown tie to match my suit, I returned to the kitchen and downed a much needed up of battery acid. Finally feeling clear-eyed and bushy tailed, I picked up my nickel lighter and lit a smoke. Cigarette burning in the corner of my mouth, I stuffed the fresh deck of Luckies, my keys, and my wallet with my P.I. license into my pocket then darted off to my car parked in the rear of the building.

The morning spring air blew cold over me as I bent over the wheel of the car sending the vehicle through the streets with a sense of urgency. Questions raced through my head, but I pushed them out to concentrate on maintaining the speed I was driving without piling myself into something.

Zipping down Reno, I flipped the radio onto WKY to listen to the early morning sports program. When the static cleared, I heard the distinctive voice of the station's new rookie sports reporter, Walter Cronkite.

"They can't stampede Bert Niehoff into predicting which club will finish in the approaching Texas league campaign."

"The gloomy Gils of the big league have nothing on the Tribal chief. Neihoff refuses to come out with a flat-footed claim for the 1936 pennant, but the big chief has his ideas when he explained it to this reporter."

"It's much more difficult to pick the Texas league finish than in some of the other leagues, particularly the Southern association. Where the league has three clubs controlled by the majors, they can turn the standings upside down in a week. But I thought we looked exceptionally good against the Cardinals behind good pitching. That always makes a club look good. Still, the boys had a lot of spirit out there."

Neihoff went on to tell this reporter, "As I see it, the only clubs in the league that have been materially strengthened are Dallas and Tulsa. Dallas looked mighty powerful to me in the games we played in Shreveport. It's a question of whether the Steers have the pitching."

"You can't tell about the other clubs, particularly Beaumont, Houston and San Antonio. You know one thing; their big league papas don't want losers on their hands."

Cronkite droned on. Scores of insects got plastered into my grill on the empty stretch of road between the edge of town and the farm house out on Reno where Jackson was waiting. I could hold back the questions no longer.

Where was Nancy's brother and why hadn't he called his sister if he was still alive? Was there connection between his disappearance and the recent deaths of the two young men in the 3rd Ward? And if there was. How and why? Was there a connection between the deceased artist Warren and the recent murders and what was it?

The questions where like the bugs out in the darkness. Scattered but yet still forming a swarm. No answered presented themselves so I concentrated on the road.

chapter twenty-five

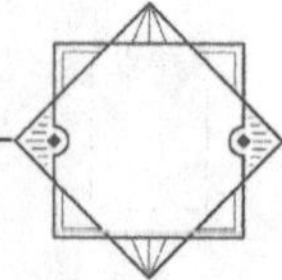

I watched the needle on the speedometer flicker it's way up to 45 mph as I cleared the city limits. When I finally passed over County Line Road I spotted the county meat wagon and the sheriff's patrol cars parked in the drive of a lone, wood framed house. It had a slightly tarnished look, like an over-aged rodeo clown. I pulled in behind the county prowler with the sheriff's decal on the door and red lights mounted on the top and shut down the little V-6.

A large silver Packard sedan was also parked in the lane. I knew it belonged to the poor bastard who had pulled coroner duty this month. The county didn't employ full-time, formal medical examiners, but rather depended on local physicians to each volunteer for one month shift each year. The Packard belonged to Doc Rowell so there was hope I would learn something.

White beams light sprayed out across the lawn as I approached. It originated from the ajar front door where two of Jackson's deputies stood on the porch, dressed out in their brown uniforms under their Stetson cowboy hats, each with their gun hand on the butt of their six-shooters. As I got closer, I recognized the two deputies— Tom Miller, a tow-headed youngster of twenty-five or six, with all the nerve in the world, and Al Croak, a quiet but intelligent youth that even Brice suspected of having ambitions above his current station.

Seeing me, Miller moved toward me and stuck his hand onto my chest. "What do you think you're going, bub?"

"Glad to see you too, fellas. I'm Lou Nayland. Brice Jackson phoned me."

The deputy's arm went down as he stepped back. "Sorry, I didn't know you at first. Well, they are all inside. Go on in." He jerked a thumb over his shoulder and mumbled, "Lousy business."

"Always is," I agreed, and strode between them and through the front door.

A small circle of men stood in the front room over the body of the deceased. Under-Sheriff Brice Jackson, wide-brimmed Stetson tilted back, gazed down at the body, with a set of eyes that had seen too much nastiness and heard too many lies. His placid demeanor was a downright lie. It is false front he has schooled himself to present to the world, concealing an iron will and a dynamic, almost effervescent personality.

I suppose I'm one of the few living men who know Brice wrongfully killed a man in a sudden flare of temper when he was young. We've never discussed it, but I know the tragic incident lives vividly in his memory and must be a strong influence behind the almost super-human self-control he exercises at all times. Although sometimes when he thinks you're not paying attention, he'll slip in some dark humor.

Doc Rowell knelt on the floor next to the corpse. Brice appeared to be questioning Doc on some point, with his hands on his hips. The flaps of his woolen Filson jacket pulled apart exposing his ivory handled .45 Long Colt stuck in an engraved leather holster on his right hip. As I came to a stop on the outside of the circle, the harsh bitter scent of death reached my nostrils. I felt dizzy and little sick, but I knew from experience the feeling would pass. It always does. I ought to know. I'd had enough. I took a breath and asked with fake levity, "What's the word on your stiff here?

"Appears to be stone dead," Jackson growled. "What's your thought, Doc?"

Doc shook his head and gave an ironic chuckle at the sheriff's attempt at humor. Then he looked at me with tinged lines of wisdom around his eyes and smirked. "He appears to be dead, and if our good county attorney has his way his Facilis Descensus Averno."

I ignored the pair's attempts at graveside humor and asked, "Who found him?"

Brice straightened up and stated, "Miller and Croak saw the front door open with all the lights on in the house. They investigated and found him lyin' here on the floor, waitin' for his seat next to God."

I nodded. "Know who killed him?"

"I suspect the same fella that killed the other two. They're all about the same age, but they've all been murdered in a different manner. I suspect there's some connection tween them."

I stood there staring stupidly down at the dead man. The corpse was laid out on his back with his legs spread eagle on a ruffled carpet where the struggle must have occurred. One knee was still cocked at a forty-five degree angle in what appeared to be the victim's vain attempt to remain standing. The right foot wore a slipper. The other slipper lay pathetically on its side a couple of feet away from the bare foot. Both his hands were caught under a strand of silk stocking. His mouth was open, tongue swollen and protruding through his teeth. The face was a bright red in color. His head was tilted to the side, frozen in a death stare, which only enhanced the effect of the eyes appearing to leave their socket. There was no doubt about the cause of death, but I asked Doc anyway. "How'd this one go?"

Doc pushed air out of his lungs in a huff which made no sound except the sound made by the air passing his teeth and nostrils. Then spoke to us both in a calm, detached manner. "His cause of death was asphyxiation due to strangulation brought about by the increasing pressure of the ligature around his neck. Several of his fingers appear to be dislocated as well. This was a result of his struggle to loosen the strap, I suspect in his panic to breath. The silk stocking constricted the blood flow to his brain and ruptured his cerebral vessels like small balloons. Theirs is petechial hemorrhaging in the conjunctivae, and the facial and neck skin. In words that Lou can understand, it means a rupture of the small, superficial vessels of the eyes and face. This is caused by cervical occlusion of the jugular veins due to the ligature around his neck. The more our victim struggled, the more the knotted silk strands tightened around his throat. Until he blacked out for the last time and died. I suspect his death was quick. But here's the gruesome part."

Doc pulled a metal probe from his bag and pointed to the area around the victim's lower rib cage and droned on in his solemn, professionally tone. "See this small amount of blood between the third and fourth ribs." Brice and I both nodded. Steve exposed a puncture wound about an inch wide between the ribs. "Usually I would tell you that this knife wound was the cause of death and that it was done professional. But it's on the wrong side. An effective killer would have struck from the left to hit the heart." As Doc spoke as I noticed the subsequent signs of death were already appearing as fine white film had begun to form over the corpe's bulging eyes. "Also, based on the amount of blood loss, I would classify this injury as perimortem, meaning that it was afflicted around the time of death and most likely after he had succumbed to strangulation. He bled very little into the surrounding tissue after the assault with the knife. He was likely already dead."

"How long has he been dead?" Brice asked.

"I wouldn't know."

Brice looked at him sharply and tiled his hat back. "A corner's man that can't guess within five minute has me beat."

Doc grinned sourly and clipped his pen back in his suit pocket. "If he ate dinner last night, I'll be able to tell what time he ate it. But not within five minutes."

The small circle stepped back for the sheriff's photographer. He began snapping shots of the corpse from all angles and took close ups on the mutilations.

Jackson and I walked back out onto the front porch as he thumbed his deputies to go inside. "Sorry to drag you out here so early in the morning, it seems like we're developing a habit of viewing corpses together at sunrise. I have questions that need answers, and I was hoping you could fill that order."

"Sure you do," I said, shrugging my shoulders. "Though I'm not sure why you called. I've got nothing, unless you have discovered a thread that connects this killing to the other two and my current case?"

Jackson shifted his weight to his other foot. "Thought you might have recognized him on your recent travels in the 3rd ward."

"Sorry, no," I told him.

Brice looked down and rubbed some mud off the tip of his boot with the back of his pants leg. "How does your client figure in?"

"I would guess wonderful in a Catalina swimsuit, but she's not mixed up with this. I'm starting to suspect her brother and his relationship with that sodomite artist, Warren, is connected somehow to these recent murders, but I haven't yet put my finger on it. I did recently discover that two of the victims also had a relationship with Warren. If I were a gambling man, I'd suspect the stiff inside did as well. But dead men tell no tales. Either way, I believe Warren's the key. I just don't know which door it fits into."

"But ain't he dead?"

"Yeah, but I didn't say a dead man did it. Just that he's the key somehow. Do you know the name of the deceased inside?"

"His driver license says Jimmy O'Donnell. But keep that under your hat because we haven't confirmed it."

"Will do," I said. "And you'll let me know if Doc finds anything further during the autopsy."

Brice lit a cigarette and threw the match onto the ground. "I will if it helps, but remember, it's a two-way street. If you dig up any red points you give them to me first. And don't give me any of your guff about professional ethics—you know, the thing about relations between client and private dicks. That matters diddly squat to me. I need facts to shut this killer down."

I acknowledged his words with a nod and replied, "I hear ya. But I think I'll still go dig around the Warren angle, whether he's dead or alive." I headed for my car.

"Okay, but remember something else," Brice continued. "The world is made up of two classes of people, hunters and huntees. Luckily for the populous of this little burg, you and I are hunters. But so is our prey. So watch yourself, Lou. Doc may not be able to sew you up next time." A gleam of satisfaction crossed his lips.

"I'll see you around, Brice," I said over my shoulder as I piled into the coupe and gunned her for town.

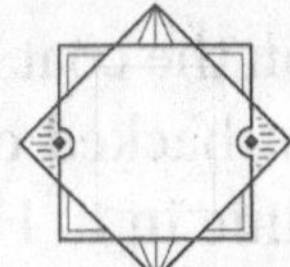

chapter twenty-six

It was still raining the next morning, the kind of steady rain that makes you think it will never stop. I raised the living room window and inhaled the cool morning breeze. I'd gotten into this mess on account of a pretty face. The Trojans had been sucked into a ten-year war for the same reason. And they didn't regret it any more than I did. I was getting nowhere in locating my client's brother. The murders of his fellow Gardenia members didn't appear to have any connection to Paige's disappearance other than they all appeared to know the James Warren. I decided to overlook that fact he was reported dead in Mexico and pursue the thin thread of their mutual association and investigate Warren and his apparent death with renewed vigor.

I headed into the shower, shaved quickly, and pulled on my slightly soiled grey suit. Then I headed to the Greyhound bus station café for a grilled cheese sandwich and a coffee. After paying for lunch, I strolled towards the offices of the Daily Oklahoman.

The Oklahoman Building was located at Fourth and Broadway in Midtown. It's one of those old office buildings built around the time Teddy Roosevelt was sworn into the White House. One of these days they're going to tear it down for a parking lot. A typist sat at the reception desk, tapping frantically at the keys of a noiseless typewriter. In the corner of the room, behind a desk with three telephones sat a rather stern-faced but pretty secretary. I walked past both of them and climbed the stairs to the second floor and went straight to Harry Gundecker's office.

I knocked on his door and a sloppy thirtyish man in a brown suit and sweater vest stuck his head out. "Lou Nayland, ain't this a pleasant surprise. Come on in and have a seat." I followed him into the cave like office, hung my overcoat and hat on the coat rack next to the desk and took a seat in a lonely straight-backed oak chair. The office looked as though he spent a lot of time in it. Harry had the look of a man who took himself and his business seriously.

Harry's office was a ten-by-twelve cube without carpet or a window. On the plain golden-gloss oaken desk sat a telephone, a steno pad, and a Remington Standard typewriter. Aside from his desk, a worktable was mounded with stacks of files, paper and a dozen or more old newspapers. A bulletin board on the inside wall was plastered with notes, sports photos, and clippings. A dozen or so copies of the Sporting News, The Ring, and Boxing Monthly haphazardly covered a smaller desk sat against the wall. Gundecker parked his expanding butt in the chair behind the desk, pushed wire-rimmed glasses from his slightly crossed eyes to the top of his head and asked wistfully, "What do I owe the pleasure?"

"I need some information on a guy, and I figured you might have the dope on him," I stated.

Gundecker reared back in his swivel chair. The effort forced his coat jacket open, disclosing a wrinkled, mustard-stained vest and a shirt, soggy with perspiration. "I just might. But I require a little quid pro quo." The corners of his mouth drew up in a devilish grin.

"What do you have in mind, Harry?"

"I want the true story behind the shooting in Deep Deuce last fall that involving the Camp woman and her brother."

I remained silent for more than a minute. "I tell you what Harry. If your information pans out, I'll give you the story. With one exception."

"That being…"

I stared straight into his dark browns. "You leave the Camp woman and her husband out of the story. You concentrate on the players involved from Deep Deuce and her brother, but that's all."

"But she's the most interesting player in that little drama," he declared.

"Those are my terms. And now that you're being shady about it, I'll leave her part of the story out."

"That ain't right, Lou."

"Those are my terms," I said as I maintained my poker face. "Take it or leave it."

"I'll take what you got then," Gundecker grumbled. "What do you need to know?"

"I need all you got on this local artist, James "Cowboy" Warren."

His eyebrows jumped towards the glasses perched on his head. "What's the case?"

I rolled my eyes. "You know I can't discuss an active case when I have clients to protect. I'll tell you what. If your information helps out and in exchange for leaving the Camp's out of the story, I'll owe you. I'll give you the whole thing on the recent murders."

"Is your client involved?" he asked, his enthusiasm growing.

"Only in passing. I have all the stuff the cops have, and I'll pass it on when they nab the guy."

"Damn! Alright, I'll wait on both. You sit there a moment while I go to the archives."

Harry was gone for twenty-five minutes before he reappeared carrying a thick brown folder. He plopped into his chair and flipped open the file. "This is what we have—he was born in Danville, Illinois in 1889. He's the youngest of a self-made man by the name of Howard Warren who moved to southwest Oklahoma before statehood and made his fortune as a cotton miller. At age thirteen, James left school and joined his father and older brother in the business. The whole family was civic-minded and greatly involved in local politics and municipal administration of Fredrick, Oklahoma and the surrounding community." I listening intently, letting him continue to speak in his even, well-formed sentences, hoping to discover a clue or two. "In 1909 he married Bertha Francis Howard, whom the family called Bertie. Apparently, it was well known in the community his father was greatly relieved, believing his youngest had tendencies towards being a sissy. He gave the young couple Grove Hall and 80 acres of surrounding ground as a wedding present. The farm had been the childhood home of James' mother's family. The young Warrens rarely socialized and had few friends. Life for the young couple revolved around the family cotton mill, a substantial employer in the Frederick area. James's father a miserly and humorless man, contributing to James's growing dissatisfaction."

The couple lost their only son to the influenza epidemic of 1919 and shortly thereafter he left his wife and family, moving to Kansas City to study art. After graduation, James traveled the Southwest working as a cowhand and acquiring the nickname "Cowboy." In the early 20s, he rose to fame due to his interesting and introspective paintings and sketches of Indians, cowboys, and oil field workers in Osage County and subsequently in the Borger, Texas oil fields." Harry looked up at me.

"That's all fine for the man's biography, but what'd you got on him that's more recent?"

Gundecker shuffled through the file folder. "Not much if you leave out all the articles and magazine stories on his artistic life. If you want me to include gossip and rumor, I can tell you what I've heard."

"That's why I'm here," I told him. "So let's have the lot."

Harry leaned back in his chair, eyes snapping, and gave a bark of enthusiasm. He leaned forward again and said, "The reason he left his wife was on account of him being queer."

I interrupted him. "What happened to the wife?"

"I'm not sure. He never legally divorced her, so they're still married. I assume she still lives in Frederick, but it seems he's never spoken to or seen her or his family since the day he left seventeen years ago."

I was getting impatient. "Okay, what else have you heard?"

Harry couldn't hide his sudden glee. "The man's a queer and quite a highstepper at that. Seems he goes for young men in their twenties. And from what I've gathered, there's been quite a string of them. Some are professionals, but the vast number are laborers. Seems he prefers them Irish. Apparently, he has a real thing for the brogue. But he never keeps them long."

"Anything else?" I asked. "Like a name or something."

Harry again flipped through the Warren file and pulled out a photo. "This might help. It's couple of years old, but it's a good likeness of him." He slid the photo towards me across the desk.

I picked it up and slipped into my suit pocket. "Anything else?"

"Like I said, most of them are laborers. With Grigsby currently sniffing around in search of sodomy convictions, the community has mostly gone silent. But I have one name. A young lawyer by the name of Paige something or another. Apparently, this Warren preferred him as a model and kept him around longer than most, but apparently he moved on from him around the first of the year. The rest you probably already know. Like the fact that he died in Tijuana six or eight weeks ago from a heart attack, laying on a lounge chair next to the pool at the Agua Valiente Casino Hotel."

"Yeah, I heard that on the radio. Anything else?"

"Just one other small thing—he might be a member of something called the "Gardenia Club," but no one in this office can pin down its existence or who any of the members are."

I stood and stuck out my hand. "Well, if that's all I'll shove off now."

Harry reached across his desk and shook my hand as if we liked each other, and reminded me, "Don't forget. You owe me two stories now."

"Yeah, I won't forget." I shrugged into my overcoat and placed my Wilton firmly on my head. Closing the door behind me, I thought to myself, fat chance that newshound will ever get the complete story from me regarding the Camp's connection to the shootings last fall. My visit with Gundecker hadn't been a total trip for biscuits. The Gardenia Club had come up again and the photo he'd provided had the potential to prove useful."

The round ornate pillar clock in front of BC Clark's Jewelers announced the time to be just shy of 2 o'clock when I got out of the Oklahoman Building. I walked down Broadway to the Playmore Bowling alley. The aroma of stale beer and dust motes danced in the air. The overhead lights were wreathed in cigar and cigarette smoke. The unmistakable sound of bowling balls rolling over highly polished floors along with the distinct echo of pins falling carried across the mostly deserted room. I passed the alleys to the bar in the rear.

The burly Irish bartender placed large rough hands atop of the bar. The red hair that covered his knuckles ran all the way up his arm until disappearing under his rolled-up sleeves. "What ya have?"

"Scotch, no ice." The big Irishman poured one into a dirty shooter from a bottle with an Antiquary label. After I tossed it back, he stepped back over and poured another hooker. Clearly he had seen in my eyes that I had required two. "Beer chaser, Mack." When the cold liquid hit my throat, my mind was already back on the case.

Since becoming a private dick, this missing Swalia kid set up was the screwiest I've ever run across. Too many unconnected turns of events. Multiple bizarre murders, seemingly unconnected, occurring several days apart but in the same part of town, each one slightly similar yet different from the others. And a dead artist in Mexico along with a list of his former poof lovers, that may or may not be a clue to the deaths of the others. And three of those on the list having had been brutally murdered and the forth still missing.

If ever there was a mess, this was it. Everything was out of place and out of focus. The ends of the threads didn't even try to meet. Hell, they were snaggled up so completely that nothing made sense. Except maybe a vague association between the three deceased pansies, Nancy's missing brother, and them all being former lovers of "Cowboy" Warren. Since he died several months before the murders began, he seemed a most unlikely link between the murders. But there it was—Warren had known them all and I needed to confirm "The Cowboy" had died in Mexico, and if possible, the current whereabouts of his body.

So, Mexico it was.

But I needed travel money. I knew of only one way to raise it quickly, and I had only used such means on three or four occasions in my life. I'd have to win the prize money in an illegal bare-knuckle fight. I placed some kale on the bar and walked to the phone booth by the bathrooms. Oban Chester Patterson had two listings in the phone book. One for the office, and the other in the fancy residential section of Heritage Hills. I dropped a nickel and dialed the number to the residence. A butler with a weak British accent answered and told me that Mr. Patterson left shortly after lunch to return to his office. Would I like to leave a message? I told him never mind and hung up. I dropped another nickel and dialed the number to the office.

I was about to replace the receiver in its cradle when a secretary answered in a crisply efficient voice. "Mr. Patterson's office. How may I help you?"

"Is Chester in? Tell him Lou Nayland would like a word."

"Please hold."

Chester is a well-mannered, distinguished man with a finely trimmed chestnut beard, manicured nails and always dressed togged to the bricks in a dark grey, custom made, three-piece suit. His cold dark eyes are the type usually only found on death row, and all his oily charm and fine clothing can't disguise the menacing, cruel personality lurking behind them. Not only is he wealthy, he is a man of considerable influence and power. He holds no public office, but participates in many elections and almost invariably backs the winning candidate.

In the first months of my new PI practice, Chester came to engage me in investigating the death of one of his money lenders who had been shot in the head in his small apartment in cowtown. I was unable to gather enough evidence to have a wop by the name of De'Aprili charged for the murder, but Patterson hadn't begrudged me that. In fact, he paid my expenses and daily rate in full. Strangely enough, De'Aprili was discovered dead several months later, apparently the victim of a hit and run. Many others had received such treatment but Chester always treated me square. And I sometimes found him useful as well.

Three minutes later the firm gruff voice of Patterson came over the horn. "Aren't you a blast from the past. What can I do for you, Lou?"

"I need to raise some funds, Chester. Can you put me in a fight this week?"

"Call me back in ten minutes," he said coolly.

I lit a cigarette and waited. When the butt burned down to my fingers, I dropped another nickel and called Chester back. "What do you have for me, Chester?"

Chester chuckled. "A little bit of good news and a little bit of bad news."

"Give me the good news first then."

"I've got you a fight tomorrow afternoon," Patterson stated firmly.

"And the bad news?"

"If you want the match, you'll have to fight up a class. Heavyweight."

"Shit!" I exclaimed.

"Sorry, but that's the best I can do on short notice."

"Who's the pug?" I asked.

"Bull Flannigan." He chuckled again.

I'd heard of Flannigan. He wasn't only big; he was mean and fought dirty in the ring. I knew I had reach on him, as well as better sparring skills. "All right, I'll take it. When and where?"

"The cattle yards in lot E, after the shift ends tomorrow around six o'clock," he stated professionally. The he added, "You want me to place a bet?"

I opened my wallet. I had a hundred from the theater owner and sixty in loose bills. "Put me down for a hundred and fifty."

"Should I place it on you or Flannigan?" he questioned gleefully.

"Me, to win, you ass."

"I was just checking where I should place my own money," he stated, "and whether you intend to win or take a fall."

"It's always a pleasure doing business with you Chester." I heard a deep roar of laughter as I hung up.

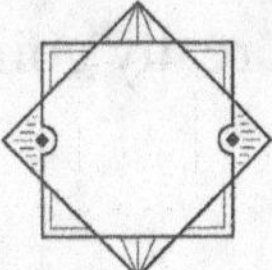

chapter twenty-seven

The alarm clock showed 7 a.m. as the first slanting rays of sun crept through my windows and found me lying in bed watching the last few droplets of rain from the previous night's storm roll off the gutters. As I considered my fate in the forthcoming fight this evening, my thoughts were interrupted by the sharp ring of the telephone. Rolling over, I picked up the receiver and slurred out, "Hello."

"Top o' the morning, Mr. Nayland. It's Danny O'Brien."

"Morning, Danny. What can I do for you?"

"Flatten tells me you're going to fight in a bare knuckler tonight," he said with excitement.

"Maybe," I retorted.

"He also told me you had arranged it yourself with Patterson. Said you needed to raise a sufficient wad of travel money to conclude your current case and that I should call and volunteer my services to keep you alive."

"He's always thoughtful that Flatten. How'd he know about the fight so quickly?"

"You haven't figured that out? David knows all the unsavory doings of this dusty town. It's also fair to say that if he's helping you now or he's helped you in the past, he only gave you fifty percent of what he'd learned or he knew on that particular subject. If you sat in his barber chair and he actually gave you everything he knew about any given subject, you'd be able to solve all your cases from his very shop."

"He's that well informed is he?"

"Aye," he said firmly. "Far more than anybody knows." In an attempt to change the subject, Danny put heavier weight into his heavy Irish brogue. "Faith an' be-Jaysus! Are ya really goin' to enter a bare knuckler?"

"I am," I said with not much conviction.

"Have you ever battled in the ring before?" Danny asked.

"Three or four times…when I needed cash. But they weren't held in any official ring," I said. "It was after the Kaiser fell and before Uncle Sam could ship me home. That I was involved in several money fights. The first was in Paris against a frog sergeant. I knocked him out in the fifth after he'd cut the bridge of my nose with his service ring. I cleared nearly two hundred francs. That covered my liquor cost until I returned state side. The other times were down in Fort Worth when I was a beat cop. Our desk sergeant arranged the fights against contenders from the fire department or the local champion of the railroad or oil company. I remain undefeated." I concluded with pride.

"Impressive, but I didn't call to get your fight history. I called to offer my skills as your corner man in tonight's bout."

"Do you have any experience?"

"Aye, that I have," drawled Danny. " I have a few bouts under my belt me'self. All told I've stepped into the ring in twenty-three gloved matches. I won ten by knock-out, nine by decision, one called a draw, and three I loss by decision. I've also been in dozens of pub fights here and back in the old country."

"Can you handle cuts?" I inquired.

"Aye, I can grease them or stitch them. Whichever one is required."

"I think you'll do then."

"But I've got to be honest with you, Mr. Nayland. I don't know any of the rules in bare knuckle fighting, or even if there are any."

"There's a few, but not many." I spent the next ten minutes giving Danny a brief explanation of the rules of bare knuckle fighting, the most important of which is that the official rules of Queensbury don't apply. "See, Danny, it's illegal in this country to arrange, or participate in, unsanctioned bare-knuckle fights for money. That's why they're kept secret and conducted in out of the way locations."

"Aye, I figured as much."

"The fighters come to the middle of a circle to the scratch line. There is one referee waiting there to start the match. There are no other judges. The sole referee is the only determinant of the winner. You fight with no gloves, only bare knuckles. There's no set time limit for a round. A round lasts until somebody gets thrown to the ground or knocked down by a punch. And there are no specific number of rounds. Throwing and grabbing your opponent are both legal. In fact, if the opportunity arises and you acquire a headlock on your foe, you can legally continue to throw punches at his face and head. If the fighter goes to the ground he has 10 seconds to rise or the fight's over. If he does stand in the stated time, the round's over and he goes to his corner. Sometimes a round only lasts seconds because one fighter sits on the ground for a rest. There's no rule against it, so it ends the round."

"So there be not many rules involved then?"

"The only real rule in bare-knuckle fighting, curiously enough, is that you can't hit your opponent when he is on the ground. In reality, a fair share do get kicked when down. The fight ends when either man knocks out his opponent or his opponent doesn't respond to the bell to come out of his corner."

"Sounds like a hell of a way to make money, if you be asking me," said danny. "But it's your neck and I would like to help if I can."

"I appreciate the offer and gladly accept your assistance. Meet me in the stockades behind Kamp's at 5 o'clock. And Danny, thanks." I hung the phone and headed to the bathroom for a shower.

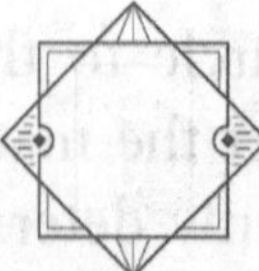# chapter twenty-eight

After I'd toweled off, I poured a double scotch and soda—the soda because it was still before noon—I called the answering service. Nothing important. Just a call from Brett Thomas. He probably wanted to know if I had anything on his wife yet.

Brett was preparing to take a new bride. The one major obstacle to this most worthy and romantic aim was he was having trouble disposing of the old, worn-out model. I hated to disappoint, but the current Mrs. Thomas was not only irrevocably opposed to the divorce, but being a nice Irish girl, she adhered unconditionally to the Oklahoma state law regarding adultery. I followed her for two weeks, but I have to tell you, my heart wasn't in it. Mrs. Thomas was an attractive, if not glamorous, woman of around thirty, of tasteful but conservative dress, and as far as I could see, the very model of propriety. She was a perfectly nice, respectable woman and I concluded that Sharon was 100 percent pure, except for a wild interlude one afternoon when she struck up a conversation with a sex-driven, sixty-six-year-old Episcopal preacher.

This being, of course, the one drawback to being a private detective, because I had got into the P.I. business with the crazy notion I would be able to do good. While I never believed I was cupid, helping true love along the way, I hadn't expected to hinder it either. Yet my investigation put one roadblock after another to romance in poor old Brett's way. When you really look at it, though, it was his wife's fault. She just hadn't come to terms with this brave new world.

I called and consoled Brett, then walked out the rear door of my building intent on investigating Warren's apartment before the evening activities. A southern mockingbird flew out of the red-berried holly bush next to my parked coupe, sailed up to the roof, and yelled curses at me. A large black tom cat sprinted from under my car, settled on the back steps, and gave me that look only cats possess. I shrugged at both disgruntled neighbors, unlocked the Ford, fell in behind the wheel and started up the little V-6.

I drove through midtown, past the Warner Theater. The marquee's white bulbs twinkled on and off. The large black letters a blaze in the center of the marquee announced William Powell and Myrna Loy were starring in After the Thin Man, Disorder in the Court, with the Three Stooges, was showing as the matinee according to the smaller lettering. I drove towards Reno to Warren's last known address. There was no traffic, the only activity was the red and green street lights changing and changing on a mostly deserted street. The traffic lights looked queerly out of place, as if the world had died around them, leaving only the memories of life. I smoothly turned onto Broadway and kept the speedometer needle below the posted speed limit, continuing south towards the Victoria. But an uneasiness came over me.

I checked my mirrors and realized I had picked up a tail. I wondered who it might be. No local police force likes to be queered out of a deal in their own back yard. And if they can move in, orders or not, they are going to give it a big try. If Brice had set the tail, it would have been hard to spot. But District Attorney was too ambitious to figure out there were civilian-type pros in the detective business too.

I turned onto Second Street and headed into the Deuce. For an hour I let my uninvited guest wait outside Ruby's while I had a sandwich and a beer. I stepped back into the bright light of day and headed down the street to the John A. Brown's department store. I fooled for a while picking up a few goodies, then slipped out the side door and walked to the Playmore Bowling Alley and went in the front door. Dashed through the place to the back door behind the pinsetters and slipped into the alley. Certain my tail was inside searching the tables and bathroom, I was back in my car before headed to the Victoria. I parked in the back lot.

Going through Warren's place was only a matter of curiosity. I doubted it would provide me with any clues as the man had been dead for months now. I knocked on the door with no response. So I stepped inside into the main hallway. A middle aged landlady who had grown plump and grandmotherly in the service of the hotel stood dusting the worn wooden railing of the stairs that led to the second floor. "Excuse me. Maybe you can help?"

She waddled towards me over the worn runner on the floor. When she stopped I showed her by badge quickly before she could get a clear look at it. "I need to get into James Warren's apartment. Can you let me in?"

"Nope, because it's already open," she said in a custodial manner. "According to the lease I'm still supposed to clean it once a week. I unlocked it earlier and just haven't got to it yet. Its room twenty above."

"Thanks," I said as I stepped towards the stairs.

"Hey, aren't you cops supposed to flash a warrant or something to enter a residence."

"Not for dead people," I said as I took two steps at time up.

The door was still unlocked. I stepped inside cautiously and listening. It was silent in the apartment. I closed the door softly and followed the hall to the living room. The unit was on the second floor in the rear. It was a set of small, but well decorated, rooms, furnished in excellent taste. It looked lived in, yet everything was in order. It wasn't exceptionally large; then too it had no reason to be. Living mostly alone, a few rooms were all that were necessary.

There were dozens of paintings, some unfinished, leaning against walls, and below shelves well stocked with books of all kinds. I noticed one bookcase that held nothing but volumes of psychology. An oak easel stood near the east window, probably to catch the morning light that most painters preferred to work with. Several good paintings adorned the walls. I looked at them all politely, like they were other people's children. Some of the canvases were vivid with color, bright and glowing and warm. Others were dark and sad. A large couch faced the fireplace where the mantel clock no longer kept time. Above the clock was a painting of a red-haired young man who looked distinctly like Nancy. Clearly this was a portrait of Paige done by Warren. But why was it hanging here. Could it be the missing painting from Paige's apartment?

A wide hallway opened off the living room and led to a bedroom and a small kitchen, with a bathroom opposite. The bedroom contained a large full size bed with no sheets or blankets. Two flashy suits hung inside the closet, nothing more. I checked the nightstands and the dresser. There were no papers in the nightstand. Nothing, in fact, except a soiled deck of cards.

I walked back out to the main room where the middle aged landlady stood in the doorway impatiently waiting for me to finish. I had flashed her my P.I. buzzer to get in, but I suspected she was starting to doubt I was a real cop.

"I'm curious as to why Mr. Warren's property is still here," I asked.

"Mr. Warren paid a year in advance."

"Was he in the habit of disappearing?" I inquired.

"Mr. Warren's business was his own, but he was gone for weeks on end in the past. And all he told me was he was out in the field drawing."

"I see." I continued around the room opening drawers and looking over the writing desk set in the front window. All produced nothing.

The drooping flesh around her eyes and mouth slanted upward in lines of impatience. "He's been a tenant for seven months and never caused any trouble and paid his rent up front like I said."

It was clear she had no more patience for cops. So I thanked her with a phoniness she had no ear to catch and walked out as she locked the door behind us.

Before I left the building, I knocked on some of the closest units and questioned those inside regarding their knowledge of James "Cowboy" Warren. The neighbors, all young bachelors, didn't know anything about Warren, or at least weren't telling for fear of any connections with a known queer. As a whole, the afternoon had been a trip for biscuits.

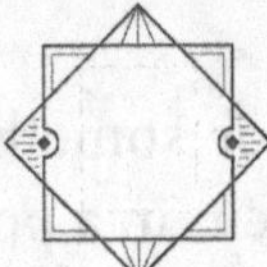

As the 5 o'clock whistle at the slaughterhouse tolled quitting time. I was sitting on a small stool inside the wooden stockade stripped down to nothing but a pair of pants. The distinct smell of cattle droppings enveloped me. I had removed my shoes. The fight promoter had raked down the yard, but there was still the chance of slipping in the manure. Instead, I laced up a pair of high-topped shoes Danny had brought along. They had steel cleats embedded into the soles to help get traction in the dirt.

Danny stood behind me, spit bucket and towel at the ready. Danny had rubbed me down with oil hoping to prevent Bull Flannigan from getting a firm grip on me and pummeling me from the inside. Because of his size I was at a huge disadvantage. Flannigan's corner was doing the same on the other side of the stockade.

Spectators drifted in. Two well-dressed men entered the arena and appeared to be looking for someone. They caught walked directly to my corner. The larger of the two spoke first. "You Nayland?"

"That's me."

"Patterson says you're a square bet and I've got money on you. And I never lose. So you better win, kid. Also, a word of advice-- finish this fight fast. Even if you're as good as Patterson says, you can't go deep against this brute." He tipped his hat and walked away with his companionto get one of the few seats above the arena.

"Who the hell is that?" I asked Danny.

"You don't know?" Danny's Irish-grey eyes hardened a trifle. "That's Alvin "Titanic" Thompson, professional grifter, gambler and golfer."

"Never heard of him," I said.

"Danny smirked. "Do you live in a cave or something? He's the gambler that brought down Arnold Rothstein in a poker game in '28. He travels the country wagering on cards, dice, shooting, billiards, fights, and golf. Some say he's the greatest gambler of the century. He's also a buddy of Minnesota Fats. They say he's a genius at figuring out the odds on almost anyway. Then betting that way, heavily."

"So why's he betting on me if he's so smart."

"My guess is he knows something about how Flannigan fights. And that you can win if you take him out early. I would follow his advice if I were you."

"Who's the guy with him?"

"That'd be Ben Hogan, the professional golfer."

"Why's he hanging with Titanic?"

Danny chuckled. "They travel together hustling golf matches against local pros in the off season. I heard that Thompson can golf ambidextrous. They challenge these local pros to play right-handed then double down if they switch to left. Apparently, they have cleaned the courses here all week."

"Nice guys." Just then a large bald man with an auburn beard entered the corral and stood in the center of the arena. "Who's the referee?" I asked Danny.

"That be James J. Braddock, pride of the Irish, Cinderella man, ex Irish heavyweight champion, and current world champion. Titanic must have brought him in to keep the fight square. Must be big money riding on this fight today on account of Thompson being involved. How are you feeling, you ready?"

"I'm copacetic Danny boy. Let's get this thing started."

A makeshift bell rang, and Braddock called the fighters to the scratch line in the middle of the ring. The pugilists stood stripped to the waist. We were very different, both in form and feature.

The expression on my opponent's face was fierce with intensity. Though I was two inches taller than him, he had four inches on me in shoulder width. His back and chest muscles stood out prominently all over his torso. His muscular effect made me look like an overgrown schoolboy that had been poorly fed and more poorly taken care of. Braddock briefed us on the rules, sparse as they were, and sent us to our corners. When Braddock shouted, "Time!" my fifth professional fight began.

Flannigan and I advanced quickly from our corners, reached the scratch and eyed each other briefly. He took an awkward boxing stance and raised his balled fists. Fortunately both of us fought with dominant right hands. I kept my distance and worked to his left with multiple jabs to his face and ears. Becoming annoyed with my tactics, Flannigan suddenly reached up, grabbed me around the neck, and threw me down. The round lasted 20 seconds.

I backed up and took a seat on the stool while Danny toweled me down. "You've got reach on him. Keep working to his left and use your legs to keep him at distance. When you come in, work his belly."

The bell rang and Flannigan and I came out smiling from our corners. After some nervous sparring, I again pushed to his left with constant jabs using my legs to avoid another headlock. Disgruntled, Flannigan left his side unprotected, and I stepped in and delivered three or four rib roasters to his stomach and kidneys. Flannigan replied quickly on the conk, with multiple haymakers aimed at my head. I deflected them with my fists and caught him in the left optic, materially interfering with that organ's ability to function effectively causing Flannigan to go to the dirt.

Back in the corner, Danny coached. "Keep working the left side, especially now. That left eye is going to close up shortly, creating a blind spot. Keep working the belly. You can't take him yet so stay outside his reach."

Braddock stepped to the center, yelled "time," and Flannigan came straight for me from across the ring. With a smart little dance move I avoided his head long attack and worked to the center of the ring. Flannigan advanced and aimed a blow for my nose. But it fell short, and we clinched. We pushed each other into the hard wood panels of the arena. The crowd began to boo, so Braddock stepped forward and pulled us apart, motioning us back to the middle of the ring. Bull bestowed his attention on my face, while I was content to shower quick hot shots to the big man's ribs, breast, and kidneys. Suddenly I was caught by a blow to my left ear from Flannigan's roundhouse. As the stars cleared, I found myself on my ass in the dirt. Flannigan had already returned to his stool. I stood and wobbled to my own corner.

Danny shoved me onto the stool. "I told you to keep your distance. He's as strong as an ox. You can't take too many of those haymakers and expect to prevail."

"That's your great insight, Danny? Kind of figured that one out on my own." Danny used his index finger to spread grease over my eyebrows to prevent cutting.

I answered the call of time, but resorted to considerable feinting when I reached the scratch line. Flannigan attempted to use his legs to protect his left side, especially now that his eye was now swollen closed. I danced and slowly retreated until I came upon the railings enclosing the corral. Flannigan bore down on me. I grabbed hold of the rail with my right hand, and with this leverage, swung myself around and with my left hand, a double severe blow to Flannigan's throat. Immediately blood gushed in torrents from the big man's mouth and I instantly followed up with a sharp blow with my right hand to Flannigan's left eye, he fell on impact. Braddock called out, "First blood, Nayland," and money exchanged hands in the stands as bets were settled. Bull rose quickly however and returned to his corner. He washed out his with water and sat into a bucket but it continued to bleed in excess.

The fight odds had been 3 to 1 against myself at the beginning of the fight, but as we watched Flannigan's corner attempt to refresh their fighter with wet handkerchiefs, Danny leaned in and said, "The odds are now 2 to 1 in your favor."

Braddock returned to the center of the ring and called "Time." Flannigan commenced into the ring cautiously, but resorted to considerable feinting when he reached the mark. He sent a good punch to my mid-section, but I stopped it neatly with an elbow block, and jabbed to his left eye. Bull stepped in big, pulled me into a clinch and stepped on my foot, accidentally or otherwise. His steel cleats punctured the top of my shoe. I felt the distinct flow of hot blood seeping around my foot.

Braddock broke the clinch. Flannigan led off and planted a terrific blow to my forehead. I returned one onto his cheek and two to his mouth. He rushed me again attempting to tackle me to the dirt, but I side-stepped his rush and danced myself back to the center. The rest of the round was a repeat of the first until jabbed him in the left temple and he fell back onto the dirt.

Sitting in my corner watching the Bull in his corner, Danny spoke softly into my ear. "It's time Lou. Concentrate on that left eye."

Braddock called "time." Bull Flannigan walked slowly to the scratch line. I reached the center, touched his upraised hands, and began working to his left with short jabs to his blackened closed left eye. He pulled his hands in so close that his knuckles appeared to be buried in his nose. So I worked his belly with multiple blows from my right and left, until he was forced to lower his hands, exposing his face. Two quick blows to his nose and left eye and Flannigan still would not fall. I delivered a sharp blow to his left temple and ear, blood rushed out of his ear and his mouth, he finally fell.

Danny ran the cold wet sponge over my shoulders, but when time was called for the next round, Flannigan's corner man threw up a white handkerchief in token of his principal's defeat. Danny climbed over the rail and held my right arm high and turned us in a circle to face the spectators. Every man in the crowd cheered the victor. At least the ones that had bet on me. When he let me go, I limped over to Flannigan's corner, shook his hand, and thanked him for the fight.

Later, removing the high-tops Danny had lent me, Titanic, and Hogan came over to my corner. "Great fight kid. I told you to finish him early." He reached through the rails and handed me $300 dollars. "This should cover your bet at the final odds of 2 to 1 kid."

"Why are you paying me?" I asked. "I placed that bet with

Patterson."

"Because he placed it with me. And he said you might be in a hurry after the fight. So I'm covering for him."

"Thanks."

"No, thank you, kid. I just made two grand on you." As Hurricane and his golfing partner walked away to their car I caught a glimpse of man leaning on a corral post. He wore a black fedora bulled down and his coat collar turned up. He had a rolled up sporting magazine under his left arm. When our eyes meet he nodded his head at men and then turned and melding into the crowed exiting the arena. He reminded me of the man that had stood on the street outside the Century rooms, but I couldn't be sure. Was he tailing me or was he just one of Patterson's hoods keeping an eye on the outcome of the fight? I shrugged and handed Danny his fighting shoes along with fifty of the dollars Thompson had given me. "Thanks, kid, for the shoes and your support."

Danny grinned. "You be welcome, I enjoyed the show. I've got something for you from Flatten. He said to pass it on if you won tonight." He handed me a piece of stained folded paper.

I unfolded the paper and read the note inside.

Lou,

I've learned that Paige may still be alive and is currently hiding out in Juarez, Mexico. To find the answers you seek go to the El Gato Café in Juarez which is a block and half south on the other side of the Santa Fe Bridge. There is a waiter there by the name of Pepe. He works the day shift. I've been told he knows the parties involved. I recommend you stay at the El Casa Del Lago Hotel. A mutual friend uses the place for business south of the border and it also so happens to be the hotel that Warren supposedly worked out of when he painted in Mexico these last three or four winters.

I slid the note into my hip pocket, climbed out of the arena, and we headed to the parking lot.

"You should get that foot looked at from where the Bull cleated you," Danny said as we walked.

"I will, son." I limped out to my coupe parked behind Cattlemen's, and headed over to Doc's office to have a proper professional look at my foot.

chapter thirty

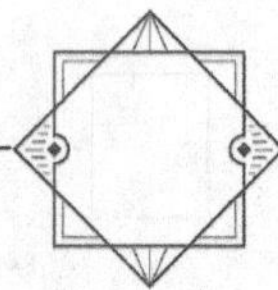

"Lou, your line of work is going to kill you!" said Doc as he cleaned the blood off my foot. "How the hell did you get a dozen puncture wounds in your foot?"

"If I told you, you wouldn't believe me."

"Try me."

"I fought in an illegal bare-knuckle match to raise enough money to search for the Swalia boy."

Doc snorted. "You're right, I don't believe you. But speaking of the missing young man, let me run something by you. What if I told you I've found a connection in the Galligan, MacDougall and O'Donnell slayings?"

"Out with it, McDuff," I said, suddenly interested. "Tell me what you have learned."

"You remember when you sat in on the Galligan autopsy and I suggested that the young man had been sexually active, but not with a woman?"

"Yes…"

"Well, I found that applies to all three of our victims."

I grimaced as he swabbed the punctures on my foot with alcohol. "Sorry to tell you, Doc, but I'd already discovered all three were involved intimately with Warren."

"Then that part is conclusive," he said, and tossed a used swab into the trashcan. "I also believe that even though they were all killed by different means, the same assailant committed all three murders. The brutality and precision of the crimes leads me to that conclusion."

"How do you mean, Doc?"

"From medically calculating their times of death and my review of statements made in the police reports, all three deaths occurred within minutes of midnight. And I do believe the precise timing of these murders is connected to a significant event in the killer's history. I would go as far as to suggest the event that enraged our killer occurred at midnight. Most likely some form of rejection."

"A childhood thing you think?"

"No. I think his anger comes from a relationship that ended poorly, and our murderer is now taking revenge on everyone he's been intimate with, whether they rejected him or not. He might have a disease, or he might just be cold-blooded and smart as hell. If he is an older man, maybe the rejection contributed to his feeling of hopelessness. I'm just theorizing there, because I have no way of calculating the killer's age. Anyway, I think whoever this guy is he would fool some pretty smart psychiatrists."

"If my guesses are correct, I would say that your theory is accurate." I paused to gather my thoughts. "I believe that Warren is somehow connected with these deaths. I know he's supposed to be dead, but I believe he may still be alive and holed up here in the city, or more likely, has returned to Mexico. That's why I needed money—to go to Mexico and check it out. Hope it was worth it."

Doc carefully applied the last bandage to my wounds. "Well, keep me posted on what you find out. Come the first of the week I to have to call Jackson with my conclusion that all three deaths are connected. I'll let him sort out who handles the case, his office or the city bulls."

I drove back to my apartment for some much needed sleep. I knew it wouldn't come easy, because even though I was dead tired, my body had begun to ache in spots I didn't remember having.

chapter thirty-one

I only get philosophical once in a coon's age, but after my visit with Doc, I paced my apartment feeling suddenly alone, out of touch and communion with the world. The way it happens sometimes. I brewed some coffee and smoked a few cigarettes. Then I went to the bedroom and picked up a book on the nightstand. I read a few lines, like my life depended on reading 'em right. I wondered where in the hell I got that idea from; I knew my life didn't depend on anything that made sense, I felt even more alone.

I wanted to call somebody. Anybody. Maybe rush out and knock on Mrs. Giannasi's door to make sure there was somebody else in the world. Only I didn't. I'm not that crazy. Right? Maybe I'm afraid that when her door opens there really won't be anybody there. But this was one of those nights when I damn sure didn't enjoy my solitude, when I really didn't want to be alone. I'm usually able to shake the feeling with a drive around town. When I was done, I'd come home, take a warm shower, and have several stiff drinks of scotch and sleep until noon. But I had plans tomorrow. I was getting on a plane to Juarez, Mexico.

I went into the kitchen and whipped up some scrambled eggs with peppers. I finished it almost without tasting it. That used up some time, but not enough. I thought about calling Irene and inviting myself over for a drink or vice versa. But I knew Irene better than that. No matter how we felt about one another, calling at 9:30 to suggest she take me in for the evening might antagonize her, being it wasn't a Friday. Women are funny about things like that. They don't like you presuming they aren't booked solid weeks in advance. Or they think you're coming over to propose. And then there's hell to pay when they discover you're "only interested in one thing."

I picked up the book I had been reading. What had interested me the night before was now dull. I was itchy, restless, nerve ends twitching and temples throbbing. I prowled the apartment, opening and shutting drawers for no reason, looking into cabinets without really seeing or being aware of what I was doing. Anything to keep from thinking about Irene or my loneliness.

This was just one of those "nowhere" nights. Only I didn't want to stand still long enough to ask myself the same old question. Why bother? I already knew the answer.

I had another drink and tried to think about something else. That made it worse. Anne, a beautiful dame I once knew in Ft. Worth, and hadn't been able to forget, came to mind. She was a tall, quiet gal with curly brunette hair and legs that ran to the sea. We'd had one of those wild affairs that we both knew from the start wasn't going to work out. I was crazy about her, the way you get only once in a lifetime if you're lucky. The only thing that mattered was being with her. Everything else was a waste of time.

But scotch and kisses weren't enough for either of us. We were two ships that passed in the night and all that crap. Though I thought I would marry her, she ran off with a two-bit con man I was trying to nail on a check kiting scheme. She needed more thrills than I was able to provide, evidently. So much for true love?

It had been an impossible situation from the start. No logic, no reason for it. Maybe that was what made it so sweet, so much more difficult to get over.

I'd think I had it licked, or not be thinking about it at all. Like when I was watching the Indians play baseball on a Sunday afternoon, or talking to another dame. Or tonight! Then I'd be hit with the thought of her, feeling that sudden rush of emptiness in my belly, like being scared. But worse because I really couldn't defend myself or run away from it. And I'd be left drained and ashamed of being so damned vulnerable that the thought of her name and the wisp of a memory could still do so much to me.

Sometimes I fought it by turning on the radio! Invite a new female acquaintance over! Drink up! And then there were other times, the weak moments, when I let it all wash over me in waves of pity and sorrow.

Funny that it was never any momentous event, any supreme act of love or passion that came to mind. I was more likely to remember how it was getting up before dawn on a cold winter's morning. Sitting on the edge of the bed, putting on my union suit and leaning back to kiss her again at that moment when she was most desirable, sleepy, tousled and warm.

I thought about how it was to have that feeling of not wanting to go, of being a little sad because, God damn it, parting really was such sweet sorrow. It really was a little like dying, this leaving after knowing the sweetness and comfort of being able to reach out and touch someone in the darkness of the night.

Then thinking of how it was standing on the windy street corner or outside some shady cheap hotel in the cold light of morning, warmed with the thought of her. Of wanting to go back and never leave, yet knowing that there was something inside me that always had to leave, to say good-bye to the warmth of a solid woman.

But she had chosen another and I now lived the life I had chosen. Catching clerks with their hands in the till, listening to other people's conversations and following errant spouses until I caught them being naughty. Or just finding missing brothers. There was an itch in me, an itch, to travel on the night train of life without baggage and without company. There would always be just me and that client in desperate need of resolution that only I could provide. For me to stop too long was to die. Because when I did stop, I always realized I was standing apart from the crowd; the poor kid, with his nose pressed up against John A. Brown's department store window at Christmas time.

Knowing all this didn't make me the happiest guy in the world. I missed Anne, and I would probably always miss her. Yet I couldn't change, even though there were times of sadness and melancholy.

And tonight, I was drowning in it. Listening to midnight music and drinking. I don't remember whether it was four fingers in eight glasses, or eight fingers in four glasses. I don't remember going to bed. Maybe because I didn't.

All I remember is getting sadder and sadder.

chapter thirty-two

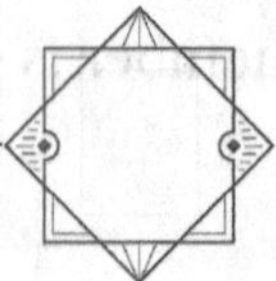

There's nothing like a good drunk. It knocks the melancholy out of you and clears the air like a summer storm. I had one hell of a headache, and the shrill jangling of the telephone at 9:15 a. m. didn't help any. All things considered though, I felt fine. Trans World Airlines was at the other end of the line confirming my flight to Tucson, Arizona, flight number 110 with a stopover in Albuquerque leaving at 11:55.

A couple hours later found me and twenty-four other passengers sitting on the tarmac at Oklahoma City Municipal Airfield. We were inside the streamlined trans-continental Douglas DC-3 under the command of what appeared to be the most affable men. My fellow passengers constituted a select and delightful mix of society. The charm of new acquaintances and amusements would make the flight pass agreeably. As the plane reached its flight altitude of 12,000 feet, we all settled in to enjoy the pleasant sensation of being separated from the world, living, as it were, on an unknown island, therefore obligated to be sociable with one another. Twenty-four hours earlier none of the airplane's occupants knew each other. But we were condensed for several hours in an aluminum wrapped craft, defying the bouncing of the air turbulence and the coldness of the altitude, which led to extreme intimacy. Perhaps those sensations are why so many ventures aboard this modern mechanical wonder with mixed feelings of pleasure and fear.

We touched down at 4:50 and after I collected my luggage, I

inquired as to the closest garage to rent a car. "Pete's Garage usually had a car to lease for reasonable rates," said the TWA ticket collector. "Walk out the front doors of the terminal, turn left and walk south for four blocks to the garage. Ask for Pete himself." After I haggled with Pete, he leased me a big Packard. I paid five days in advance and headed down state highway 90 towards Juarez.

I stared moodily through the windshield at the wide strip of concrete that was flowing rapidly backward beneath my wheels. When I neared the halfway point to the Mexican border, I stumbled upon the worst driver in the world. He was driving a tan and red 1931 Maclaughlin-Buick convertible coupe with the rag up as if he were tacking a sailboat on the sea. The heavy car wove back and forth across the freeway, across both lanes and sometimes the gravel skirt. It was late, and I felt the need to sleep soon. I started to pass the convertible on the right, as it was riding the double line. The Buick drifted towards me like a steer trying to push the cowboy and his horse into a barbed wire fence. I was forced me off the road into a screeching skid. I hit all sixes in an attempt to pass the big convertible on the left. Simultaneously, the driver of the breezer accelerated. My speed couldn't match his. We raced neck and neck down the middle of the road. I wondered if he was drunk, crazy, both, or just after me.

The road narrowed. I was doing seventy-five on the wrong side of a two-lane highway, and a truck came over the rise ahead like a bull out of the gate. I pushed the pedal to the floor and yanked the wheel sharply to the right, threatening the Buick and its driver. In the approaching headlights I could see his face was tight in fierce competition, with black holes for eyes. He glanced over and recognition sparkled in those eyes.

As the truck closed in, honking angrily, he slowed enough to let me get slid into the right lane. The truck eased off onto the skirt of gravel. I braked gradually, hoping to force the Buick to stop. But it swung past me in a looping arc, tires skittering, and then faded away into the twilight.

When I finally came to a stop, I pried my fingers off the wheel and wonder if the driver was drunk or was connected to my investigation, threatening me to give up. After smoking several cigarettes my nerves calmed down. I drove on south until midnight, when I pulled over to a roadside campsite and tried to sleep the remainder of the night.

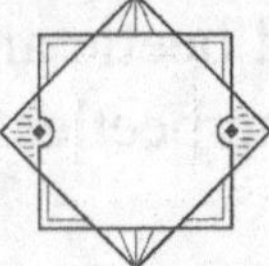

chapter thirty-three

The morning sun beating through the front windshield woke me. My mouth was sticky and my throat dry from the half a pack of cigarettes I'd smoked the previous evening. I climbed out of the Packard and walked to the water spigots provided by the state. I took a whore's bath.

While drying my face with a handkerchief I noticed a big pandenus scorpion emerging with a dry rustle from the finger-sized whole under a finely polished pebble, its two black fighting claws held forward like a wrestler's arms. The scorpion danced to the center of a small patch of hard flat sand outside the hole and stood motionless on the tips of its four pairs of legs, its nerves and muscles braced for a quick retreat as its senses quested for minute vibrations which would decide its next move. The early morning sun, glittering down through a mesquite tree, threw sapphire highlights off the hard black polish of the five-inch body and glistened brightly on the moist white sting which protruded from the last segment of the tail, curved over parallel with the scorpion's flat back.

A foot away, at the bottom of a slope of sand, that had been created by the wind against the base of the tree, a small greenish beetle concerned only with trudging onwards to better pastures than he'd found under the mesquite bush. The swift rush of the scorpion gave him no time to open his wings to escape. Flipped onto its back, the beetle's legs waved in protest as the scorpion's sharp claws clamped around his body, and then its stinger lanced into him from over the scorpion's head and he was instantly dead.

After killing the beetle, the scorpion stood motionless, testing the ground and air for hostile vibrations. Reassured, its fighting claws withdrew from the half-severed beetle and its two small feeding pincers reached out and into the beetle's flesh and fastidiously ate its victim.

I walked back to the car and retrieved a clean shirt from my suitcase, attempted to comb my hair in the car's rear-view mirror, gave up, and jammed my Wilton back on for the hour drive into Juarez.

The broad ribbon of the Rio Grande gleamed in the morning sun. As I approached the border, vagrant lights flickered atop the International Bridge. I came to a stop at the checkpoint. A man in a khaki uniform emerged from a small, framed hut and bustled forward to meet me. As he circled the car, I began to doubt my ability to cross the border. I'd had negative experiences before at other border crossings and I knew the authorities on both sides were, at times, inflexible about what time they closed and opened the bridge. But he soon approached my open window, asked me for my ID, read it briefly, handed it back and beckoned me to drive on. I was halted briefly on the Mexican side but the Mexican officer courteously waved me through.

I smiled at the sign the Juarez Chamber of Commerce had installed on the side of the road.

You are Now Nearing
JUAREZ, MEXICO
Pop. 39,699
WATCH US GROW

The traffic on Juarez Avenue grew heavier as neared the center of the city. I turned onto a main street, pushed down on the accelerator directing the nose of the car towards the towers surrounding the main plaza. I rolled by the Lobby Café and the Crystal Palace, both still dark and shuttered and passed the local police station. The muggy Mexican spring air blew through the car's chromed vents in a vain attempt to cool the interior, but it was losing the battle.

Juarez is different from an American city, of course. Circulars published by the Juarez Chamber of Commerce describe the border city as having a "delightfully quaint, old-world charm." I wouldn't have chosen those words. The streets are narrow, and the pavement is in poor condition. Business and homes are built of adobe, or flimsy frame construction, and are either incredibly old and weathered or flamboyantly flaunt new paint. Ragged children crowd the streets, ganging up on American tourists to beg for centavos, or they furtively offer to guide males to the infamous Calle de Diablo where women in cribs sell their services for practically whatever one wishes to pay.

Once in the plaza I expertly maneuvered the big Packard into a narrow parking space in front of a small hotel. The display above the door flashed with red and green lights. In large red letters the sign read La Fonda Motel. I smiled. La fonda means "the hotel" in Spanish, which makes the name ridiculous—the Hotel Motel— when translated. I suspected the original owner had been an American.

I grabbed my luggage in an attempt to look the part of a touristas and walked to the post office for directions. Inside I found a large, lightly complected man with thick black hair cut at the collar in a brown government issued shirt and pants along with the standard black cloth tie. "Bueno dias, senor."

"Bueno dias," he replied.

"Donde hay esta El Gato Café?"

"Esta cerca de la Plaza Sendro Las Torres en Av de Las Torres."

"Muchas gracias, senor." I stepped back out into the sizzling Mexican sun. The now sizzling temperature penetrated the back of my summer wool suit. I watched shawled women and sombreroed men walking along the sidewalks. Some of the women carried large clay pots balanced perfectly on their heads. The scene clearly reflected the Commerce's promise of a city with quaint old-world charm. I admired the local scenery briefly then strode towards the rental car.

I noticed the El Gato Pobre was open for business. Danny had told me it was always open and it was the best cantina for local ethnic cuisine id I needed some comfort food. Most of the joints in Juarez depended entirely on American patronage, but Danny swore the El Gato Pobre wasn't one of those dives because the tourist hadn't discovered it yet.

As I stood looking at the café, a local man wearing a white suit and matching straw hat rushed up to me. He was almost as tall as I, but thinner, his olive face marked by twin creases from cheekbone to chin, above deep-sunken brown eyes with laugh lines radiating from the edges, and dominated by a thick, black, neatly trimmed mustache riding on his lips that were thick, moist looking, and curiously scarred in the center. "Taxi, senor, taxi? I speak English, mister, and I have a fine automobile."

"No, thanks," I told him as I tried to slip by.

"I can drive you anywhere," he persisted. "I can show you the sights, but good."

"That's what I'm afraid of so, sorry, I don't need a guide."

"Why do you repulse me, senor? Mexico is heaven, but without me she's a disappointment."

"No doubt," I tried to conclude the discussion by walking over to a small girl in a beautifully colored dress selling flowers on the corner. Her large brown eyes and face lit up as I approached. I took a bouquet of flowers and handed her two US quarters and thanked her in Spanish.

The taxi driver sidled up. "I think you will need me here in Juarez. Are you here on business or pleasure, senor?"

"Pleasure."

"You in luck, senor, pleasure is my business. Names Ricardo Guzman, whatever you need, look no farther, I'm your man."

I really didn't need a taxi with my Packard sitting across the street, but I thought I might be less obvious if I did use the taxi. "Alright, Ricardo. Lead the way."

Ricardo picked up my case and continued his sales pitch. "You want the best Mexican cooking? My cousin Hector has the best cantina in the city. Night life? You can't beat my cousin Juan's

Crystal Palace."

"How many cousins do you have?"

"How many do you need? So, what is it, senor, music, booze, food, a senora to keep you company?"

"Don't tell me the senora is your cousin, Ricardo?"

"No, she's not my cousin, but she is a close friend of my cousin."

I gave him a knowing smile. "No, Ricardo. I don't think I need to meet the friend of your cousin today. I thought I would just look around the city today. A friend told me to check out a place called the El Gato Café."

"I know the place, senor, back towards the border. It has lots of tourists."

"Let's try it anyway."

We walked to his taxi where a young boy sat in the front seat. "This is my son Poncho."

"Bueno dias, senor," the young man said as his father threw my case into the backseat and slid in behind the wheel.

I stood there inspecting the car, "What's this?"

"I own the Tradino, senor."

"A Tardine?"

"Si, si, senor, you want a better car you trade in an old car for a new one. Get in, get in senor. You're in good hands now. By the way I didn't catch your name."

"Nayland, Lou Nayland," I told him as I hopped into the backseat next to my case.

We headed off down the street and Ricardo continued his monologue. "That's Alda Maria Park. She is very historical."

"Very nice, Ricardo," I interrupted. "Did you notice that another taxi has been following us?" I watched the pursuing taxi weave in and out of the flow of traffic, attempting to keep us in sight.

"Yes, I notice that now."

"Is there any chance you could lose them?"

"Don't worry, senor. Nobody knows the Mexican police like Ricardo. You don't think I'm going to lose a good passenger, eh?"

"Why would the police be following us in a taxi though?"

"Many reasons, senor. Maybe when you crossed the border

you raised suspicion, or maybe somebody knows you're in Juarez on secret business and they paid them to keep an eye on you, or maybe they are bored and just tailing you to see what an American is doing in their city. There can be many reasons or no reason in Mexico." Ricardo shrugged his shoulders and continued as a tour guide. "On the left is Caballito's. If you get lost sometime, you come here, Ricardo will find you."

Poncho jumped in, "Hey senor, you want to make a circle around?"

"Not just now, but look, the sooner that we lose them the better."

"And the slower, the surer, don't worry we still have a way to go." Ricardo added.

As the taxi approached the northern part of the city the car began to smoke. "The motor she don't run so good now," stated Ricardo.

"Every plaza we come to she gets worse." Poncho injected.

I turned to check on the taxi following us. It was nowhere to be seen. "Turn off there, Ricardo. Up that alleyway." Ricardo quickly braked and swung onto the deserted side street. After I observed the trailing taxi go by, we all exited the vehicle, lifted the hood and inspected the smoking engine. "What seems to be the matter?" I asked.

"Everything, senor. Someday I get mad and turn this car in for junk." Ricardo walked off around the corner.

Poncho handed me some tools. "Maybe you can do something, senor?"

Twenty minutes later as Poncho and I leaned against the smoking car, Ricardo reappeared driving a new four door Ford. "Get your luggage and come on, senor."

"What's this? Another Tardine?"

Ricardo chuckled. "No, senor. She's a sixteen cylinder down payment."

"Never heard of it."

"Down payment and they take that car as a down payment on this one."

"Okay, but from here on you need to stay on the back roads."

"No senor, that's where you make a mistake. Your pursuer don't look for this car, whoever they may be."

"You seemed to know the police pretty well," I suggested.

"Not really, senor, but when they look for the old car and find out what's happen, Poof!, we will be gone."

Fifteen minutes later we parked in front of the El Gato Café.

chapter thirty-four

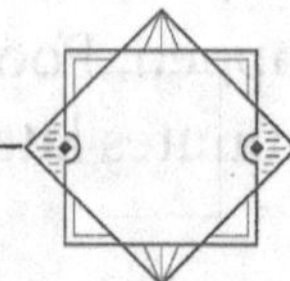

Ricardo and I looked over the interior of the café. It was not your typical border cabaret. Fifty wooden tables covered with Mexican flag styled tablecloths filled the low-ceilinged room and intimate dining nook in the rear. Only half were occupied at this early hour. A few diners were Americans, the remainder prosperous-appearing Mexicans.

Two Mexicans sat on their stools and drank cervezas in front of the long oak bar. Behind them was the traditional frosted mirror and long rows of bottles. Glasses and spoons littered the far end of the bar near a fair sized dance floor. There was a small raised platform set against the wall. I assumed a band played on it in the evenings. A square-shouldered, semi-bald man plied a bar rag with what amounted to violence and one look at him left no doubt concerning his origin. He was one of those American bartenders driven to Mexico by prohibition who had never returned.

Ricardo and I walked to a table in the corner and sat. A heavy pall of smoke hung over the room, and the chatter of Mexican conversation was ceaseless. Two drunken American couples sat two tables away directly in front of us. They'd evidently missed getting across the bridge before it closed the night before and had obviously made a night and morning of it. Otherwise, the clientele was as sedate and well-mannered as that of any first-class American restaurant.

A Mexican waiter came toward us in a rumpled vest and apron.

"Que desean ustedes?"

"Dos cervezas y dos huevos revueltos con chile, por favor."

When the waiter was out of hearing I told Ricardo that a friend of a friend worked here."

"What is the name of your friend of a friend, senor?"

"His name is Pepe."

"Pepe Guzman?"

"I don't know for sure. My friend just gave me his first name and said I should speak to him."

"Pepe is my cousin, senor. He is a very nice boy, though it's been said that he wields a stiletto and runs marijuana across the border." Ricardo shrugged. "You know, young men. But I'm sure he'll be glad to see his friend of a friend."

Our beer was good. There is none better than Modelo. We drank it slowly from our mugs and waited for breakfast. The diners were gradually leaving the café. The two American couples started an acrimonious drunken argument which ended with the smaller of the men taking a wild swing at his companion, missing, and landing under the table. The trio went on drinking and left him there.

The waiter returned as we finished our mugs of beer. Ricardo ordered more as well as questioning our waiter, "Dos cervezas y una informacion, por favor."

"Si lo puedo, senor."

"Pepe esta aqui hoy?" Ricardo inquired.

"Si, senor. El esta en la cocina." The waiter affirmed that Pepe was in the kitchen.

"Puedes pedirle que venga a hablar con nostros. Dile que su primo esta aqui."

Ricardo leaned over and said, "I told the waiter to have Pepe join us."

Soon a tall Mexican wearing a vest and apron threaded his way between the tables toward us. Dank black hair fell forward over his brown cheeks. His dark brown eyes were fixed on us as he made his way toward the table. He couldn't have been more than twenty. He carried himself with arrogance, seemingly put on to conceal an inward weakness.

I lit a cigarette and puffed on it, watching the red-grey ashes move down toward my fingers as we waited. The young man stopped by my chair. "Hola, primo."

"Hello, cousin," Ricardo replied brusquely, when he sensed the youth's suspicion of my presence. "This is my new friend, Lou Nayland."

Pepe's eyes flickered over me as he extended his right hand. "Nice to meet you, Mr. Nayland."

"And you, Pepe." I shook his hand.

Ricardo pushed out the empty chair at our table. "Please sit down. My friend would like to ask you a few questions and you will tell us what you know, si?"

"Si." He sat down just as our waiter placed the scrambled eggs and beans on the table.

"Flatten sends his good wishes," I said. "He also hinted that you might be able to help me out while I'm in the country, in exchange for that favor he did for your brother."

The young man's gaze flickered uneasily. "I will be happy to, if I can."

I reached into my vest and pulled out the picture of Paige. "Have you ever seen this man?"

Pepe looked closely at the picture for a moment. "Yes, senor. I saw him in Juarez several weeks ago. I had gone to the El Casa Del Lago Hotel to pick up my sister. She works there as a bellhop. Anyway, when Senor Flatten called me, he asked me to keep a look out for two Americans. One a young man, most likely well dressed with bright red hair, the other man being Senor Warren. I knew the man I saw in the lobby with red hair was his man. So I sent him a telegram saying I'd seen the young man."

"You're sure that the man you saw at the hotel that day is the same one as the one in the picture I just showed you?"

"Si, senor," he said, fiddling with his glass with the dark fingers of his left hand.

"Have you seen him around since?"

"No, senor, but I can talk to my sister to see if he has been in the hotel lately. I will call you and tell you tonight."

"It's better that I call you, Pepe. I'm not sure where I'll be staying."

"Si, senor," Pepe said. He took a pencil out of his pocket, wrote his number on a piece of paper, then slid it across the table to me.

I placed the number in my pocket. "How would you know if James Warren was, or wasn't, in town, Pepe?"

His slight frame tensed as he leaned back in his chair. "Everyone in Juarez knows Senor Warren. He is a very generous tipper, especially to young men working as waiters and bartenders."

"I understand. And when was the last time you saw or heard Mr. Warren in Juarez?"

"It was the week before Christmas." He spoke deliberately, as though each word took distinct effort. "Now, senor, if that is all, I must get back to the kitchen."

"Gracias, Pepe."

Ricardo frowned and looked me in the eye. "I thought you were here for pleasure, senor?"

"I am, Ricardo, but I was asked to find and speak to Paige Swalia for his sister if I ran into him while I was down here on vacation."

"I see, senor."

We finished our breakfast in silence, after which I paid for us both and asked Ricardo to drive me to the Hotel El Casa Del Largo.

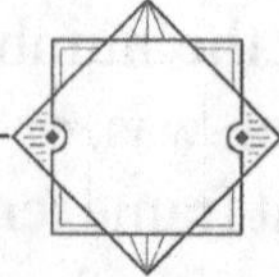

chapter thirty-five

Ricardo and his son, Poncho, drove back to the center of the city. The sun was high and bright, effectively turning the whole city griddle hot. After circling the plaza twice Ricardo pulled up in front of the only open cantina and asked two old timers selling fruit from a cart for better directions to the hotel. "Bueno tardes? Donde hay esta Hotel El Casa Del Lago?"

"Ir tres cuadras girar a la izquierda, estra en el derecho."

Poncho said, "Mucho gracias."

"Por nada."

Ricardo pulled Poncho back into the car. "You let me give thanks for my own questions."

Five minutes later Ricardo pulled his taxi through the stone stucco archway into the courtyard of the Hotel El Casa Del Lago. A neon vacancy sign, with a Mexican sleeping under a sombrero, flashed luminously above the office door. The main structure of the hotel was a three-story building with an orange tiled roof. There were two wings to the hotel that ran to the east and west of the main hotel, each a two-story stucco edifice with exterior hallways and wrought iron rails. A three-tier water fountain burbled in the center of the courtyard, small rainbows dancing in the spray.

I gazed at my new digs and stated to no one in particular, "So this is Hotel El Casa Del Lago?"

"Si, senor."

"Isn't this where the artist James Warren did most of his painting when in Mexico?"

Ricardo shrugged. "Quien sabe? If it is, I'll find out for you which room he worked and slept in and you can sleep in the same bed, no?"

"No." I entered the lobby through the glass panel front door. The small lobby inside was pleasantly furnished with rattan and chintz with two large oil paintings of bullfighters hanging on the walls.

Ricardo followed me and continued talking to the back of my neck. "No, okay. But I still ask questions about him for you, senor."

As we walked to the main desk, a beautiful woman, with jet black hair that spread like silken corn hairs across her shoulders, walked in from the courtyard. She wore a yellow and green cotton dress of with a rather demure neckline and no sleeves. Her legs were bare, and she wore strappy leather sandals. Though she was probably twenty-six or so, she seemed child-like, her eyes large and brown with glints of green, appeared apprehensive. She wore no noticeable perfume, but there was a sort of powdered, delicately feminine aroma about her, clean and fresh as a tropical night on the water and as sensual as a roomful of dancing girls.

I tipped my hat to her as she passed. "Buenos tardes, senorita."

"Good day, senor," she said in perfect English with a hint of a Mexican accent. Her voice was as soft as a whispered "kiss me."

I traipsed across the well-worn Navajo rugs covering the lobby floor to the main desk, where a matronly woman flipped through the day's mail. Her face was gouged and eroded by years of trouble. Black hair, shot with grey, hung in straight limp bangs over her forehead. Large, tarnished silver rings dangled from her earlobes. Several silver chains circled her withered neck, the longest having a large turquoise stone pendant on the end. They all tinkled when she looked up at me. "What can I do for you?" If there was a lilt of coquetry in the question, I don't think it was meant for me. It was simply there, a surplus from her youth.

"I would like to register, please," I stated with a sincere smile.

In a voice a few degrees colder than absolute zero, she replied, "I'm sorry, senor, but the rooms are all taken."

"Who's in thirteen?" I asked, noticing that the mail slot behind the desk had a key in it and no mail like the others.

"I'm sorry, senor, but that's reserved for one of our oldest guests."

"Oh, that explains it. Oban Patterson reserved it for me," I stated with confidence. I leaned closer. "But don't breathe a word of this. Mr. Patterson sent me down here on a confidential mission. Do I need to say anymore?"

She gave me a peculiar look, neither hard nor soft, but mixed. "He didn't mention your name in his last telegram, senor."

"Of course not. He's much too clever for that. Now where is this room?"

"I suppose if you want to rent a room, I can't stop you. Only please don't imagine you're making an impression on me. You're not." Her hand went to her hair, then she reached for the register book, rotated it and allowed me to sign in. Finally she handed me a key. "Breakfast is served from seven to nine in the morning. You are welcome to use the pool and spa. Your room is located directly above us in the main building."

The four floor to ceiling glass windows gave an excellent view of the crystal blue double oval pool surrounded by palms. It was early, but three young couples lounged on white recliners around the pool. I assumed the one-story stucco building at the rear was the spa.

Poncho slid up beside me with my luggage and took the key from my hand. "I can handle this for you, senor," He headed up the tiled staircase, I imagine, to stow my case and check out the room.

Ricardo smiled. "See, senor, I fix it up for you, eh? You ask Ricardo, he pull the strings."

Poncho returned and I tipped him a couple of quarters and thanked Ricardo for his assistance.

After they left, I went to my room and plopped onto the bed. I called room service and ordered a bottle of scotch and a bucket of ice. I stripped to my pants and turned the shower on as hot as it would go. I had learned, the hotter the shower, the quicker you can cool down and sleep. When the bottle and ice arrived, I filled a glass to the rim with ice and added three fingers of scotch. I removed my pants and with my drink stepped into the shower. I stayed until my drink was finished.

I toweled off, shaved and with a towel wrapped around my waist, poured another drink, laid on the bed and sipped my scotch, watching the ceiling fan rhythmically attempt to circulate the thick air in the room. Sometime later, I dropped off to sleep.

chapter thirty-six

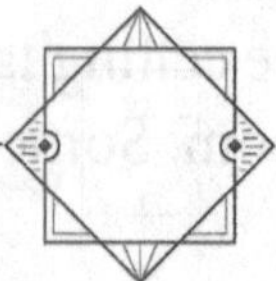

Though exhausted from the previous night's drive and the uncomfortable night in the front seat, I woke suddenly, felt sluggish and uncertain. My dreams had been confusing and fragmented, with people moving in and out of focus so fast that they became blurred double images of themselves. I couldn't pin them down or connect how they were related. I sat up and rolled my feet off the edge of the bed, yawned a couple of times until the fog disappeared from my brain. I checked my watch—6:30 p.m. The phone was only for in hotel service, so I dressed quickly and walked down to the main desk in the lobby.

"Are there any pay phones available?" I asked the woman working the front desk. She was older than the previous clerk.

She pushed a rotary phone around across the desk in my direction. "I guess it's all right for you to use this one, as long as it isn't a toll call."

"Aren't there any other phones?" I didn't relish having a private conversation in the middle of the lobby.

"Not on this floor, senor."

I picked up the receiver and dialed Pepe's number. On the third ring someone with a heavy accent picked up and answered. "Hola."

"Pepe?"

"Si."

"Its Naylan. What did you learn from your sister?"

"A couple of things, senor, but I can't discuss them on the phone.

I'm off at eight o'clock. You can meet me back here at El Gato then?"

"I'll be there," I told him, and returned the receiver to its cradle.

When I got back to my room, I unlocked the door and stepped in. Ricardo was searching through my luggage with, Colt 38 special in his left hand. "What do you think you're doing?"

"I unpack the luggage so the senor does not get wrinkles.

"What gave you the idea I'd hired you as a valet?"

"I gave myself the idea, senor. I double up the job and undouble the clothes."

"I've thought for a while that you were up to something."

"Me, senor?"

"Look, you're not a taxi driver and you're certainly not a guide. Who are you?"

"I am anything you want. I am the best corpse guard, chauffeur, waiter, butler, mechanic, downstairs man and upstairs man, gardener, handyman—"

"—You're all fired."

"I think not, senor."

"Why's that, Ricardo?"

"I think you need a corpse guard."

"You mean a bodyguard."

"That's right, senor, I take care of your body."

"I don't need a bodyguard, but I do need a ride back to the El Gato. And leave the Colt in the luggage."

"Very good, senor. Now we go visit my cousin, eh?"

"Yes, Ricardo."

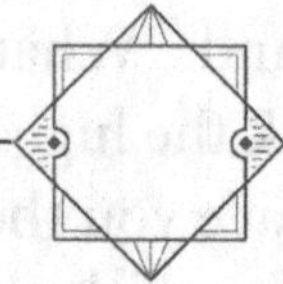

chapter thirty-seven

It was dark outside, but the lights of the café spilled out onto the street where Saturday party goers were dancing and drinking. I told Ricardo to wait for me in the car, strolled inside, and walked up to the bar.

The place was livelier now than at breakfast. Ceiling fans roiled the smoke-laden atmosphere. Three men were seated at one of the few tables next to the dance floor with poker chips and cards in front of them. One of the three players was dark, half Mexican, I guessed. He seemed to be losing and didn't like it. The man on his left was called John from what I gathered from the loser's comments. He was a large Caucasian with brutal features, large ears that pointed out at a ninety-degree angle from his head, and big hands that were surprisingly deft in manipulating cards and chips. The other player was a well-dressed Mexican with the most expressionless face I'd ever seen on a human being. The others called him Manuel, and he seemed to not speak except when it was strictly necessary. The half-Mex finally scared the other two of a seventy or eighty peso pot. Feeling benevolent, he got up and came to the bar and ordered drinks for the boys at the table.

As he waited for his order he asked, "You new in town, senor?" His broad smile revealed two gold front teeth.

"I've just arrived from Tucson to look over some property opportunities," I responded. "But they were a bust, so I'll probably drive back tomorrow morning."

He nodded in acknowledgment and picked up his order and headed back to the poker table. I watched the play a little, ordered a beer, and asked the bartender if Pepe was still around. He stepped to the service window, yelled for Pepe, then returned to washing out glasses.

A mariachi band dressed in charro outfits was giving a lively rendition of La Cucaracha on the orchestra dais, a camp song of that immortal renegade, Pancho Villa. They finished and were rewarded with loud applause. It was expected. La Cucaracha is a sort of provincial national song. It brought back flashing memories of the Chihuahua stable cleaner who later flung his defiance in the teeth of the government: "Que chico se me hace el mar para hacer un buche de agua…I'll use the ocean to gargle!"

A lanky sunburned girl came out next and sang a plaintive folk song. Her colorful dress of thin cotton clung to her because of the heat inside the bar with the effect of dampness. The singer was greeted with the sound of mild applause and she began another song as I finished the dregs of my beer.

When I attempted to get the barkeep's attention for another, I saw Pepe walk out from the kitchen. He stopped at my stool and leaned in. "It may be best that we go outside to speak, senor."

A pair of tiny muscles beside my spine twitched. It wasn't a new sensation. Twice before I had felt those tiny insidious vibrations and both times, minutes later, I was being shot at. But I ignored my body's intuition and dropped a couple of pesos on the bar. I followed Pepe out the side door to the alley and the darkness beyond.

While waiting for my eyes to become accustomed to the darkness. It was a fine night, soft breeze and stars, glinting brass-button bright in the navy blue sky. The type of spring night when you sense nothing can go wrong.

Outside Pepe lit a cigarette and leaned against the wall. I lit a fag for myself and asked, "Well, Pepe, what did your sister have to report?"

As the last word echoed down the passage, the three poker players appeared. I'd failed to notice the poker players push themselves back from the table and follow us out. The two larger goons stepped to my sides and took hold. The half-Mexican's grip on my arm was like a tourniquet. I peered into his eyes. They were shallow and glazed, with no light behind them.

I jerked suddenly at the arms holding me. "Just a minute," I yelled. "What's this about?" Neither of the torpedoes said anything. They tightened their grips on my arms and roughly shoved all one hundred and eighty pounds of me towards their short companion.

The smaller well-groomed Mexican spoke with a cultivated accent. "Senor Nayland, I would like to have a word with you." His English was better than I had expected, as well as charmingly effeminate.

I dropped the cigarette still gripped between my fingers and put it out with my foot. I flipped open the front of my suit coat and pretended to peer down the front of my pants before suggesting, "I have plans tonight. Maybe you can have a word with me tomorrow."

"No, senor, that will not do. You see, it's time for you to return to your own country and give up this business you have involved yourself in. To stay any longer would be hazardous to your health."

"Okay. Have your party, boys. But I'll tell you now, I don't like your methods." I added slowly, "And I'll do my damnedest to make us even." Neither of the three acted as if they'd heard me.

Then the ugly white dude, eyes dancing, asked, "Where would you like it?"

I just looked at him. There is no answer to a question like that. I didn't see the first blow coming but I sure felt it land. I bent forward and nearly puked. I hadn't half straightened up again when the half Mexican with a thick black mustache busted me in the guts. There is nothing tougher than a tough Mexican, nothing more honest than an honest Mexican, just as there is nothing gentler than a gentle Mexican, and above all nothing sadder than a sad Mexican. The half Mexican was one of the tough ones. They don't come any harder anywhere.

My heart started palpitating and I wondered if a heart attack would get me out of this jam. Probably not, I concluded, before the notion occurred to me that if I was in a book or a movie, the hero would have a snappy comeback, joking bravely in face of fear. My response fell short. "I'm just a tourist."

"No, senor, we both know that is not true. And it's been said that a wise guy never fools anybody but himself." He pulled his coat back to reveal a snub nose .38 in his waistband. "Don't get smart with me. You've now been told, and you got told nicely. When I take the trouble to call around personally and tell a character to lay off, he lays off. Or else he lays down. And he doesn't get up." His right hand caressed the small revolver as he spoke.

Ricardo stepped out of the shadows holding a revolver in front of him like a dangerous gift pointed at my three new friends. He was as calm as an adobe wall in the moonlight. "You best leave that there, senor." The other two released my arms as he spoke.

The effeminate Mexican moved his hand slowly towards the waist pistol. Ricardo failed to observe the suddenly moving mass of nickel metal that seemed to leave a blur as it streaked. I stepped quickly and backhanded the pistol skyward. A shot rang out, hitting a piece of roof tile above. I turned and dived for the weapon, pinned the little man's wrist, and got cuffed in the ear by his other free hand. I ignored it and closed my other hand around his arm. We circled in a slow, straining dance, while I pulled at the elbow, attempting to twist the pistol free with the other. The waltz continued until I got behind the gunsel, and wrenched his wrist further back.

"Detener! Me estas rompiendo el brazo, eres grande bruto!"

I leaned over the gunsel like a prosecutor as he sat bent over double, the hammer-lock wrist now shoved near the nape of his neck. Only then did his pain-wracked fingers let go, the gun falling forward in front of him instead of behind. He made a grab for it, but I quickly knee socked him in the chest. I then picked up the gun, a nickel .38 that had been fired, but never cleaned.

Pepe started to slink away. "No cousin I think it best you stay with us. I don't like to shoot men in the back. You others keep your hands up, please." I noticed Ricardo's English had suddenly gotten better. "You wish me to kill them, senor?" His face darkened as I caught a glimpse of the red fires banked within.

"Who said anything about killing someone? By the way, nice work, Ricardo."

The effeminate Mexican, still rubbing his wrist, spoke up. "You cannot just shoot us. We have done nothing wrong other than have a conversation with this American tourist."

Ricardo snorted. "Sometimes bad men talk, but they don't say anything. Isn't that true, Senor Lou? Maybe we give them the four degrees?"

"It's true, but I don't think we should give them the third degree. But I do have a few questions for them. Like who hired them?"

"Senor Nayland asked you a question. Speak up!"

Well-groomed Mexican hesitated, and then spoke. "We don't know the man. He just came into the bar the other night and sat down at our game. After a while he suggested he needed some muscle to push off an American debt collector. We told him for the right of cash we could handle the job. He gave us all a hundred dollars and your description."

"That's it?"

"He said to just scare you a little and send you back across the border. We swear, senor that is all. We never even caught his name."

"What do you say, Ricardo?"

"I think we may get more if I give them the third degree."

"Maybe, but I doubt it. Best we let these three get back to their poker game now."

"If you say so, senor." Ricardo spat some Mexican words at the three and waved his gun at them. The three disappeared back into the bar. Ricardo grinned. "What do you say? This Ricardo comes in handy, eh? I work for you some more now?"

I shook my head. "Your salary starts the moment you put that rod away."

"I will be your corpse guard now. We don't know if they may come back."

I walked over to Pepe and asked, "Alright ,Pepe. What you got for me?"

"Not much, senor. I call my sister like I said. She says the red-head man was there at the hotel a little while back."

"You're not telling me anything new, Pepe."

Ricardo spat some Mexican words at him.

Pepe jabbered excitedly in Mexican and then nervously said, "Si, senor, but my sister she does not know much."

"Did she say how long the man stayed there?"

"Si, senor, she tell me that he only stayed in hotel for two nights."

"Did she say whether he met or spoke to anyone?

"She saw no such thing, senor. She says he was alone by the pool most of the time."

"Did she learn anything else?"

"Maybe. She tell me she overheard him when he was checking out. He tell the desk clerk that if anyone should call he could be reached at the Hotel Agua Valiente Casino in Tijuana."

I handed him five bucks. "That's fine, Pepe. You can go."

When Pepe had gone back into the café I grabbed Ricardo's arm. "Just a moment. I've a few questions for you Ricardo."

"Si, senor. How may I help?"

I lit a cigarette, cupped it in my hands the way we used to do in the infantry, and said, "I noticed your English was excellent when you spoke to those three trigger-men."

"Que?"

"You know what I'm asking. You're too good with that pistol. And the way you handled those three like you've done it before? It's something an ex-cop notices."

He reached into his rear pocket and pulled out a small bi-fold wallet and flipped it open. From the light blinking over the side door I could clearly make out the badge of the Mexican Federal Police. "That real, or are you setting a gringo up to be rolled?"

"That real? Or are you setting a gringo up to be rolled?"

"It is very real, senor," answered Ricardo with conviction.

I suddenly became aware of how Ricardo looked like what he was—a straight cop. Nature had molded him for the task. Years in the harness had sculped his face in deep, seamed lines. He was broad and strong, built close to the ground, with a powerful neck and iron-hard fists, the better to fight when the going was rough. His crag of a jaw might represent bull-headed aggressiveness, or perhaps just strength of character. I leaned towards the latter. "Then why are you huffing as a taxi driver and trailing me so close?" I asked.

"It may interest you to know that you have been watched since the minute you arrived in Mexico, by orders of the Federal Police."

"I see now why you're such an authority on police matters."

"I believe a man by the name of James Warren from your Oklahoma City is the man we want for the death of a hotel employee in Tijuana four weeks ago. When I called up to your authorities to check on his background, I spoke to a sheriff by the name of Brice Jackson. He sounded like a good cop, by the way."

"He is," I replied.

"That is good to hear. Anyway, he told me about the three murders of similar aged men in the last month in your city and that you were looking into the disappearance of a fourth. And who you and he both believe had connections to the three deceased men. It is one of the strangest cases I have ever been on. A series of murders that occurred in your country, and one, maybe more, in mine, presumably by a man who is supposed to be dead."

"Can you prove he isn't?" I asked.

"The facts indicate it. You know Warren's reputation, one romantic adventure after another."

"He's not the first painter to be a romanticist, but it hardly explains the murders."

"True, but when Warren's true identity was discovered by the bell hop at the casino, and he had already committed murder back in the states he felt he had to kill anyone who could possibly testify he was still alive. But we will see. Once we arrest Warren we will have our answer."

"Possibly, but what's that got to do with me here in Juarez?"

"I'm looking for a connection between the investigation Senor Jackson told me you were currently involved in, and the murder of a young bell hop who worked at the Hotel Agua Valiente Casino in Tijuana. I believe Senor Warren is that connection."

Brice had obviously made the connection before Doc dropped that bombshell into his lap. "What he told you is true. But as you must have gathered, I still haven't located my missing person. Now I have a question for you—why do you think Warren is alive and our man for the murders?"

Ricardo held out a box of cigarettes. "Try one of mine."

I shook my head. "Too strong for me. Nicaraguan cigarettes I like. Cuban cigarettes are murder."

"Suit yourself, senor." He removed a pill from the box, lit it and blew smoke before answering. "The famous Senor Warren is known to many of us down here. He is also well known to be an adventurous maricon and, yes I know, he was supposed to have died several months ago. But there is something unusual about his illness. The hotel staffs say that over the month he stayed there his health gradually declined until the day he was found dead by the pool by one of the waiters. Their descriptions of his health and treatment didn't add up to a heart attack to me."

"That all falls in line from what I've learned, but what has you here in Juarez?"

"I have established that Senor Warren saw no doctors during his stay here in Mexico, and that he was only cared for by a privately hired nurse. She gave a statement to the local police that she only gave him medications prescribed by his American doctor. What they were I do not know, but I'm suspicious when an ailing man sees no doctors. When I called your city, the doctor's name listed for the prescriptions didn't exist. Add to that the fact that we do not embalm our dead in this country, so he was quickly buried without an autopsy. Such things make me suspicious," he said, pointing to his nose. "Especially when that man is a person of interest in an unsolved murder. Because, senor, even in Mexico, we like to do things right."

"Interesting, but why are you here in Juarez and not in Tijuana?"

"All trails of my investigation have gone dead in Tijuana. So when Senor Jackson told me you were coming down here to investigate, I come here also. But the trail appears to have gone dead here as well. So I will return to Tijuana tomorrow and begin again. What will you do, senor?"

"Drive back to Tucson, return my rental, and then find

transportation to Tijuana. Although this trail has gone cold, the clues, and my instinct, all point to your hometown. And, by the way, thank you for what you did for me back there with the goons, Ricardo."

"No problem. I wish us both well on our investigations. Adios, Senor Nayland."

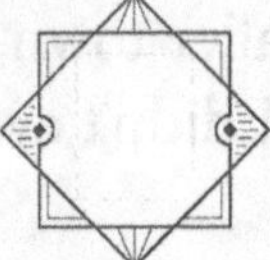

chapter thirty-eight

I checked out of the Hotel El Casa Del Lago early the next morning and took a taxi into town. The wind blew strong from the south and desert grit peppered the side of my face as I crossed the street from the taxi stop to where I had parked the Packard. The clock in front of the bank showed it was nearly eight, so I threw my case in the backseat, slid in, and headed out of the city, north to Tucson.

When I approached the international bridge over the Rio Grande I was the only traffic in sight. The two khaki-clad border guards were leaning on the rail that blocked the road, dragging on a couple of cigarettes. Neither looked impatient. Mexicans seldom are. The border guards looked briefly at my credentials then waved me across the border.

In Tucson I returned the Packard to Pete's garage. Pete expertly counted out the money of my deposit and two days rental fees. Then he gave me a ride to the terminal where I caught a TWA flight to Los Angeles.

The plane banked in towards the shoreline and began to descend. Mountains detached themselves from the blue distance, and civilization appeared between the sea and the mountains, a city made of cubes. The cubes increased in size. Cars crawled like colored beetles between the buildings, and matchstick figures hustled along the pavement. A few minutes later I was one of them.

An hour later, in another rental car, a Chrysler this time, I headed south to Tijuana on the coastal highway. It's a long drive from Los Angeles to Tijuana, so I drove fast but not fast enough to get tagged. The southern run to the border is as monotonous as a Catholic mass in Latin. You drive through a beach town, around a curve, along a stretch of beach, through a smaller town, up a hill, along another stretch of beach, ad nauseum. I didn't even stop to eat. My time was running short in this case.

Preferring to fill the car with gas on the U.S. side of the border, I swung the Chrysler through the large concrete arch that told the world, YOU ARE NOW ENTERING VISTA BEACH. Vista is a small, isolated settlement south of the City of Angels. I drove through the entrance arch toward the village below. Under the slanting brown bluffs of the coastal mountains stood a dozen houses, a gas station and a small grocery store huddled together as if for protection against the ocean. It was a warm clear day. The dull red sun balanced like a glowing cigar on the rim of the hills above town. The sky was a paler reflection of the churning sea. The beach was quiet except for the boom of the surf as the waves surged high up on the beach, then lost their energy at the deck posts of the outermost homes.

Vista Beach, or at least this section of it, is probably the most exclusive real estate in California. Beside it Malibu is Coney Island itself. Even the gas station is plush. Squat barrel palms, hibiscus bushes and poinsettias bordered the entrance all the way to the light pink and yellow stucco filling station. I pulled up to the pumps, stepped out of the car, and told the kid to fill it up. Across the road, a large sign announced Josie's Bar and Bait Shop were open for business. I walked out back to look at the water and stretch my legs. A wooden gangway ran from the parking area along the rear of the filling station, by some homes, down to the beach, and out onto a short pier. The ocean glinted brightly as it roared up onto the beach. I could see half dozen boys huddled around a small fire. Most of them were bare-backed, one or two of them were wearing sweatshirts. Their surfboards encircled them on the sand.

Such settings always reminded me of something I had come to learn, if not accept in my years as a PI. Once you go beyond the manicured lawns, beautiful adorned houses and the loving family façade, you'll usually find neurosis, sociopathy and murder.

After I paid the attendant, I started the car, turned on the radio. I tuned it to KHJ out of Los Angeles just as Bing Crosby began to sing Robins and Roses. I thought about my destination. Tijuana is not Mexico and no border town is anything but a border town, just as no oceanfront is anything but waterfront. The citizens just really want to make a peso, or better yet, an American dollar. A Mexican border town has too many children begging in the streets and too many women of questionable virtue selling their wares to be called a real town.

Soon I was back on the international border where a Mexican policeman dressed in a wrinkled khaki uniform checked out my car and credentials. If he had been more thorough, he would have known I had crossed the border twice in two different cars, at two separate crossings, in the past 48 hours. Such behavior, if known to the authorities on either side of the border, usually got you a seventy-two hour stay in an unpleasant cell.

The haze of twilight was deepening towards the edge of darkness in the mountain valley a few minutes after eight o'clock when I pulled into the courtyard of the Hotel Agua Valiente Casio. I parked diagonally in the flagstone parking lot where a little stone angel fountain gurgled pleasantly, flinging small lariats of spray into the warm air. The hotel was an interesting combination of Mexican colonial, California mission, and neo-Islamic design with over three hundred rooms. The 85-foot Campanile ("bell tower") served at least four purposes: bell tower, beacon for the air strip, entrance sign to the hotel from the road, and an icon of the resort. The canteen is also famous for their medicinal hot springs, therapeutic pools and spa. Its chief attraction to wealthy Americans is the luxurious casino, greyhound races, and elegant full-service cocktail bar that provides Hollywood entertainment on the weekends. In fact, the actress Rita Hayward had only last year been found singing and dancing with her father in the main lounge.

A small Mexican boy about fourteen years of age wearing a

large, floppy sombrero raced down the stone steps to my car. "One dime, senor, and I carry your bags inside the hotel." The boy's voice sounded familiar.

I stepped out of the car and noticed that my cotton white dress shirt was now sweaty and clung firmly to my shoulders and back. I pulled it away from my skin as I spoke to the boy. "Don't young men with manners remove their hats when they speak to a stranger for the first time?" I asked the lad.

"Si, senor, my apologies," he responded. He removed his hat and held it crushed with both hands to his chest.

"Hello, Poncho. A long way from home, aren't you?"

"Si, but I am here on a mission."

"May I ask you what your mission is?"

"Oh, si! I am here to carry your bags into the hotel. Like mi padre. I am your man, senor."

"Okay, Poncho, you can carry in my bag."

"Oh, senor, I almost forget. Once you are checked into the hotel mi padre would like to speak to you."

"Where may I find him, Poncho?" I inquired.

"He's working as the bartender here, senor. It very hush-hush but if you go and buy a drink from him, he will speak to you." I gave him some spare pesos and watched him carry my bag inside.

I walked up the dozen marble steps and through the padded leather doors that swung inward when I pushed them. I passed through the lobby with a glass roof, which contained a jungle of banana trees. The main room was decorated with tinted desert photomurals. Looking through the glass doors beyond I could make out a rattan bar with a grass canopy, and a white-coated bartender, drying shot-glasses with a bar towel. It was Ricardo.

I returned to the main desk where the hotel clerk, a small olive colored man wearing a plain, tan, single breasted suit, busily worked. With his rapid fire chatter and quick, darting movements, he seemed like a human dynamo. He gave me the impression of a man who would walk down the stairs instead of using the elevator. As I approached, he waved a sheet of paper with his left hand and nervously snapped the fingers of his right hand at the bellhops, using up some of his excessive energy. He greeted me. "Good day, senor. How may I help you?"

"A room, please." He pushed a card towards me and I registered, thanked him, then picked up my key and headed towards the main elevator.

When the brass doors slid open a teenage boy appeared and asked, "Which floor, senor?"

"Three please." When the doors closed, the young man slid the brass operating lever to three. "I'm looking for a friend of mine who is supposed to be staying here. Can you help me out?"

"That is possible, senor. What is your friend's name?"

"Paige. He's a young man about thirty with bright red hair. You couldn't miss him."

He didn't even look at the folded bill I slipped him. He smiled a grin of appreciation and replied, "Sorry, senor, but no man by that name or description has been at this hotel."

The doors slid open. I thanked him and walked down a long hall carpeted in green and paneled in ivory. A cool breeze blew through the hall from open windows to the fire escape. I enjoyed it briefly, and then I inserted the key into the brass door lock and stepped into my room. My muscles ached. Too much time driving, and cramped airplane seats had caught up with me. I quickly undressed and took a cold shower. Towel wrapped around my waist, I pulled the covers down and dropped into the cool sheets and drifted off.

chapter thirty-nine

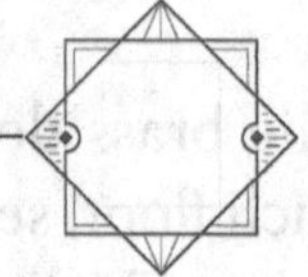

When I woke the next morning, hot sunbeams danced through the beads of sweat on my chest and a large fly was buzzing my face. Even for April the humidity in the room caused the sheets to stick to my naked body. I rolled over and watched the ceiling fan turn slowly. I began to notice intermediate flashes of light appear, and disappear, on the fan blades. As my head cleared, I determined there was a pattern to the flashes. I began to count their duration; 20, 15, then a short break before they appeared again; 15, 2, 19, 5, 18, 22, 5. Then the flashes disappeared for a few moments, before starting a new sequence; 8, 1, 22, 5. Another break, then 12, 15, 3, 1, 20, 5, 4 and so on, until I recognized the last two sets of numbers were a repeat of the original set.

I grabbed a pencil and a piece of hotel stationary. When flashes reappeared on the ceiling, I began to scribble the lengths of time of each flash. When the sequence concluded on the same 15, 2, 19, 5, 18, 22, 5 I slipped out of bed and approached the window, tilted the slats of the blind slightly and peered down into the garden below. The zinnia and yucca flowers were in full bloom and evenly spaced before a stand of palms. No one was in sight. Then I noticed a shadowy figure behind a palm with what appeared to be a pocket mirror in his hand. Catching the sunlight, he flashed it up towards the wall of the hotel. With the final flash the figured pulled back and disappeared into the trees.

I returned to the small desk and looked down at the numbers

I had written down. At first, I thought maybe it was nothing more than children playing a game. Then I realized it was a simple cipher. I corresponded numbers to letters of the alphabet. Once that was established, I put a letter under each number I had written down previously. Then I read it back to myself.

> Have located our Man
> Living next to the beach
> Will continue to observe

I looked over at the small clock next to the bed. The little hand was on the seven and the big hand was pointing straight down. I rubbed my face with my hands. My stomach rumbled angrily at me. I hadn't eaten since I had consumed that thing they call a sandwich on airplane the day before. I got a cigarette off the night table and lit it. It tasted like old inner tubes. I had smoked the last of my American cigarettes trying to unwind the night before. I hadn't unpacked my suitcase, so I pulled it out from under the bed and retrieved clean underwear and socks. I decided to hell with a suit in this heat chose a white short-sleeved shirt instead. I quickly showered and dressed.

I closed the door and slipped the hotel key into my pocket as I moved down the corridor toward the elevator, the second door down from mine, on the same side of the hall, opened for a moment as I went by. Before I reached the turn of the hall, something made me glance back. Maybe the fact that it hadn't immediately closed again caught my attention. But as I turned, I spied the outline of a dark haired woman.

I shrugged and continued down the stairs and through the brightly decorated lobby to the hotel café for some breakfast. After finishing off my plate of huevos rancheros and frijoles, I stuck my head inside the hotel bar. The place was empty.

A young man stood behind the bar pensively cleaning his nails with a penknife but quickly became very businesslike when our eyes met. "May I get you a drink, senor?"

"It's a little earlier, so I'll pass."

"Very good, senor," he replied and began to wipe down the bar with a linen towel.

I trekked to the backside of the hotel and out the sliding glass doors to the pool area. The sun burned bright in the sky and white gulls circled above. Purple and white flowers flowed over the lips of their large terracotta pots, emitting an aroma like a slow breath of sunlight. The pool was surrounded by tall palms and hibiscus bushes with a small stucco building at the far end, which I assumed was the spa. A paved path ran along the brightly painted building and under a eucalyptus tree toward the luxurious private cottages surrounding a smaller private pool. Another path led off towards the resort's famous tennis courts.

It was still early. Few people were out yet, except for an older couple wrapped in hotel robes, playing checkers. The woman wore a large straw hat and a heavy string of pearls rested against her crepe bosom. Across the pool a girl was sunbathing on a white lounge chair. Two Turkish towels draped across her body to meet the minimum demands of modesty and to protect sensitive areas from the sun. She had long black hair and was tanned and as darkly complected as the natives. The morning sun highlighted features that were young, lovely, and sweet. There was no discernible polish on her nails. Her face was finely chiseled, firm and sensitive. Large dark sunglasses hid her eyes, leaving them to one's imagination to fill in the blanks. She had a hint of Latin in the face, possibly French or Spanish or even southern Italian, not a foreign face though. And unlike most of the women I've met over the years, she would become better looking with the passing of years.

I made a snap decision, the kind you usually live to regret, and strolled around the pool to where she lay. I stopped near, she didn't stir. Then I stepped closer. She still didn't stir. She had a mole on one side of her naval, a scar on the other; both, I thought, were equally attractive. But I could smell danger mingled with her perfume. To someone else it could have been frightening, I enjoyed it. It added spice to the forthcoming encounter. She must have heard me cross the patio, even if she hadn't seen me. When lying down, most people will flinch or sit up if a stranger comes walking directly toward them. But she hadn't moved a muscle with my approach. "Excuse me," I said, "but—"

The woman studied me for several seconds as she bit her lower lip. Her lips were pale and unlipsticked, but firm and nicely shaped when they spoke. "Estes es un hotel privado."

"I know," I answered solemnly. "But I'm a private detective, so that's all right. What I wanted to say was—"

"I won't burn in the sun, but mucho gracias for worrying about me, Senor Nayland," she stated loudly with a heavy Mexican accent. The elderly couple turned their heads and stared briefly, then paid no further attention.

"How do you know my name?"

Her face remained smooth, immobile, as if she were dead. Only a tiny twitch at the corner of the full-lipped mouth betrayed a touch of inner amusement. "One asks questions about newcomers. It is one of our simpler forms of entertainment here in the hotel."

"Two to nothing to your side," I growled. "Which one of us is the detective?"

"Just you, senor." Her eyes remained shut, or where they? I couldn't be sure below the dark glasses.

I paused for a moment to give my words significance. "I was going to point out that the Mexican sun isn't like anywhere else."

"Ten minutes today, five minutes yesterday. Fifteen minutes tomorrow. Five minutes more each day until I reach the tan I desire. Does that reassure you, senor?" She wasn't using charm as much as she simply possessed it.

I wandered to the edge of the pool and stood looking at the chlorine-green water smooth as polished agate in the windless morning. I turned and caught her admiring me. "If it doesn't interfere with your tanning, may I ask you a few questions?"

"If you must, senor," she said giving me a small smile that didn't touch her eyes.

"How long have you been here at the hotel?"

"Just a few days."

"I'm supposed to meet a friend here, maybe you've seen him. He's got bright red hair, slim, about thirty years of age." I could see a tiny blue pulse beating in the hollow of her temple.

She tensed. "I'm sorry, senor, but I have not seen any man here that fits that description and now my ten minutes are up." She swiftly stood up, holding the towels in their respective zones and quickly slipped into a white beach robe. She quickly pulled one of the towels out from beneath her covering to dry her hair while letting the second fall to the ground. There was something familiar about her. When she turned her head, to rub it dry with the towel the sun hit it just right, revealing a glint of redness between the strands.

She walked towards the large glass doors leading back inside. I said, "Nice chatting with you," while still watching the rhythm of her hips under her beach robe as she walked up the stone stairs into the hotel. We'd been getting along fairly well, I thought, and then suddenly we weren't. I hoped I wasn't losing my interrogatory touch. I grinned to myself and thought, there was definitely something familiar about her.

As I walked to the stairs, I saw Ricardo watching me, eyebrows lifted. "No luck, senor? Maybe nice Mexican ladies don't prefer nosey Americans."

"That's one possibility," I responded.

"It is good to have you here in our fine city, Mr. Nayland. Now maybe we can solve these strange circumstances."

"What have you learned, Ricardo?"

"Sorry to say, not much. But I have a lead for you to follow since I am, how do you say it, undercover."

"Tell me what you need then."

"There is a house detective that works the hotel by the name Pedro Rodriguez. He's an ex-cop, but he's a solid fellow. I believe he may possess information regarding Senor Warren. He may be able to provide us with information—things like when he saw Warren here, the condition of his health and possibly the circumstances surrounding his supposed death. You can usually find him in the casino after 10:00 a.m."

"Anything else?"

"Si, I suggest you speak to the hotel manager, as well. I've been told a local politician has instructed Mr. Zueger to cooperate with the American investigator when he arrives."

"You didn't happen to speak to this politician before I arrived, did you?"

"It is a possibility, senor. Either way, come speak with me after you have spoken to him.

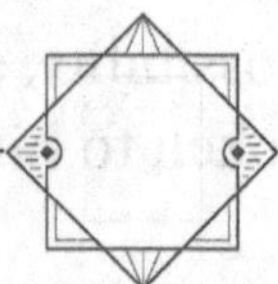

I found the manager in his office behind the reception desk. The walnut paneled walls were hung with photographs of parties, famous Hollywood guests and tennis matches. The name plate on his desk said Myles Zueger, Manager.

Zueger looked like he could still hold his own on the court. He was handsome in the slightly effeminate fashion of some male actors, but there was nothing actually effeminate about him. Though over-dressed for the heat, he was well built with strong shoulders and a thin waist. His smile, composed of even, white teeth and full lips, was both infectious and charming. His face was open and honest. He had the grace of a pleaser and pleaser's lack of permanence.

I flashed him my buzzer.

Cordially he stated, "Sit down, Mr. Nayland. I hope you are enjoying your stay," he said with a faint German accent. He carefully pulled up his trouser legs to preserve the knifelike crease and eased back gracefully into the swivel chair behind his desk. "What can I do for you?"

I sat down facing him across his highly polished desk. "I've been told you can tell me about Mr. James Warren. And that you may have had some trouble with him."

Zueger slid a cigarette from a hammered-gold case on his desk and lit it with a ribbed gold lighter. He appeared to like gold, as do most of his countrymen. He blew smoke upward and spoke calmly. "A little, yes, but it is in the past. Let bygones be bygones, and especially when one speaks of the deceased."

"Did you ask him to leave?"

Zueger spread his well-manicured hands over the front of his tailored double-breasted waistcoat covering his flat stomach. "No, I didn't ask him to leave on account of the incident, but I should have."

"May I ask why?"

I observed him clinch, but he contain himself. "The man was a powder keg. Even with the state of his health he could grow volatile at any moment. You see, Mr. Nayland ,we like a quiet, friendly atmosphere in our club."

I leaned back giving the expression of staying. "Tell me about the trouble you had with him. It may be important. What did he do?"

"He offered to kill me." Zueger paused, then asked, "You want the whole story from the beginning?"

"Please."

"It occurred just after the first of the year. Mr. Warren ordered a drink to his poolside cabana, coffee with rum. The bar boy was busy, so I took it to his cabana myself. I sometimes do that as a special courtesy. But as I drew close, I noticed he was talking with the bellboy, the same one they found murdered on the beach not long ago. Good manners required that I wait outside the curtains. I wasn't consciously eavesdropping." Zueger signed heavily. "But Warren seemed to think I was spying on them so he jumped up and attacked me."

"With his fists?"

"With his cane." His hand unconsciously trailed to his shoulder. "It was made of some black ebony wood topped with brass and — how do you say it?—a wild horse's head."

"You mean like a mustang head with a trailing mane?"

"Yes, that is it, precisely."

"Did he strike you?"

"No, but he drove the head of the cane into my shoulder. Fortunately, the bell boy calmed him down and he apologized. But

I was never at ease with him in the club again."

"What were they talking about when you overheard them?"

"The young man seemed to be doing all the talking. It sounded to me like some kind of philosophy. He was saying how some author believed that original thought was the basis for everything. But Warren said the author was wrong and that reality didn't come into being until two people thought together. So the basis for everything was love." The corners of Zueger's mouth turned down. "It didn't make sense to me."

"Did it to him?"

"But of course, he was making love to him. That was the point. He was angry because I'd interrupted him in the middle of his spiel. As I think back to the episode now I believe the man was psychotic. Normal men don't get so agitated over such little things."

He clinched both his fists. "I should have advised him to give up his guest privileges then and there."

"I'm surprised you didn't."

Zueger blushed. "Well, you know he was a sickly man and I didn't want to make a scene in front of the other guests. I consider my essential role to be a buffer." He gazed past me out the windows to the gardens beyond as if the God of innkeepers was watching over him. "I try to buffer my guests from the unpleasantness of the outside world."

"You're very good at it, I'm sure."

He accepted the compliment with a nod of his head. "Thank you, Mr. Nayland. Our resort is known in the trade as one of the better run clubs. I've given it fifteen years of my life. I was trained in the hotel schools of Zurich and London."

I nodded my head in respect. "Can you tell me anything about the day Mr. Warren died?"

"A little. He was being cared for by his private nurse, but I never saw an actual doctor attend to him while he was in the hotel. From what I observed after our encounter at the pool, his health deteriorated fairly quickly. He appeared to be losing weight and his skin developed a pasty coloring. He ceased any attempts at interactions with any of the guests and spent most of the time either in his room or wrapped in layers of towels in the sun by the pool. Like an orchid in a hot house."

"And the day he died?"

"Like most days, he was laying by the pool. Around noon his nurse came out to the pool to give him his medication. He failed to respond so a doctor was called. But by the time he arrived Mr. Warren was already dead. The doctor diagnosed it as a heart attack due to his weakened condition. The coroner came shortly after and took him away to the morgue. That is all I know."

"It's enough," I said. I thanked him, and he showed me out with a bow.

chapter forty-one

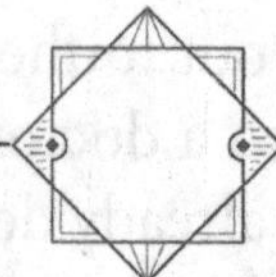

At 10:30 I followed a bevy of expensive looking people into the casino and listened to the contingent of slots getting some early morning play. Bright multi-colored lights blinked from each of the one-armed bandits lining the wall; their whirling ring of clicks, clunks, and small bells dominated the noises of the main room. A gold framed placard described the twenty-four hostesses of the casino as glorious, glittering, and glamorous. Not even the girls believed that.

I enjoy casinos—the hum of conversations, the dry riffle of the cards, the click-clack of the ball on the roulette wheel, dice rattling before they are thrown, a glass of scotch at one's elbow, and the quiet unhurried attention of a good waiter. The atmosphere of strain and tense expectancy is contagious and pulse quickening. Above all, I like the unbending fact that in gambling, everything is one's own fault. Only oneself to praise or blame. Luck is a servant, not a master. Luck has to be accepted with a shrug or taken up to the hilt. But it has to be understood and recognized for what it is and not confused with a faulty appreciation of the odds. When gambling, the deadly sin is to mistake bad play for bad luck. And luck in all of its moods had to be loved and not feared. For luck is a woman, to be softly wooed, never pandered to or pursued.

I stood and watched the fleeting expressions on the faces of the gamblers as the ball or dice stopped. Gambling requires focus, but it's a certain kind of focus requiring one part mathematical thinking and another part natural intuitiveness. The gambler must also maintain a slow pulse and sanguine temperament. The total of which are essential equipment for any gambler who is set on winning.

Amidst the activities of the room didn't keep me from noticing a man in an unkempt suit with a stringy black tie. The cuff of his left sleeve was folded under and pinned to the side of his coat with a big black safety-pin. He evidenced a degree of nervousness as he surveyed the room from his post at the top of a small set of steps that led to the cashier windows. The man was of medium height, solidly built, with black hair, with oily black hair, drooping across his forehead giving him a low-browed appearance. His dark brown eyes were emotional and sullen. Giving the pretense of the ability of thought which he was currently not using.

I found a loose cigarette in my pocket, lit it, and walked over to the house dick. When I came to a stop in front of him, the man's face didn't changed. He continued to observe the room. He brought a cigarette up in his right hand from behind his back and put it slowly between his tight brown lips. A puff of smoke came towards me, and behind it words in a cool, unhurried voice, without inflection, "What do you want, Mack?"

"I'd like to ask you a few questions about a guest who stayed here. If you have the time?"

"Don't get the idea that I play stoolie for just anybody, but the brass upstairs told me to cooperate with the American detective. So I can spare you a few minutes. What do you need?"

"I'm inquiring into the whereabouts and activity of a James Warren."

He smirked. "Have you tried the local graveyard? I hear he acquired a plot of land beneath a large oak tree."

I let that knuckleball go by before diving back into my questions. "I heard that too, but what about his time here in the hotel?"

"Not much to tell. I never spoke to him personally; he was sickly from what I gathered and spent most of his time next to the pool or in his room."

"I was told the same. Anything else?"

His eyes didn't shift from his surveillance. "He did spend some time with a local artist who paints those really bad, highly colorful paintings that are sold in the square to the American tourists."

"What's this street painter's name?"

"His name is Cisco, Cisco Leyva. I was told they had been friends for several years. Maybe he can tell you about Senor Warren. He lives down on the beach in a little adobe house. It's just a 30-minute drive south from the hotel. Take the main coastal highway south until you come to a small village named Santa Teresa. Take a right and drive until you come to the beach. From there you'll have to walk down the beach a mile or so until you come to a small house painted dark green."

I wouldn't say the pieces were beginning to fit into place, but at least they were beginning to look like the same puzzle. I thanked him and headed to the bar. I had a very satisfied feeling all the sudden. I mentally patted myself on the back and thought; I'm acting like a detective for a change.

Ricardo was busy serving drinks to two couples dressed in white tennis wear. I remembered there was a telephone booth in the lobby, so I went to it and dialed my answering service. Several seconds later the clear firm voice of Vicki's clear firm say, "Lou Nayland's office. How may I help you?"

"It's me gorgeous. You got anything for me?' I asked.

"It's nice to hear your voice, Lou. I was starting to miss the sound of it."

"I would miss it too, if I didn't hear it in my head every minute." I said sarcastically.

Vicki chuckled then told me, "You've got just one message, Lou. It came in about an hour ago from Sheriff Jackson. He said to call him if you had anything new on the murders."

"If he calls, tell him I'm following up on a lead on Warren and that I'll call him tonight with the details. See you soon."

"Bye, Lou, and be careful." I heard her say as I hung up the receiver.

I walked back into the bar. Ricardo was alone so I sat on a stool at the far end. He drew me a beer and brought it over. "What have you learned so far, senor?"

"Not much other than Warren had a temper and physically attacked the hotel manager with a cane, and the manager believed him to be unhinged."

"That's not much, senor."

"No, but the house dick gave me the name of a local man acquainted with Warren. He lives down on the beach, somewhere just south of here."

"Did he give you the man's name?" Ricardo asked.

"Yes, one Cisco Levya, a local painter who sells his work to tourists."

Ricardo scratch his chin. "I have heard of this man, but we have never met."

"Well, I'm driving down now to see what he knows. Care to come along?"

"Do you believe he may be dangerous?"

I shook my head lifting my elbows off the bar, "No, but I could use the company and I could give you a full account of my interviews on the drive."

Ricardo began wiping the oak counter with his bar towel. "I still have another hour on my shift, but when I get off, I will come and find you at this Cisco Levya's house. Will that be fine?"

"Yeah, I'll see you then." I downed the last of the beer and headed out to my car.

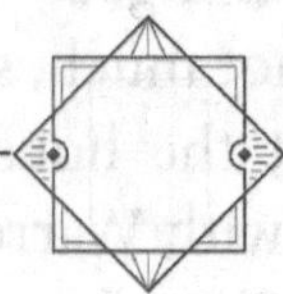

chapter forty-two

An hour later, and two stops for directions, I pulled up to the house on the beach. A well-dressed Mexican sat next to an open window smoking a brown cigarette. It smelled strong even from distance. He was very slender and, in a way, very elegant. He had dark hair, a neat beard, and a fawn-colored suit of some loosely woven material. He stood up politely as I exited the car and inquired, "Senor Levya?"

"Si, I am Cisco Levya. What can I do for you?"

I flashed my buzzer. "My name is Lou Nayland and I have a few questions regarding..." I paused. "Have we met before?"

"No, I don't believe so, Mr. Nayland. Maybe we've passed one another on the street."

"That's possible," I said. But images flashed through my mind—a convertible Buick, a middle-aged man reading a paper outside the New Century rooms, and a distinguished looking spectator leaning against the post at the end of the fight Thursday night. I focused. "But I don't recall, Anyway I would like to ask you a few questions regarding, Senor James Warren

"Ah, Senor Warren. It is very, very sad. I miss him very much."

"I'm sure you do. Can we talk about him?"

"Si. Why don't you have a seat here in the shade and I'll get us something cool to drink."

As he walked past, I caught a whiff of perfume. I also noticed his eyebrows were awfully plucked and dainty. And against the trim of the door leaned a black ebony cane with a brass mustang head.

Returning with two margaritas, he handed one to me before reclining in a wicker lounge chair. "Now, Mr. Nayland, how can I help you?"

"You can start by dropping the pretense, Mr. Warren."

Surprise flashed across his face. "How'd you…?"

"Clues were adding up, but it was the cane. It was the same cane you used to threaten the hotel manager."

He took a slow sip of his margarita. "Stupid sentimental mistake on my part. It belonged to my grandfather. I couldn't leave it behind."

"Now that we have established your true identity, I have a few questions for you. Just to satisfy my personal curiosity."

"Go ahead, Mr. Nayland. I have nothing to hide any longer."

"How did you appear so ill?" The question flicked out like a hook on the end of a long line.

"Appearances can be modified at will. For instance, a hypodermic injection of paraffin will puff up the skin at the desired spot. Pyrogallic acid will change your skin to the dark complexion of a Mexican. The juice of the greater colander will adorn you with the most beautiful eruptions and tumors. Another chemical affects the growth of beard and hair; another changes the tone of your voice. Add to that months of dieting, exercises repeated hundreds of times in my room at night to enable me to hold my features in a certain grimace, to carry my head at a certain inclination, and adapt my back and shoulders to a stooping posture. And finally, five drops of atropine in the eyes to make them haggard and wild, and the trick is done."

I dug further. "How did you fool the nurse and the staff?"

"The change was progressive. The evolution was so gradual they failed to notice it. Most people fail to see what is right before them."

"How about giving me the facts surrounding the events of your own death?"

"Simple enough," he said. "I took an herbal mix that day. The mix slows the heart down and before the doctor arrived, I'd placed a tennis ball under my arm and squeezed on it a few minutes before the doctor searched for my pulse. The pressure stops the beating of one's heart briefly. You have to time it perfectly, but as history now shows, I pulled it off brilliantly."

"Okay, but what about the morgue?"

"That was simpler because this is Mexico. When they left me that first evening, I moved an elderly man's corpse to my slab, put my toe tag on him, slipped his in my pocket, pushed his slab to the corner, empty, and walked out."

I shook my head. "Amazing." Now something a little tougher—why did you kill all those young men?"

He smiled at me, his lack of expression more terrible than anger. "They had betrayed me. They broke my heart, then laughed at my age and foolishness for falling in love with them. They were shallow beings who only cared about their own needs."

I grunted noncommittally, and forcibly restrained my tongue from running out to moisten my dry lips, "I understand that, but are you done killing then?"

"No, I have one more betrayer, Paige Swalia. But he has unfortunately disappeared. So, for now I'm on a hiatus."

The surrealness of the moment stunned me. "Do you really believe you'll get away with it? I understand there's a dead boy here in Mexico, too, and the cop on the case, will never close the file."

Warren took another sip of his margarita. "There's no connection between us other than that day by the pool. Even your cop friend can't make enough out of that to charge me."

I grimaced slightly because I knew he was right. "There are the dead bodies in Oklahoma."

"The narrow-minded people of Oklahoma will not give a flying flip about three dead queers. And besides the cops up there have me listed as legally dead. Nobody cares."

"Yeah, nobody but me." I finally took a sip of the now lukewarm margarita.

"Yeah, that's you Mr. Nayland. You'll never learn. I'm dead and home free now."

A flash of orange and a sound, sharp like a cough, erupted from the doorway. Warren tumbled to the ground in a heap, legs in the sand, head and out flung arms on the paving stones. The report of the weapon had forced me down on the ground next to the corpse. I quickly slid up to my knees and saw Warren's dark brown eyes became sightless as the life poured out from his mouth in the form of dark red ooze. I mind swirled attempting to determine where the shot had come from. I was in a hell of a spot out in the open.

But as I stood and tried to center myself, a tall dark haired woman stepped out from behind the foliage lining the sides of Warren's little house. She was squeezing a pearl handled Iver Johnson 32 caliber revolver in her hand. She trembled, her nostrils dilated and she turned pale as a ghost as she caught a whiff of cordite and death hanging in the air.

Tears of relief flowed down her bronzed face as I stepped forward and carefully removed the revolver from her trembling hand. Her mouth went soft. She looked remarkably young and virginal. I knew she was neither. She was too spent to resist. I bent down, and placed the still smoking gun in Warren's outstretched left hand. The Mexican woman removed her sunglasses and spoke. "Thanks Lou." I immediately recognized Nancy Swalia. My gorgeous, redheaded client had dyed her hair black. I realized it had been her tanning by the pool earlier today. How had I missed that?

Then I reminded myself that murder and redheads were my business and the one sometimes blinded me the truth of the other. "Why, Nancy?"

Her gaze, blue and remote, swung back to me. "He's been pursuing Paige for several months. I had to protect him," she said in a low voice. "Just like when we were kids."

I stared into her eyes searching for a tinge of veracity. "Did you know that when you hired me?"

"No, Lou, I honestly didn't. But a few days later, after the second young man from the Gardenia Club was murdered, Paige called me and told me why he was hiding. The last time he had seen Warren it had gone badly, and Paige realized Warren was off his hinges. The death of his friends only cemented that realization." As she spoke she had a drawn look that made her more beautiful because it made her look more delicate.

"Why didn't you tell me he'd contacted you?"

"We both believed it was too dangerous and that our only hope was to find Warren before he found Paige. I'm sorry, Lou, but the best way to do that was to have you continue to search for Paige."

"I might have continued anyway if you had just explained this when we spoke on the phone. Anyway, how did you find me here in sun drenched Tijuana?"

"You're so simple sometimes, Mr. Nayland. Did it never occur to you the Gardenia Club might be in other cities and other countries?"

"I have to admit, it hadn't occurred to me."

"Well, it does. And Paige's friends kept us posted of your movements. But to be honest we suspected Warren was in Tijuana while you were still in Juarez. I came to the hotel disguised before you arrived."

"You could have said something at the pool."

"I might have, but I believed you might be too righteous to aid in our scheme."

"Thanks for the compliment, but I'm not sure you analyzed me correctly. I'm not always a Boy Scout."

While Nancy stood looking down at Warren's body I noticed a lone male walking down the beach towards us. As he drew closer his bright red hair flashed in the sun like the tip of a 4th of July Roman candle. He had the manner of one whose self-confidence is complete and not altogether unjustified. He was a rather nice-looking lad. The family resemblances being unmistakable as I watched Nancy rushed over to him and gave him a hug. After they separated they both returned to stand next to me."

"Mr. Nayland, this is my little brother, Paige." He stretched out his hand and I shook it.

Paige then excused himself and walked into the little house. A few moments later he emerged carrying what appeared to be a rolled-up canvas painting. "It's of me, so I guess it's mine now. Sorry for the subterfuge Mr. Nayland."

"Not a problem son. I understand why you did it."

"I'm sorry Lou, but we must leave. But please look me up when you return to the city." She took Paige's hand and they walked off in the other direction along the beach.

My heart no longer palpated at her nearness, not after what had just happened, but then I thought I should have recalled sooner that beauty and brains can make a deadly weapon. I looked back at Warren's corpse. Warren and I had both forgotten that, but Warren's fate had been sealed when he had failed to recognize the first rule of the jungle—the top and most ruthless predator is the female of the species.

I couldn't prevent from smiling as my eyes watched Nancy's high slim shoulders and tight-sheathed hips walk away beside her brother as their forms grew smaller and smaller and began to shimmer in the haze of the evening sun. I felt a little sorry for the slew of men who had warmed themselves, or been burned, at that secret electricity. I guess I was now one of the burned ones, but in a different way because I should have remembered what Bert had once told me. "Son, women have been fooling men ever since Eve opened the first fruit stand."

◁○▷

I was still smiling when a large four door sedan roared up to where I stood. Ricardo stepped out. "Have you found who you looking for, Senor Nayland?"

"We have, but when I confronted him, he pulled out a gun and shot himself." The blow flies were starting to gather on the dead body.

"That is too bad. I would have liked to see that one hang."

"I believed he deserved to finish up that way," I stated solemnly. "But the almighty has intervened."

After Ricardo called for the ambulance, I asked him, "Would you care to watch the Tijuana Colts play baseball against Mexico City tonight?"

"I would enjoy that very much, Senor Nayland," he said as he loaded himself into his car.

"Well then, let us go forth a while and get better air in our lungs. Let us leave this foul death within these closed rooms. For the game of baseball is glorious."[1]

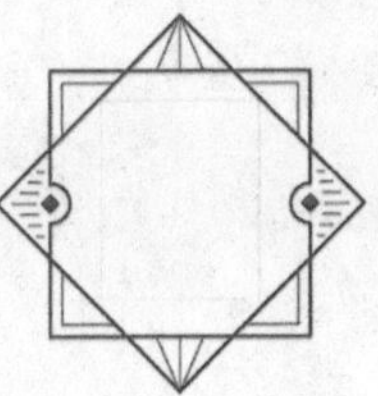

Scott R. Hartshorn

Scott R. Harshorn is an attorney with degrees in history, politics and law. He has been a prosecutor and criminal defense attorney for the past thirty years. He and his wife have been married 34 years and have two children.

Hartshorn is a member of the Private Eye Writers of America, Mystery Writers of America, the Historical Novel Society, and Sisters in Crime Writers Society.

◁○▷

SPECIAL THANKS TO LAURA YATES, JAY WEBER, AND MARLA JONES
FOR THEIR INSIGHT AND ASSISTANCE IN COMPLETING THIS BOOK.
S.R.H.

www.ingramcontent.com/pod-product-compliance
Lightning Source LLC
Chambersburg PA
CBHW011928300726

48970CB00008B/2613